# THE GRAY SHIP

## RUSSELL F MORAN

Coddington Press
PO Box 419
East Islip, NY 11730
Copyright © 2013 by Russell F. Moran
All rights reserved.

ISBN: 0989554600
ISBN 13: 9780989554602
Library of Congress Control Number: 2013910857
Coddington Press, Islip, NY

# Preface

A story begins with an idea, which then develops into a concept that eventually becomes the story. Like most of my work, this book began with conversations with my wife, Lynda. I have always been a Civil War buff, fascinated by its grandeur and its horror. The idea of a modern warship in the Civil War popped into my mind during one of those conversations. To pull that off, of course, I knew that the book would be based on the science fiction sub-genre of time travel. That's the only way I could get a nuclear powered cruiser to 1861. I enjoyed *The Final Countdown* by Martin Caidan, the 1980 novel about the *USS Nimitz* getting caught in a time portal during a freak electric storm and time travelling to Pearl Harbor on the eve of the attack. Lynda and I talked for hours about the captain and his (or her) character. Ashley Patterson became part of the concept.

This is a work of fiction, and any similarity between a character and a living person is a coincidence. There are, however, historical figures in the book, including Abraham Lincoln, Jefferson Davis and President Barack Obama. Although these are real people, the scenes in which they appear came out of my head.

# Acknowledgments

An author can't be his own editor. You're too close to the subject. You skip over the grammar and punctuation because you're concentrating on *The Story*. No matter how many revisions you go through, you are bound to miss a lot of errors. An editor looks for grammatical and punctuation errors, but he also brings a fresh eye to the story itself and spots inconsistencies. I thank my friends Bill Holland from Olympia, Washington and Nick Wartella from Sayville, New York for their bicoastal efforts. I also thank my wife Lynda for her countless hours of input into this novel.

I also thank my friend Lloyd (Hoss) Miller, Rear Admiral, Retired, United States Navy. Admiral Miller was the first commanding officer of the *USS California*, the ship that plays the pivotal role in the story. His technical input was invaluable, but I must emphasize something here. This is a work of fiction, and because it's a novel, I changed some facts to serve the story. For one thing, I had to bring the *California* out of mothballs for *The Gray Ship* because the ship had been decommissioned in 1999. Although the historic *California* didn't carry them, I added Tomahawk cruise missiles to the ship's arsenal. I also disabled the ship's inertial navigation system to serve the story.

Admiral Miller makes a cameo appearance in the book, but obviously the scene is fictional. I won't tell you why it's obvious. You'll find out. In the scene, Admiral Miller is a strong leader, a gentleman, and a very likeable person. That's not fiction. That's the truth.

I hope you have as much fun reading this book as I had writing it.

# Chapter 1

"Captain, we have a problem."

Captain Patterson hit the reply button on the intercom next to her bed.

"What is it, Lieutenant?"

"It feels like we're going aground, ma'am."

Because the captain's sea cabin is only 10 feet away, Captain Patterson is on the bridge in seconds. She always wore fresh fatigues to bed so she can respond to an emergency in uniform, not a bathrobe. It is 0307 (3:07 A.M.).

The ship went through a strange turbulence, an underwater commotion the likes of which no one on the ship had ever experienced, a soft bumping sensation, not like waves, but more like the ship was riding over a herd of whales. In 30 seconds, the bumping stopped.

"What's our depth, Lieutenant?"

"Sonar shows 200 feet, Captain."

"Any sign of marine life?"

"No, ma'am. Sonar shows nothing between us and the bottom except water."

"Damage control report?"

"Nothing so far Captain except for a few broken dishes in the mess hall."

What happened next was an event that would forever change the lives of the crew of the *USS California*. At 0309, the dark night changed to a bright noon. The sun was high in the sky, and the sweet smell of ozone, when the bright sun mingles with the ocean, was as pleasant as it was terrifying.

All departments reported to the bridge in order of protocol.

"Captain, we've received reports from almost every department," said the officer of the deck. "Engine room, AOK; reactor room, AOK; after-steering station, AOK..."

"Lieutenant, please tell me what's wrong, not what's right."

"Aye, Captain. We've lost all GPS navigation, ship-to-shore communications, and ship-to-ship communications. We have no Internet connections, email, or cell phone service."

* * *

Petty Officer Third Class Andrea Dunne was exchanging text messages with her mother in Norfolk, Virginia. Her mother has liver cancer, and she is getting worse every day.

"Mom, please tell me the truth. Don't try to make me feel better, I want *you* to feel better."

"Well, honey, the doctor was just here and he said..." There was no more message. Dunne was frantic. Her mother was about to tell her something important and the message stopped. She tried to send email, but the send command didn't work. The message on her IPhone said that there was no cellular network available. She tried to phone, but got the same message: no cellular network available.

* * *

Lieutenant Kevin Fitzpatrick stood watch in the Combat Information Center doing a routine check of satellite positions. The software displayed a computer simulation of satellites in range of the *California*. Suddenly, all satellite images disappeared from his screen. He tried to "ping" the code for each satellite. Not one responded. He assumed it was a software malfunction. Dozens of satellites can't just disappear, Fitzpatrick thought.

\* \* \*

At the Pentagon, Lieutenant Fran Talierco was on watch at the Office of Naval Operations, NavOps. Her job, as deputy watch officer, was to monitor the positions of all Navy ships in the Eastern Atlantic via Global Positioning System or GPS.

"Oh my God," yelled Talierco, "where's the *California?*"

Lt. Commander Frank Orzo, the Duty Officer, hurried to Talierco's station. "What happened Fran?"

"The *California* just disappeared," said Talierco. Because every ship had multiple redundant GPS devices aboard, they both knew it was impossible for a ship's position to disappear if one malfunctioned. That could only happen if a ship sank.

"Call them by phone," said Orzo. Talierco called the satellite number for Captain Ashley Patterson, the CO of the *California*. A recorded message said, "The number you are calling is not in service at this time." She tried the number of the Executive Officer of the *California*. Same message.

"I'll try the *Ticonderoga* to see if they can get the *California* on radio," Talierco said. The *USS Ticonderoga* steamed twenty miles east of the *California*'s last position. Talierco spoke to the Officer of the Deck (OOD) on the *Ticonderoga* who immediately radioed the *California*.

"I get no response, Lieutenant," said the OOD on the *Ticonderoga*.

"Get Admiral Friese on the phone, Fran," Orzo said. Talierco hit the emergency line for the Deputy Chief of Naval Operations.

\* \* \*

Lt. Commander Dominic Valente, the *California's* Supply Officer, arose early so he could get some work done without interruption. He ordered supplies for the next two months using newly installed supply software. He went through the on-screen menu of items, which calculated the amount needed based on the size of the crew and the length of deployment. Valente loved that the software was "cloud based," meaning that the data was on a distant server farm somewhere in the Midwest and could be updated instantly. His screen flashed the message that the network wasn't responding. This is crazy, thought Valente. We must have a dozen different Internet connections on this ship. But his workstation could not pick up one of the ship's networks. Wow, thought Valente. We're totally off the Web. He called Lieutenant Jason Terhune, the ship's IT officer.

"Any idea what's going on, Lieutenant?"

"Beats the hell out of me, Commander. The whole ship seems to be out."

\* \* \*

At 0309 Petty Officer Third Class James Randolph sat on a gun turret looking at the sky, playing with a new IPad app to learn astronomy. The screen was darkened, a great idea because if it were backlit it would be no good for viewing at night. A tiny point of light represented each star, with the star's name appearing at the bottom of the screen when he tapped on the image. He committed himself to learn astronomy, something he could share with his seven year-old son. He looked at the sky, trying to match the star to what he saw on the IPad screen. Suddenly, the sun appeared where his eyes were focused. With a shout he covered his eyes, shaking his head from the sudden pain.

\* \* \*

"When was our last good fix, Lieutenant?" Captain Patterson asked.

"At 0250, about 30 minutes before the event, Captain. The quarter-master of the watch tried to get a position right after the event, but that's when he learned that our navigation systems are out."

"Well let's get a land fix now, Lieutenant. I can see the shore lights from here."

"It gets worse, Captain. The navigator tried to get a fix using the charted landmarks, but the landmarks and buoys aren't where they should be. We got a position line from the flagpole at Fort Sumter, but that's it. Our charted buoys and towers just aren't visible."

Piloting, or what some call close-in navigation, is a simple matter. You look through a telescope on an instrument called an alidade. You line up your "target," say a lighthouse, and read the bearing from the ring at the base of the alidade. You then take a parallel ruler, line it up to the bearing on a compass rose on the chart, which is a circle with all points of the compass. Next, you take the parallel ruler and "walk" it over to the dot you've made, and then draw a line on the chart on that bearing. One line is not a fix, because your position can be anywhere along the line. With a second line from another known target, you have a fix, but not a great one. Once you have a third line from yet another target, and all three lines intersect, you now have a good fix, or navigational position. All you need are updated charts and a good alidade. If your charts don't conform to the targets you're looking at, you can't get a fix. And that was the *California's* problem.

"How's radar and sonar?" asked Captain Patterson.

"They appear to be working, Captain, but what we see on the scopes isn't what we expect to see when we look at our charts. Based on the harbor chart, there should be eight buoys in sight or visible from radar, but we can only see three, and they aren't where should be. We know our approximate position based on our last fix, but another thing looks weird. Our depth readings from sonar are way off. We should be in 200 feet of water according to our charts, but sonar thinks we have only 160 feet under us."

"Sound General Quarters, Lieutenant."

"Aye aye, Captain."

The ear splitting clang of the general quarters alarm sounded in every space on the ship, followed by the announcement, "General Quarters, General Quarters, All Hands Man Your Battle Stations. This is not a drill. Repeat, this is not a drill."

"Order right full rudder and come to course 090, Lieutenant. Until we can figure out what the hell is going on, I want some sea between me and the land."

"Aye aye, Captain. Right full rudder, steer course zero niner zero."

* * *

At the Pentagon, Duty Officer Frank Orzo was on the phone with Rear Admiral Robert Friese, the Deputy Chief of Naval operations. "Admiral this is Lieutenant Commander Orzo, Duty Officer at NavOps. We've lost all contact with one of our ships, the *California*, off the coast of South Carolina."

Friese had been celebrating his wife's birthday all evening and was quite drunk.

"Lizzen up, Luzzenum Cabana Orbo, you're just not (hiccup) lookin' hard enough." Orzo tapped the phone and said, "I'm sorry sir, but we seem to have a bad connection. I'll call you later." He heard a loud snore just before he hit the end button. Orzo then called Admiral Gary Roughead, Chief of Naval Operations.

"I tried to call Admiral Friese, sir, but we were unable to communicate." (A very true statement, thought Orzo). Roughead asked, "Did any nearby ships report an explosion?"

"Negative, sir. We've contacted all ships within 20 miles of the *California*, and no one saw or heard an explosion."

"Call the Coast Guard command in Charleston," Roughead said to Orzo. "Give them the last known position of the *California*. Tell them to launch helicopters and begin a sea rescue operation immediately."

"Aye aye, sir" said Orzo.

Admiral Roughead worked up the chain of command and called the Secretary of the Navy, who then called the called the Secretary of Defense, who placed a call to the White House.

As the phone rang, Roughead wondered how the hell a cruiser could just disappear?

The *California* has been missing for seven minutes.

# Chapter 2

The nuclear guided missile cruiser *USS California* (CGN 36) had been taken out of mothballs and recommissioned as the Navy's only nuclear powered surface ship except for aircraft carriers. The ship launched in 1971 and was commissioned in 1974.

On the morning of April 10, 2013, under the command of Captain Ashley Patterson, the ship left its homeport in Norfolk, Virginia and steamed toward Charleston, South Carolina. The ship would anchor near Fort Sumter for a ceremony commemorating the first battle of the Civil War on April 12, 1861, the bombardment of Fort Sumter. Civil War reenactors from around the country would be on hand for the ceremonies. The *California* was scheduled to deploy to the Persian Gulf after the ceremony at Charleston.

The ship has enough fire power to unleash Biblical hell on an enemy. Her armaments include: Harpoon anti-ship missiles; five inch, forty-five caliber Mark 45 guns; the Phalanx anti-ship missile defense system; an ASROC anti-submarine missile system; two Mark 13 guided missile launch systems; Mark 46 anti-submarine torpedoes, and 12 newly installed Tomahawk Cruise Missiles. She is also equipped with an Apache attack helicopter and two unmanned drone helicopters, both for surveillance and attack. The *USS California* was designed to instill fear in an enemy, and if fear didn't work, to destroy it.

Besides a platoon of 16 SEALs, there is also a platoon of 16 marines scheduled to disembark the *California* when they arrive in the Gulf. Counting the SEAL and Marine platoons, the ship has a complement of 630 crew members, including 31 officers.

With its nuclear power plant, the *USS California* can stay at sea for years. The only tether to the world beyond the ship is its need for supplies. The *USS California* is a key in projecting American power in the world.

On the morning of April 10, 2013, the *California* was on its own.

# *Chapter 3*

shley Patterson was scared. Her years in the Navy exposed her to countless challenges, all of which she handled. She had graduated fifth in her class from the United States Naval Academy in 1999. At age 36, as Captain of the *USS California*, she is the youngest commanding officer in the fleet, and the first African American woman to command a nuclear combat ship. She is six feet tall and strikingly beautiful. During a CBS *60 Minutes* segment on women in the military, Ashley was featured. Captain Patterson is a rising star in the Navy, and she's on a lot of short lists to make admiral.

But on the morning of April 10, Ashley didn't feel like a rising star. She always had a concern, although she never let it show, that she was not up to the task, that she was in over her head, that her station in life had gotten ahead of her. Why couldn't she be a math professor at a small college in the Midwest, her original career goal? There is a petulant little girl inside of her who wants to be coddled, who wants someone else to make decisions, who just wants to be left alone. She calls this little girl "Splashy," a nickname given to her when she was eight years old by a little friend missing her front teeth, who found it impossible to pronounce Ashley.

* * *

When the ship was 10 miles offshore, Captain Patterson ordered a change in course to head north along the coast and dropped the speed to a modest 10 knots. This was the nautical equivalent of taking a walk around the block to clear one's head. Take it slow, sort things out.

"Lieutenant Bellamy, take the con," Captain Patterson said to the officer of the deck. "Steer the current course and maintain speed until further orders."

"Aye aye, Captain."

She also told him to cancel the General Quarters status, thinking it unnecessary to add to everyone's stress by keeping them at battle stations.

She turned to Commander Philip Bradley, the Executive Officer.

"Phil, gather all department heads in the wardroom right now, please. We're going to look for answers."

*Answers to what?* she wondered. *What, precisely, is the question? We've gone from reality to science fiction in a matter of minutes and I'm calling a goddam meeting. Get a grip girl. This is your ship, your responsibility, your problem.*

# Chapter 4

The wardroom, the place where the ship's officers take their meals, is a modest-sized space at 22 by 28 feet. An industrial green carpet covers its deck, complementing the typical gray walls or bulkheads. On the bulkheads hang prints of famous naval battles of World War II. The dining table accommodates 18 people, which works because there are 31 officers on the ship, many of whom would be on watch at mealtimes. Two round tables at the far end can sit an additional 12 diners.

The captain is seated at the far end of the table. Ashley Patterson runs a tight meeting. She asks questions, listens to the answers, and will not tolerate political sideswiping. Over the years she had attended enough gatherings run by pompous assholes that convinced her that running an efficient meeting is a matter of personal pride. Every attendee has the confidence that he can speak without fear of having a foot shoved in his mouth.

"It's been 35 minutes since the *Daylight Event,* as people are starting to call it," Ashley said. "I think it's safe to say that everyone in this room is baffled." Heads nodded. "We went from an uneventful cruise to an amazing event that we can't explain. But it's not our job to stand around with our mouths open and scratch our heads, although that may be our inclination."

The captain's job, and theirs, is to handle the situation, make rational decisions and, well, do something. But what? What are they up against?

"Phil please bring us up to date."

\* \* \*

Commander Philip Bradley is a mystery to Ashley. He's been her Executive Officer for just over eight months, but she never felt the bonding that occurs between a commanding officer and the second in command. There's something in his attitude that she can't put her finger on. He's smart, competent, and professional, but she isn't sure she can trust him, a feeling that she doesn't like.

\* \* \*

Bradley began his briefing. "At 0309 we experienced the *Daylight Event*. We went from a dark night to a bright day in an instant. We've lost all satellite navigation, Internet connection, cell phone reception, and all communication with air, sea and shore. Our two-way radios work but we get no response from the shore or other ships. We know that the *USS Ticonderoga* was steaming 20 miles from us, and I spoke to the OOD on her bridge a few minutes before the event. She hasn't answered repeated attempts to raise her. We were also in communication with the Office of Naval Operations at 0230. We can't raise them either. Since the *Daylight Event* we've received no communication from anyone, including the weather service. We've tried to raise the Port of Charleston, our destination, but we're as cut off from them as we are from everyone else. All of our shipboard systems appear to be working. We have radar, sonar, and communications with every space on the ship. Our inertial navigation system is malfunctioning as we all know. There's a problem with the gyrocompass. One of our main jobs in Charleston was to meet with engineers from the manufacturer to get it up and running. As a result we've relied on GPS positions backed up by celestial fixes and positions from shore sightings. Because we lost satellite navigation we've relied on our paper charts and fixes by visual and radar. The problem is that none of the navigational aids, including buoys, are in the right place. The only visual object that conforms to the charts is the flagpole at Fort Sumter at the entrance to the harbor. There's another problem. The depth readings are way off by as much as 40 feet. To summarize, we appear to be cut off from the world beyond the *USS California.*"

Captain Patterson took over.

"Thank you, Commander. Folks, it may sound like a hackneyed phrase but we need to think outside the box. We *are* outside the box, so we may as well think that way. I've considered just steaming into Charleston Harbor, but I don't want to put the ship at risk with depth soundings we can't count on. Also, I don't like navigating among buoys that are out of place. If we slip outside the channel we're aground. I won't risk it. Any comments?"

"What if we head north and return to port in Norfolk?" said Lieutenant Commander Nick Wartella, the engineering officer.

"Remember, we can't raise Norfolk either," Ashley said. "Something's very wrong, and I don't think location makes much of a difference."

Ivan Campbell, the navigator, said, "Why don't we send in the motor launch, tie up to shore and find out what's going on?"

"I've thought of that Ivan," said the Captain, "but I have a concern, one that I can't explain. Maybe one of you can explain it to me. We find ourselves in a very strange situation, and I believe we all agree." Heads nodded. "Something tells me that stealth is in order. Again, I don't know why, but it seems the safest choice."

Lt. Commander John White, the ship's Communications Officer, spoke. "We have a detachment of SEALs aboard. They not only think outside the box, they trained outside the box. Weird situation management is in their blood. They're not just tough, they're smart, and they know a thing or two about stealth. They can hit the ground, recon the area and talk to people. Why don't we send a SEAL group ashore this evening to see what the hell is going on and report back?" The face of every officer in the wardroom told Ashley Patterson that John White had just nailed the answer.

"Phil, call Lt. Conroy and tell him to come here immediately."

# Chapter 5

Lt. Frank Conroy commanded a platoon of 16 SEALs, part of Seal Team 10, headquartered in Little Creek, Virginia. The platoon was assigned to the *USS California* as part of her deployment to the Middle East. They were scheduled to disembark from the *California* at a secret location in the Persian Gulf region.

Navy SEALs are legendary as a unique fighting force. SEAL is an acronym for Sea, Air and Land. The training is the most demanding military preparedness in the world, consisting of six months of grueling physical and mental stress. During "hell week," SEALs spend their time swimming in cold water, crawling through mud, climbing trees and tall obstacles, and jumping out of airplanes from impossible heights like 30,000 feet. All of this is accomplished with little sleep. About 50 percent of those who start SEAL training finish. There is no other way of saying it: SEALs are tough. They are not only professional class athletes, they're also mentally disciplined and intelligent.

The idea behind SEAL training is to cheat reality of its surprises. When a SEAL is lying in a pool of mud and cold water, having not eaten for 24 hours, with two hours sleep, surrounded by a superior enemy force, he has one thought: "Been here, done this." Lt. Conroy was a typical SEAL. Six feet tall with a wiry build, Conroy was ready for anything an enemy may throw against him. After two tours in Iraq and one in Afghanistan, Conroy was a hardened combat veteran.

But nothing prepared Conroy for the *Daylight Event*, and in that regard he's just like every other human being on the *California*. He's frightened. His training prepared him for explosions, gunfire, bayonets, and all the other horrors of combat. His training did not prepare him for daylight at night.

* * *

At 0600 Lt. Conroy entered the wardroom and sprang to attention.

"At ease, Lieutenant," the Captain said. She explained to Conroy what Bradley had told them at the briefing a few minutes earlier.

"Bottom line, Lieutenant, we're out here on a nuclear powered cruiser with the best that technology has to offer, and yet we're cut off from the world. I'm sure you've noticed the lack of Internet and email."

"Yes ma'am, I've noticed. I didn't get my 0315 briefing from headquarters in Little Creek, which I can usually set my watch to."

"Lieutenant, I've decided to send a SEAL squad ashore to assess what's going on. The problem is, we don't even have a theory or a hypothesis to give you. What we need is information, and your mission is that simple, to gather information. Recon and report."

"One of my people could be our best source of information," Conroy said. "Petty Officer Smith told me that he was here in Charleston about five months ago visiting his cousin. Since he can't call her, maybe he'll just ring her doorbell."

"Who will be in charge of the mission?" Captain Patterson asked.

"I'll take the squad in myself, Captain." The CO of a SEAL platoon seldom takes command of a specially tasked squad, but would send in a senior petty officer, just as the officer in charge of an Army platoon would assign the job to a sergeant. "I like to brief my people on what to expect, and, as you said ma'am, we have no idea what we'll run into. I'll take a squad of eight, including me, just enough to fit in one of the Zodiac inflatable boats."

"Remember, Lieutenant, we've got no satellite or cell tower communication, so we'll have to rely on two-way radios. I want radio silence if possible. We don't know what we're dealing with. We'll break radio silence only for a good reason. What's the range on your radios?"

"We can get good reception up to 35 miles, Captain. If you could position the ship about 30 miles off the harbor entrance, that should be ideal. I'll dictate everything we see into my recorder. Chief Petty Officer Duane Jackson will be second in command."

"Do you want backup from the Marines?"

"No ma'am. I'd have those guys covering my back anytime and anywhere, but this will be a recon mission. The fewer the better."

\* \* \*

"The time now is 0730 hours," Captain Patterson said. "Prepare to leave tonight at 2030, about 45 minutes after sundown. There's a quarter moon so it should be very dark at that time. You'll have six hours to snoop around. Be back at the ship by 0300 or earlier if you decide that you've accomplished the mission."

"Aye aye, Captain. 2030 hours we leave, 0300 we return."

Conroy called a meeting of SEAL Squad Alpha and briefed the men on their task. He called on Petty Officer Smith and told him that he had a key role in the recon mission because of his recent visit to Charleston. He told them to get some sleep because the mission would stretch into the wee hours.

It would be a mission that none of them would ever forget.

\* \* \*

Ashley spent the day reviewing reports from all department heads. There wasn't much else to do until the SEAL squad returned to give their report the next morning. She stepped out onto the portside weather deck off the bridge to get some fresh air. The day was sunny and clear, and the temperature was 62 degrees.

From the deck below she heard shouting. She peered over the rail to see what was going on. A tall gangly kid was cornered by three other sailors. He was blond with a pallor to his skin, and his long skinny arms protruded far beyond the cuffs of his shirt. The bottom of his fatigues were a couple of inches above his ankles. He had a hard time finding uniforms that fit. He was being taunted mercilessly.

"Hey, I'm talking to you shithead. Say something," shouted one of the bullies.

"You're so fucking ugly you make a fish look good," said another.

"Hey, dickless, open your mouth before I punch it in," offered a third bully.

Ashley grabbed Ensign Martin, the Junior Officer of the Deck by the arm. "It sounds like a fight is about to start on the deck below. Go break it up and get me the name of that tall skinny kid who's being bullied."

"Aye aye, Captain," said Martin. He went below and ended the incident. Martin returned to the bridge and said, "Captain, the kid's name is Simon Planck, Seaman First Class. He's assigned to the clerk's office." Martin also handed her the names of Planck's assailants.

Ashley called Lt. Cdr. Karen Sobel, the ship's personnel officer.

"Karen, please come to the bridge. I need to talk to you about something." When Sobel appeared, Ashley told her what happened and asked if she knew Planck.

"Yes, Captain. Planck is assigned to the clerk's office and I see him often. He gets picked on a lot. I've stopped it a couple of times myself, but we can't control what happens when he's out of sight. It's a shame because he's a good kid, bright and efficient. He's just homely and insecure, and that makes him..."

"A bully magnet?" asked Ashley.

"Yes, that's a perfect way of putting it, Captain."

"Send him up to the bridge, Karen. Make up a story that he has to pick up a piece of paper from the Captain to deliver to you."

Sobel was happy that the Captain wanted to do something about this. She, like Ashley Patterson, detested bullying.

Planck appeared on the bridge and saluted his Captain.

"Good afternoon, sailor, how are you today?"

Planck couldn't believe that the Captain addressed him personally. Ashley always liked to get to the point and said, "I saw some sailors giving you a lot of shit recently. Do you have any thoughts on that?" Planck was shaken by the Captain's bluntness.

"I'm used to it, ma'am. It happens all the time. I try not to let it bother me."

"But does it bother you?" His eyes started to fill up. He's tall but Ashley's taller. She leaned over and gave him what people called an Ashley Patterson Eye Job. Ashley has large expressive eyes, eyes that can express anger, concern or, as in this case, sympathy. "Listen sailor, this is my ship and it's your ship. Nobody in my command gets treated with anything but respect."

Ashley then shared a plan with the sailor.

"SEAL Petty Officer Peter Campo is a martial arts instructor with the SEAL team. He runs a regular class for all ship's personnel twice a day. Martial arts are great training for a person's body, but it's also a way to improve your attitude. He won't turn you into a SEAL, but he'll do wonders for your head, not to mention your body. I could recommend this to you sailor, but I've decided to give you a direct order. Join Campo's class starting tomorrow." Another Eye Job: "You're a good person, Simon."

"Aye aye, Captain" said Planck.

"And ma'am..."

"Yes, Simon?"

"Thank you, Captain."

Planck felt dizzy. She even used my first name, he thought. He had told the Captain that he got used to bullying, but that was a lie. His life was a living hell. But somebody noticed, somebody didn't think that it was okay for people to treat him like a dog. Somebody cared.

Nobody tortures a wounded bird on my watch, Ashley thought, as Planck left the bridge.

# *Chapter 6*

*A*t 2030 Lieutenant Conroy and the seven other SEALs lowered their boat over the side of the ship and headed toward Charleston Harbor. Their Zodiac inflatable boat was 20 feet long and equipped with a quiet battery driven motor. The temperature was 55 degrees Fahrenheit. It was clear and the winds calm. They had no idea what they may encounter, so stealth was essential. It was also second nature to a SEAL.

At 2045 they passed Fort Sumter at the entrance to the harbor. Something wasn't right. Fort Sumter was totally dark. They expected to see a museum, and none of them could figure out why there were no lights. "Don't museums need security?" Conroy observed. "Why no floodlights?"

Smitty pointed out that when he was in Charleston five months ago, Fort Sumter was visible from the shoreline at night. "It was lit up like a carnival," Smith said.

They continued on to the main pier at Charleston Harbor. It looked nothing like the photographs they had seen. Instead of a modern dock with a steel frame and rubber cushioning devices, the pier was all wood, with the salty smell of tar and seaweed. The area was lit by what appeared to be gas lamps. A few vessels were tied up along the waterfront. They all looked like they were from the nineteenth-century, not the typical boats you expect to see tied up next to a modern pier. About a dozen workers were on the dock, all dressed in period costumes.

"These people take their historic reenactments seriously," whispered Conroy.

They motored slowly along the docks until they found a deserted area with no activity. They came to a narrow indentation in the dock, and Conroy ordered the boat to be pulled into the opening. The Zodiac fit under the dock, completely hidden.

"Okay, let's have a look around. Move out."

They wore night camouflage, which is excellent for lurking in the shadows, but if they walked among the crowd it would be obvious that they weren't part of the upcoming ceremony.

Conroy spotted a flat roofed building that was totally dark. At four stories tall it would make a good place to recon the entire area. An exterior stairway on the side of the building led up to the roof. The area was unlit, so they climbed the stairs without fear of being spotted. From the southwest corner of the roof they had a perfect line of sight to a downtown business district that bustled with activity, mainly people staggering from bar to bar. Gas lamps lit the street.

The area bustled with people and horse-drawn carriages. Everyone they saw wore a period costume.

"We're here to observe and to report," Conroy said. " 'What the fuck?' does not count as an observation."

"Okay, I want each of you to tell me what you see. I'll dictate your observations into my recorder. You guys chime in when I call on you. If you see something that you want us all to look at right away, just speak out."

Conroy spoke first. "I'm observing a scene that looks like a Hollywood set. There are no motor vehicles in sight, only horse drawn carts and carriages. I can't see anything that appears to be electric light, only gas lamps.

Although the Civil War reenactment ceremonies don't begin until the day after tomorrow, all personnel in view are wearing nineteenth-century costumes. Anything look familiar, Smitty?"

"Yes and no, sir. My cousin lives right near the waterfront, but almost everything looks different. I see two buildings that I remember from my visit, but they're painted different colors. I saw a whole bunch of modern buildings, the kind you see in any city. But they're not here now. What really blows me away is that I can't see the Cooper River Bridge. My cousin is an engineer, and she loves that bridge. The thing was built in 2005, just eight years ago. It had these huge diamond shaped towers, and I remember her saying they were 575 feet tall. The bridge was beautiful when lit up at night. It should be right there," said Smith, pointing southeast. "It's not there. It's not fucking there."

Conroy asked Smitty if he could locate his cousin's building.

"From where we are, my cousin's apartment building is about four blocks away — I think."

They continued surveying the crowd on the street, all decked out in their nineteenth-century finest.

Petty Officer Cyrus Durbin said, "Maybe these people went to method acting school and they're just getting into their characters for the ceremony."

"I know you meant that as a joke, Durbin, but I'm willing to listen to any observation or impression you have, and that's not a bad one."

Petty Officer Rick Donnelly spoke. "The smell is incredible. It's a combination of horse shit and raw sewage. I just saw a guy dump what looked like a bed pan out a window. How authentic do you have to get?"

Petty Officer Emilio Juarez called out. "Look, here come a bunch of guys on horseback all dressed up like rebel soldiers. And check out the cannons they're dragging behind them. This is going to be one hell of a reenactment."

A cavalry unit of about 40 horsemen strode into view and paraded past the building heading toward the dock area. Behind the column were six artillery caissons each drawn by a team of two large work horses. The column passed by the building just beneath them.

Petty Officer Walter Reilly called out. "Look at the barrels on that cart. They're tied up next to a couple of goats. I can see the word 'milk' on them. Where I come from, the county health department would go ape shit over that."

Chief Jackson said, "I don't see one black face in that crowd. Will this be a reenactment for white people only?"

"Look again," said Giordano. A cart with a half dozen black men came into view. They all sat on the floor of the cart in chains. Through his binoculars Chief Jackson could see visible scars on a couple of the men. The temperature was 55 degrees Fahrenheit, but the black men were all shirtless. "I guess those guys volunteered to play the part of slaves," said Jackson. "These people are assholes."

"Okay, listen up SEALs," said Conroy. "I think it's accurate to say that none of us can figure out what's going on. Maybe Durbin is right. We're looking at a bunch of reenactors getting into their roles. But we need to go into that crowd and mingle so we can get some information. I want to know what they thought about the *Daylight Event* and whether they know something that we don't. With all of the military bases around here, I'm sure they've seen combat fatigues before, but if we just walk into the street in uniform, the conversations will turn to why we're wearing modern fatigues and not Civil War costumes. We need to blend in."

"Look at the store next to the theater," Conroy continued. "It says Morton's Dry Goods. I'd be surprised if they don't stock period clothing. The store looks closed, so we'll have to do some personal shopping. I have cash, so after we rob the place I'll just leave what we owe."

Jackson chimed in. "Better not leave any fives or fifties, Lieutenant. If these nut jobs see bills with Lincoln or Grant on them they may totally freak out. Wouldn't want to ruin their show."

"Not a bad point, Chief."

Entering a locked building is a minor challenge for a SEAL. Before breaking the lock they looked for any wires or evidence of an alarm device.

"The place doesn't have any kind of alarm system at all, Lieutenant," said Chief Jackson. "This store would never make it in South Philly."

They each picked out trousers, a shirt, a coat, boots, and a hat. The clothing didn't fit well even though the sizes were marked, but judging from the wardrobes in the crowd they should blend in perfectly.

Conroy found a cash box and withdrew the contents, about $75. "Like you said, Chief, these bozos are playing this authenticity bit so hard they even stock antique bills and coins."

"Smitty, I want you to take Reilly with you and see if you can find your cousin's apartment building. Let's hope she and her husband are home. Maybe they can explain this. If they're not home, walk around the neighborhood and record your observations."

"Okay, move out. Side arms only. Leave all rifles, grenades, and other equipment here. We'll rendezvous back here at 2300. Juarez, you'll stay here to watch our gear."

"Aye aye, sir."

They left through the back door.

"Okay SEALs, we're heading for that saloon over there, the one called Gabbey's. Order beers only and sip slowly. I want everybody's nerves and minds sharp. Here's some cash for each of you. Go in two at a time. I don't want to look like we're a group. Giordano will go in with me."

"Should we talk with southern accents Lieutenant?" asked Tony (Geo) Giordano, a native of Brooklyn.

"I wouldn't worry about it, Geo. Probably half the people we'll see are from up north, here to enjoy the reenactment. Your Brooklyn accent will do just fine."

"Fuggeddaboutit," said Giordano.

Conroy and Giordano entered the saloon. "Just act casual," said Conroy.

"How else can you act in a gin mill, Lieutenant?"

Just as on the street, everyone in the bar wore period costumes. A guy in the corner wore a straw hat and played old Dixie tunes on an upright piano. As they approached the bar, they noticed one of the customers let go of a great gob of tobacco juice into a spittoon.

Giordano leaned over to Conroy and said, "These fucking people need a life, Lieutenant."

"I think you have a point, Geo, but I want more specific observations."

The two men walked up to the bar and ordered their beers. The bartender sported a handle bar mustache, a striped shirt with garters holding up his sleeves, and a white apron. Conroy turned to a man at the bar who wore a bowler hat and well tailored clothes.

"How are you this evening?" said Conroy.

The man responded with a refined southern accent, "I'm doing just fine sir, enjoying the springtime weather. If you don't mind me asking, sir, you sound like you're a Yankee. Where are you from?"

Conroy sensed that the man was friendly so he figured he'd loosen things up with humor. "I'm from Wisconsin, and I prefer the Milwaukee Brewers." The man didn't get the joke, having never heard of the Milwaukee Brewers. "Are you from around here friend?" asked Conroy. The man told him that he was a native Charlestonian, and volunteered that he was the president of the local bank. Great, thought Conroy, a guy with his finger on the pulse of the city. Conroy decided to jump right in.

"Were you awake for that crazy light event last night?" He tried to sound casual about the most amazing thing he had ever seen.

"What light event, sir?"

"Well at about 0300, er, 3 a.m., the darkness suddenly became bright daylight. It lasted for about two minutes."

The man looked puzzled. He shouted down the bar, asking anyone in earshot if they saw the night turn to daylight in the early morning hours. Nothing but shrugs and confused looks.

Conroy decided to change the subject. "So, it looks like all you folks are ready for the big reenactment."

"Reenactment? Of what?" asked their banker friend.

"You know, the reenactment of the Battle of Fort Sumter."

"Sir," said the banker, "between the daylight at darkness and your talk of something being reenacted, you have managed to confuse me. There have been rumors, God knows, that General Beauregard intends to fire on Fort Sumter, but most of it is just irresponsible war talk."

\* \* \*

Back at Morton's Dry Goods store, Petty Officer Juarez patrolled the shop and noted his findings. He hit the record button.

"This is Petty Officer Emilio Juarez reporting from Morton's Drygoods store in Charlestown, South Carolina. The time is 2205 on April 10, 2013. Pursuant to orders from Lt. Conroy I'm recording my observations and impressions. Although the light is dim, I can see my surroundings from the gas light outside the store. As we've been saying, these reenactors take their job very seriously. This store is decked out to look like something from the Civil War era. I just can't understand why they didn't just put out some old stuff for tourists to photograph and keep the regular goods in a corner or another room. The floor creaks like you would expect from old lumber. There isn't a piece of tile or linoleum in sight. I'm now looking behind the checkout counter. I expect to see a computer or at least a laptop under the counter. None. There is no adding machine, no cash register and no electronic gear of any kind. I can't find any electric outlets either. Wait, here's a newspaper." Juarez took out his flashlight, turned off the recorder, and walked behind a wall so he wouldn't be seen from the street. The headline read:

## "War Talk Grows Louder"

The newspaper was dated April 10, 1861. Holy shit, thought Juarez. These reenactors don't miss a trick. He turned the recorder back on and dictated his findings from the newspaper, minus the "holy shit."

Petty Officers Smith and Reilly were looking for Smitty's cousin's building. Five months ago, thought Smitty, this street was absolutely charming, a typical block in a prosperous city that tried to look antique, but with all the modern amenities. Five months back, every other group of shops had a name that ended in "Mews" or "Commons."

"There it is," said Smitty. "I remember her building's next to that old firehouse. I remember the beautiful carvings."

After they passed the firehouse Smitty froze. Instead of the upscale condo building that he had visited a few months before, there was now a warehouse. He recalled his cousin telling him that condos often were built in old warehouses, a common tool of an imaginative real estate developer. The facade of the building had the same shape and stonework it did five months ago, but it wasn't modernized. He recalled polished mahogany paneling around the doorway inlaid into a stainless steel frame. Now it's just a warehouse with a plain entrance of stone. He remembered that he had a perfect view of the Cooper River Bridge from this very spot. But there is no bridge.

They continued to walk the neighborhood, snapping pictures and dictating their observations. A few of the houses had small yards. Instead of the sounds of urban traffic he heard five months ago, all they heard were cows mooing and chickens clucking. They came upon an area with a fenced-in enclosure of split rail fencing. Inside the enclosure were about a dozen passenger buggies in various states of disrepair.

"I guess this is what a used car lot used to look like 152 years ago," Reilly said.

Smitty turned on his recorder and described the "used buggy lot." He added, "I wonder why, for a reenactment, people would set out a bunch of broken down carriages." They were about to cross a street but had to stop for a large cart drawn by two huge horses that looked like they came from a Budweiser commercial. They crossed the street after the cart had passed. A man sat on a bench smoking a pipe.

"Good evening," said Smitty.

"Ready for the war, boys?" said the man.

"War?"

"Everybody's talking about it," said the man, tapping his pipe. "Wouldn't be surprised if it happens any day now."

"You don't mean the reenactment ceremony at Fort Sumter tomorrow do you?"

"Reenactment of what?"

Smitty wished the man a good evening, and the two walked on.

* * *

Jackson and Donnelly entered the bar last. Jackson noticed that he was the only black person in the place. A tall, slim man with a beard and a Stetson hat walked up to Jackson, along with two other men. Jackson imagined a movie director calling a casting agent and saying, "Send me three people who look like characters from *Deliverance*."

The tall man with the Stetson squared off in front of Chief Jackson and said, "Wachoo dewin heah boy?" SEALs are trained to act fast and think faster. They're also trained to keep their emotions to themselves and to concentrate on one thing: the mission. Jackson's first inclination was to turn this cracker's face into meatloaf, but he stopped short. He thought to himself: We've been sent here to look, observe and report. Our recon mission does not include busting up a bar. It's time to role play.

"Pahdin me, suh," said Jackson, "my massa done tole me to come here to look see if I kin find his brotha. I ain't seein him, so I'll be gittin on." He walked out the front door. Conroy had seen the encounter and motioned with a flip of his head to Donnelly, indicating that he should follow Jackson. Donnelly slipped out a side door and strolled a distance behind Jackson, who was walking back toward Morton's Dry Goods. Donnelly's eyes scanned the street to make sure that the three primitives from the bar were not in pursuit. He didn't notice that the three had run across the street behind a large cart that blocked his view. As Jackson walked down the alley toward the rear door, the three jumped out in front of him.

"Ah thought ya'll was fixin to go back to yo massa, boy. Looks lahk ya'll needin some whuppin."

Jackson stopped role playing. He said with his dialect-free voice, "Ah, Mr. Meatloaf Face, so nice to see you again."

"Wachoo call me, boy? It's time for you to meet yo maker," said the man as he drew a large hunting knife with a 6-inch blade. His companions drew theirs at the same time. Jackson realized he was about to be murdered. Suddenly, Mr. Meatloaf Face saw a dark four knuckled piston rocketing out of the darkness toward his eyes. The karate punch caved in his nose, fractured both eye sockets, and drove the resulting mass of tissue and bone into his brain. As his lifeless body fell, Jackson delivered a high arcing kick to the temple of the second man, crushing his skull and causing a massive brain hemorrhage. The third froze, as Jackson caved in his solar plexus with four rapid punches. The man was dead before he hit the ground.

Petty Officer Donnelly came running up the alley. He saw the entire confrontation even though he sprinted. "Are you okay, Chief?"

"I'm doing better than these guys." The two men dragged the bodies into a nearby clump of bushes. Hearing the commotion, Juarez ran to the alley, his M4A1 carbine at the ready.

\* \* \*

Lieutenant Conroy continued his conversation with his new banker friend at the bar. Petty Officer Durbin joined them. "So why are Yankees so unpopular around here?" Conroy asked as pleasantly as possible, looking for information.

"I have a number of Yankee friends and business associates," said the banker, "all of whom are fine people. The problem is those damn meddling Northern politicians, especially Abraham Lincoln."

Conroy and Giordano glanced at each other. Giordano chimed in. "What do you think of Barack Obama?"

"Who?" said the banker. The look on the man's face, as both Conroy and Giordano would later agree, belied any pretense, faking, lying, acting, or reenacting. This man had never heard the name Barack Obama, the President of the United States.

Petty Officer Durbin struck up a conversation with three guys who looked like fishermen, judging from their clothing and scent. One of the men asked him, "Have you seen the *Gray Ship*?"

"No I haven't," said Durbin. "What is it?"

"That thing is about 1,000 feet long," said the fisherman. "It had a big white number 36 painted on each side of her bow. I couldn't see the name on the stern because the ship was so fast."

Another fisherman spoke. "One thousand feet? Shoot, the damn thing was at least 2,000 feet long."

Durbin asked, "Was it a Navy ship or some kind of merchant?"

"That thing is definitely military," said one of the men. "It had guns that must have been 100 feet long and a foot wide."

Conroy glanced at his watch, which he kept in his pocket. It was 2245, almost time to rendezvous at Morton's. They exchanged pleasantries and departed their new banker friend. As he and Giordano walked for the door, Conroy gave a head motion to Durbin, who politely broke off his conversation with the fishermen.

The SEALs met at 2300 as planned. Chief Jackson debriefed everyone on his encounter with the thugs in the alley. Donnelly said that he had seen the entire thing and would give a written report to Conroy when they got back to the ship. They were SEALs, not cops, but they were on a surveillance mission with no clear Rules of Engagement.

"We'll change into our fatigues back at the boat," Conroy said. "Grab any other piece of clothing you can find on the shelves. Something tells me we may need a change of outfits down the road. Also bring ladies' garments. Captain Patterson or another of our female crew may visit the shore at some point. It will be tight but I want to bring as much stuff as we can fit on the Zodiac. Anything that doesn't fit we'll stash in the bushes and pick up later. I hope Mr. Morton has insurance."

"Lieutenant," Chief Jackson said, "are we going to plan to be back at the ship at 0300 or sooner?"

"We've accomplished our mission," Conroy said. "Hanging out any longer may be a problem, especially since your encounter with those thugs. The boat is about a 20 minute walk from here. On our way to the boat I want everyone to take as many photos as you can. Let's empty the shelves and move out."

Chief Petty Officer Jackson, age 32 had seen intense combat in Iraq and Afghanistan. He had been wounded and had taken many lives. But he had just gone through the most amazing experience of his life, and now his very presence was changing the mission. He grew up in a racially mixed neighborhood in Philadelphia. He had white friends and black friends, white neighbors and black. He never gave race much thought. Although he'd seen prejudice in his life, he was never obsessed with it. But he had never experienced sheer hatred as he did from those thugs in the alley. He had to kill to save his own life.

On their way back to the ship they noticed much heavier boat traffic in the harbor. "Carbines ready, lock and load." Conroy didn't want any trouble with "reenactors." He decided to break radio silence, as was his option. He didn't worry about anyone in this strange place intercepting a radio transmission. "Lima Juliette, Lima Juliette (The radio call sign of the *USS California*) this is Tango Xray.

"This is Lima Juliette, go ahead Tango Xray."

"Please advise the Captain that we're returning to the ship, ETA 20 minutes"

"Roger, Tango Xray, Lima Juliette out."

They knew they were heading for a debriefing. A debriefing that may change history, Conroy thought.

# Chapter 7

When they returned to the ship, Conroy and his fellow SEALs were ordered to report to the Captain's office. Besides the SEALs and Captain Patterson, the others present were Executive Officer Phil Bradley and all department heads. Captain Patterson also invited Commander Rick Sampson, the ship's chaplain. Ashley and Chaplain Sampson were long-time friends. He was a history buff, like her, and she wanted his input into the bizarre events of the last few hours.

"Lieutenant Conroy, please proceed and tell us about your findings ashore."

"Captain, I've assembled my notes and will write out a more detailed report, but we can give you a good idea of what happened now while it's fresh in our minds. I'm going to ask my men to jump in and add anything that I may have missed."

Conroy reviewed their few hours ashore. He discussed the period costumes, the lack of anything electrical or electronic, the absence of motor vehicles, and the architecture, which was nothing like modern photos of Charleston. He reported the burglary of the clothing which he deemed a mission necessity. He also discussed Chief Petty Officer Jackson's encounter with the attackers and his need to dispatch them. Chief Jackson answered a few questions about the incident. Conroy then handed Captain

Patterson the newspaper that Juarez found, with the headline, "War Talks Grow Louder."

"Petty Officer Smith was here in Charleston five months ago to visit his cousin," Conroy said. "I believe I mentioned that before we left. I'll ask Smitty to fill you in on what he saw today and what he saw five months ago."

Smith recounted his futile search for his cousin's apartment, telling them about the familiar building that was a condo complex five months ago and is now a warehouse. He also discussed the Cooper River Bridge, the most prominent structure in Charleston, which has simply disappeared.

"Lieutenant Conroy, please give us a one sentence conclusion of your findings," Captain Patterson said.

Conroy took a deep breath and came right to the point. "Captain, today is not April 11, 2013, but April 11, 1861." Every SEAL in the room nodded vigorously in agreement.

"Frank," the Captain said to Conroy, "I'm sure that you and your guys realize that what you just said is absurd. Science fiction is just that, fiction. We live in a real world that wants real explanations. Please defend your conclusion."

"Captain, we talked about this on our way back to the ship. We all agreed that the people we saw and met are either the greatest actors in the world, or they're for real. We wondered if we just witnessed a big conspiracy or practical joke, with everyone in on the joke except us. But one thing is beyond a doubt and has nothing to do with our opinions: those buildings that we saw in the photos of modern Charleston, which I can verify from my previous visits here, and which Petty Officer Smith confirmed from his visit five months ago, did not tear themselves down and somehow get rebuilt as nineteenth-century structures. That beautiful new bridge is nowhere to be seen. We have plenty of photos and video clips from our phones. It's simply unbelievable that the 'reenactors' could have hidden all evidence of electrical outlets and electric gear. Also, when Petty Officer Giordano and I were talking to that guy I mentioned, he had never heard of President Barack Obama. He wasn't acting; he never heard of our president."

Giordano chimed in and said that the expression on the man's face was simple honesty, not an act. Others talked about the chatter they heard referring to Abraham Lincoln.

"Captain," Conroy concluded, "tomorrow is April 12, 1861. Fort Sumter will be bombarded, and the Civil War will begin."

\* \* \*

Ashley knew that she had to communicate to the entire crew. *Scuttlebutt* is the Navy term for gossip. The word is derived from the cask of drinking water on old ships, around which sailors gathered to sip water and exchange information. Unless she talked directly to the crew there would soon be scuttlebutt that the ship went through a nuclear event or worse. She would address the crew at 0800.

The salty shrill tweet of the boatswain's pipe rang through every compartment on the ship. "Attention all hands, attention all hands, stand by for Captain Ashley Patterson."

Ashley leaned into the microphone. "Good morning. By now every crew member of the *California* has heard about the strange event that occurred early yesterday morning. You are aware that we have no Internet access or cell phone service. We've also lost satellite navigation, ship-to-ship as well as ship-to-shore communications, except for two-way radio. All other shipboard systems are operational, including radar and sonar. A few hours ago I sent a SEAL reconnaissance team ashore to investigate and report their findings. They have reported back. Based on their report, including photographic evidence, I have come to a conclusion and the heads of all departments agree: In some way that we don't understand, we find ourselves in April 11, 1861. We have gone back in time 152 years. If our conclusion is correct, tomorrow Fort Sumter will be fired on, and the Civil War will begin. I will update you as we learn more. That is all."

The ship was silent, as if in prayer.

# Chapter 8

The Chaplain of the *USS California*, Father Rick Sampson, graduated from The University of Michigan in 1989, and received a doctorate from Yale Divinity School. As an Episcopal priest he had looked forward to a parish assignment where he would enjoy a career tending to a flock in his home state of Iowa. A friend from Yale suggested that a flock that always needs tending is the one aboard a Navy ship. Father Rick decided to give it a try and first reported for duty aboard the *USS Independence* in July of 1993. He loved the Navy from the start, and agreed with his friend that sailors were a flock in need of spiritual care. Like many a Navy chaplain, Father Rick was a hit with the crew. Most of them call him *Padre* when addressing him, the traditional Navy term for chaplain. Among his many talents he plays a great guitar, and loves nothing more than jamming with the crew. Besides his friendliness, what crewmembers especially like about Father Rick is that he's a man they can confide in when they need help, that special kind of help that's needed on long tours of sea duty. He's tall, broad shouldered, burly, and has a galvanic laugh. The normal expression on his face is a smile. His rank is commander, but his personality is that of a friendly neighbor, one you can turn to. According to people who know him, Father Rick is also a student of almost everything. He doesn't so much read as devour books. His special love is history, specifically the American Civil War. He wrote two books on religious observances during the Civil War, and he's appeared as a consultant in the credits of dozens of history books.

Father Rick is also good friends with his commanding officer, Ashley Patterson. Both Episcopalians, the two officers hit it off since they first met at the Pensacola Naval Air Station in 1999. Ashley and her late husband Felix dined often with Father Rick and his wife Janet. They all shared a love of history. When Ashley Patterson took command of the *California*, she was happy to find that her long-time friend was the ship's chaplain.

\* \* \*

"So, my spiritual advisor, friend, and Civil War maven, please tell me that God spoke to you during the night, and wants you to tell your commanding officer that everything is just hunky dory."

Father Rick let out one of his famous belly laughs and said, "Hey, Captain Ashley, just because we suddenly find ourselves 152 years in the past doesn't mean it should ruin our day."

Ashley cracked up. She hadn't laughed in many an hour, and it felt strange. "Whatever you eat to get such a positive attitude, I want the recipe."

"I just eat what's there and let God handle my attitude."

\* \* \*

"Have you ever heard of The Black Swan Theory?" asked Father Rick.

"Yes," said Ashley. "Some economist came up with it. It means something big, surprising, and unpredictable that changes the shape of things. He called these things black swans because they're so rare. I remember he used it to describe the economic meltdown in 2008."

"Exactly, Captain. And what these events have in common is that they can't be predicted easily, and some not at all. There are bad Black Swans, like the Tambora Volcano eruption in Indonesia in 1815, the Tunguska Siberia asteroid hit in 1808, the terror attacks of 9/11, the Great Japanese tsunami, and the perfect financial storm of 2008. There are also positive Black Swans such as the discovery of the transistor, the microchip, or the launch of Google."

"What we have here Captain is a Black Swan, the *Daylight Event*. None of us saw it coming and we certainly couldn't have predicted it. It could have a long term impact on history, although to predict that we'd be soothsayers. So we find ourselves in the middle of the biggest Black Swan we could ever have imagined. Because we couldn't predict it, we have no idea how to handle it."

Ashley put her face close to her friend's and looked into his eyes.

"Rick. Help me, help my crew, help my country. Tell me something to point me in the right direction."

"Seaman Jack," said Father Rick.

"Who's he?"

"Seaman Jack is one of the most interesting sailors on this ship. He holds the low rank of Seaman, having recently joined the Navy, but he's about your age. He's one of the smartest people I've ever met, and he's written a slew of books. And there's another thing about him that I think you'll find interesting."

"And just what kind of interesting information could this seaman have for me, Father?"

"Seaman Jack can explain the *Daylight Event*."

# Chapter 9

shley called Lt. Commander Karen Sobel, the ship's personnel officer, and asked for the file on Seaman John Thurber. She wanted to learn about this sailor before she met with him. In what seemed like another lifetime she would have just Googled his name, but now she would have to settle for a paper file. She sat at her desk with a cup of coffee and opened the file of the sailor who so impressed Father Rick. It was not what she expected to see for a man who holds the rank of Seaman. John Thurber, or Seaman Jack as Father Rick calls him, graduated from Yale at the top of his class with a degree in history, after which he received a master's degree from the Columbia School of Journalism. He's a widower, his wife Nancy having died in a car accident in 2008. He has no children. His most recent job, prior to joining the Navy, was Feature Articles Editor for *The New York Times*. He's the author of ten non-fiction books and three novels. He won a Pulitzer Prize for a feature article in the *Los Angeles Times* entitled, "The Tonkin Gulf Affair: The Real Story."

Among his long list of accomplishments, a particular entry jumped out at Ashley. One of his non-fiction books, *Living History — Stories of Time Travel Through the Ages,* was on *The New York Times* Best Seller list for 48 weeks. This page of his personnel file would forever be marked by a dark liquid stain, a result of Ashley Patterson spitting coffee all over it.

Ashley called Corporal Arnold Nesbitt, her Marine aide, and ordered him to bring Seaman Jack to her office.

Seaman Jack Thurber entered the Captain's office wearing standard fatigues, the uniform of the day. Jack was about 6'2" with broad shoulders and an athletic build. His eyes were the color of the Caribbean on a sunny day. His eyes are beautiful, Ashley thought, but they also have a certain sadness about them. He has close cropped sandy brown hair. Ashley thought that this guy is one of the handsomest men she had ever seen, quickly reminding herself that such a thought is completely irrelevant to this meeting.

"Please have a seat, Seaman. Would you like a cup of coffee?"

"No thank you, Captain."

Ashley skipped over small talk, the usual way to start a meeting. She hated small talk, wasn't good at it, so why bother.

"Seaman Thurber, Chaplain Sampson said that I should talk to you, that you may have some information that can help us understand the strange event we've experienced. But first, I need to know something. I've read through your personnel file and noticed that you're quite an accomplished guy, to say the least. You've gotten a bachelor's and master's degree from two great universities, and you've written a lot of books and articles. You even won a Pulitzer Prize. I see that you've also served in senior editorial posts at major newspapers. Quite a distinguished career in journalism, I'd say. But what jumps from your personnel file is that you've just enlisted in the Navy at the age of 34, the maximum age permissible. I love my Navy and I don't question anyone's reasons for joining, but with your education you could have enrolled in Officer's Candidate School and joined the Navy as a commissioned officer. Why join as an enlisted man?"

"The answer is very simple, Captain. I'm writing a book about life in the Navy from an enlisted person's perspective. As a journalist I like to do research from an insider's point of view. I enlisted in the Navy to do research for my book — after hours, of course."

This explanation was one of the more interesting reasons Ashley ever heard for joining the Navy, but it made perfect sense. "I always like a straight answer to a question. Thank you Seaman."

"I guess you've figured out that I didn't call you here to talk about your career."

Jack chuckled. "No, ma'am, I didn't think that was the reason."

"Let me lay out the situation for you, Seaman Thurber. Father Rick seems to think that you will have some insights that may help us. Take a look at these."

Ashley laid out the photographs of the Charleston waterfront taken a few months ago. They were the typical pictures of a modern city, with gleaming buildings, a modern bridge and a bustling waterfront. She then showed him the photos taken by the SEALs. Instead of glass enshrouded buildings, the structures were all masonry, no taller than four stories. She then showed him photos of the street scene with people dressed in mid-nineteenth-century garb. Referring to her notes, Ashley gave him a synopsis of the debriefing from the SEALs, including their observations about the lack of electricity, modern equipment, and motor vehicles. She also discussed Petty Officer Smith's comparison of the city he visited five months ago to the way it is now.

"Here's the bottom line, Seaman Thurber, if there is a bottom line to this craziness. Lt. Conroy and every one of the SEALs on the recon squad came to the same conclusion: Today is April 11, 1861, not April 11, 2013. As I said in my announcement to the crew, we are living 152 years in the past."

Jack rubbed his face, stared at the desk, and then looked into Ashley's eyes. "I guess you want to talk to me about my book, *Living History.*"

"That would be a good guess, Seaman. When I read about it in your file I immediately went to download it onto my Kindle, but, of course, that plan didn't go too far."

"Don't worry Captain, I always carry a few copies with me. I'll be happy to give you an autographed edition."

\* \* \*

The squawk box squawked. "Captain Patterson this is Lt. Tomlinson, the Officer of the Deck on the bridge. Pick up please."

"This is the Captain, go ahead Lieutenant."

"Ma'am, the XO told me to report any suspicious sea traffic activity directly to you. There is a small fast paddle-wheel boat that's been trailing us for a few minutes. He seems very curious."

"Can you blame him Lieutenant?" said Ashley. "Keep me apprised if there's any sign of hostile intent."

"Aye aye, Captain."

Ashley turned back to Seaman Jack. "Just a sample of the strange things that have been happening."

"Jack, (it's frowned upon for officers to address enlisted sailors by their first names, but Ashley was beginning to feel very comfortable with this man) tell me about time travel. Tell me how the impossible is possible."

"Actually, Captain, time travel is *theoretically* possible. It just seems impossible to our human senses. In physics there's a theory called the Einstein-Rosen Bridge, also known as a wormhole. It's derived from Einstein's General Theory of Relativity. Wormholes, or time portals as some call them, appear throughout the literature of time travel. I'm no scientist, but I've read a lot about this. I've also discussed it with at least five physicists who are listed in the credits to my book. To sum it up, if $E=MC^2$, then it's possible for a portal or wormhole to exist in space and time. I can't say that I understand all the math, but physicists love playing with this stuff."

* * *

Although his book was 650 pages long, Jack summarized it, a talent acquired after many years of pitching manuscripts to literary agents. He told Ashley that the book had two main parts. The first part is a review of the fictional literature of time travel over the years. The second part of the book consists of interviews with people who claimed to have travelled through time. He began with the classic, *The Time Machine* by H.G. Wells written in 1894, the first book to use the term *time machine*. He also talked about *A Connecticut Yankee in King Arthur's Court*, Mark Twain's time travel classic written in 1889. He synopsized dozens of other time travel novels, as well as movies such as the comedy *Back to the Future*. Almost all of the works have one subtext in common: Don't change the past because the future may surprise you.

Jack then discussed his interviews with a dozen people who claimed to have traveled in time. "This was the hardest part of writing the book. I interviewed over a hundred 'time travelers,' but most of them were obviously imbalanced, the same kind of people who think they were abducted by aliens. The dozen who made it into the book were normal people, except they all claimed to have done the impossible." Jack explained that he brought a friend with him on these interviews, one of the book's contributors, a psychiatrist with the New York City Police Department, Dr. Benjamin Weinberg, who went by the nickname Benny. Weinberg had a rare skill in spotting lies. He was a hit with every prosecutor he ever worked with. They swore that Weinberg's testimony was better than a polygraph machine. As a joke he carried a business card that read, "Dr. Benjamin Weinberg - Bullshit Detector."

Benny Weinberg told Jack that each of the time travel interviewees was telling the truth, and any one of them would be a star on the witness stand. "These fuckers (Benny also considered himself a hardened cop, and his language showed it) are either the straightest shooting people I've ever seen, or they're a new breed of psychopath that I never encountered before."

Ashley peppered Jack with questions, especially about the personal interviews. "Did their stories have anything in common?"

"Yes. None of them started their time journeys intentionally. It just happened. Also, the time portal, or wormhole, always had a specific location. That's how they were able to get back to the present. It's also interesting that not one of them tried to go back in time once they returned to the present. A couple of them have traveled more than once, but never intentionally, except for the return trip."

Jack also told Ashley, as he had written in his book, that the times the people visited varied all over the place. One guy went back 1200 years to the Bronze Age. Another travelled back to World War I.

"One of the people," said Jack, "travelled four times. He always went back to the same period of time, twenty years in the past. He experienced all of his journeys in the mid 1980s, so his travels took him back to the mid 60s. One time he found himself in New York in 1965 on the Number 7 train heading toward Flushing, Queens. The doors opened at the 109th Street Station in Corona, and he could hear the crowd at Shea Stadium, roaring for the Beatles concert. In 1969 he found himself at Altamont Speedway for the famous Rolling Stones concert. His two other journeys also involved rock & roll, but he couldn't remember those other two bands. Doctor Benny thought he saw a clinical explanation for the phenomenon. Four time travels, four rock & roll concerts. Could it be the guy just vividly imagined things that were imbedded in his subconscious mind? On further questioning it turned out the guy was a classical music teacher who hated rock & roll, and couldn't even name one individual Beatle or Rolling Stone. He claimed that he never heard the names Paul McCartney or Mick Jagger."

Another common thread, Jack noted, was that the elapsed time between the start of the journey and the return to the present was relatively short, and never matched the time they spent in the past. "The World War I guy said that he was on the battle fields of France for over eight months. An artilleryman, he spent what seemed like ages wading through mud and hooking up horses to caissons. He recalled one incident while he sat in a trench. It was raining heavily. He faced up toward the rain and cried his eyes out, thinking he would never see his wife again. At that point he had been on the battlefield for just over seven months. When he returned to 1987, he was standing on the edge of the rear patio of his house, dressed in the same blue jeans, sneakers and a sweat shirt that he wore when he began his journey. His wife said to him, 'Where have you been? I've been looking all over the house for you for five minutes.'"

"Then there was the diner traveler," Jack said.

"Diner Traveler?" asked Ashley.

"Yeah," Jack said as he laughed. "This story is really weird. It's the only one where there were two time thresholds, hundreds of miles apart. This guy, named Phil, was sitting in a diner in Rochester, New York in July of 1983. It was 8:30 in the morning. He had just ordered his usual scrambled eggs and sausage. After he ordered, he realized he had left his wallet in his car. He excused himself and said he'd be right back. To get to his car, he took a short cut through a hedge opening, stepping on an old cement slab. Suddenly, he was standing on a street corner, in what he would soon learn was a suburb of Elkhart, Indiana. He looked down and saw that he stood on a storm grate. He had no idea where he was, only that he was in a nondescript suburban neighborhood. He looked up at the street signs to see if he recognized anything, a lucky move on his part, otherwise he would have never returned. The sign said Juniper Street and the cross sign read Elm Avenue. He began to walk. He estimated that he walked for three miles based on the elapsed time of 45 minutes, until he came to a business district. He was out of smokes, so he went to a convenience store. When he asked for a pack of Merits in a box, the proprietor said he never heard of Merits. They had Winstons, Marlboros, Luckies, Pall Malls, Chesterfields, and Camels. He asked for Marlboro Lights, and again the owner said he never heard of them. He bought a pack of regular Marlboros and grabbed a newspaper and a cup of coffee. He asked how much and the guy said that'll be 85 cents. He thought the guy was being nice because he didn't have his brand, so he just handed the guy a dollar and left, telling him to keep the change. He sat down on a park bench in a small memorial park to sip his coffee and read the newspaper. The paper was the *Elkhart, Indiana Bulletin*. Phil went back inside to ask the owner if he had anything from Rochester, New York. The owner, beginning to think Phil was a bit weird, just said, 'Don't get much call for Rochester news.' So Phil sat down with his coffee, lit up a butt and began to read. That's when the cigarette fell from his mouth into his coffee. The main headline was an update on the sinking of the cruise ship *Andrea Doria* on July 26, 1956. He looked at the date on the newspaper. It was July 27, 1956. He couldn't describe why, but, like all time travelers I've interviewed, he knew instinctively that he had to get back to the location he originally found himself. He began walking back to find the corner of Juniper and Elm. He became hopelessly lost, all of the houses appearing so similar. He finally came across a man who knew of the intersection and gave Phil instructions. After another thirty minutes of walking, he found Juniper and Elm, spotted the storm sewer grate, stepped on it, and was back in the hedge opening at the diner in Rochester, New York. He was back in 1983, after almost eight hours in the past. He noticed his wallet in his hand. He walked into the diner and sat down on the same stool he had vacated those long hours ago. The waitress put his plate in front of him and said, 'Sorry it took so long. We're training a new cook.' He looked at the clock on the wall. He had been gone for six minutes."

The longest anyone reported being away from the present was 12 hours.

"Do you know of anyone who couldn't to get back to the present?" Ashley laughed and answered her own question. "Obviously, we don't know because they were never seen again."

"That's right, and you raise an important point, Captain." Jack talked about his research for another book he wrote about crime statistics and missing persons. "Every year there are thousands of cases of missing persons that aren't solved. Most of the explanations make perfect sense: unhappy spouses, embezzling employees, military deserters, businessmen who screwed their partners, and many others who disappeared but had a motive to disappear. But there are hundreds of missing person cases every year that have no explanation at all, cases of apparently happy and contented individuals who just vanish. "We'll never know if some of these people are stuck somewhere on the wrong side of a wormhole in a different time."

"So let me ask you a blunt question, Jack. How do we get back to 2013?"

Jack asked if there was an exact navigational position recorded prior to the *Daylight Event*. When Ashley told him it was only an approximate navigational fix, Jack suggested that it may be possible to stumble into the time threshold by steaming back and forth until they hit it. Ashley noted this on her yellow pad in all caps.

"I do see a problem. All of the people I interviewed, including the crazies who didn't make the book, reported that the wormhole was a distinct place on land. I never heard of a portal located in the ocean."

\* \* \*

They had been together for over two hours, and neither wanted their time together to end. Ashley wanted to know more about this guy, and came up with a sneaky way to find out. "So, I bet your girlfriend is proud of all your success."

"I don't have a girlfriend, Captain. Since my wife died I've been dating my books." *Praise Jesus, no girlfriend.*

"I'm sorry, I know how hard it is," Ashley said. "As you may know I lost my husband a few years ago, and my ship has become my spouse. Felix was a Marine Major, killed in Afghanistan in 2008. We were classmates at Annapolis. It's not easy losing someone you love." Jack's reporter's antenna went up. Was she simply commiserating with a person who shared a similar tragedy, or was this gorgeous, charming woman opening her life to him for a reason?

More time went by as Ashley reviewed her notes and asked more questions. After each question she would sit back and gaze into his blue eyes as he answered.

"Well, Seaman Jack, this has been a terrific meeting."

Ashley noticed something about her own voice. She usually spoke in crisp military tones, common among career officers both men and women. But she noticed that as her meeting with Jack wore on, her voice softened, her commanding officer facade weakened.

Ashley said, "Is there anything else you think I should know at this point?" *Like what's your favorite type of food, drink, play, movie, song, like I want to know everything about you. Don't you want to tell me?*

"There is one thing Captain."

"Yes, Jack, what is it?" Ashley cooed. *Get a grip girl!*

"I'm going to tell you something I've only told to one other human being, my late wife." *Tell me honey, your secret's safe with me. Cut this crap out girl. NOW!*

"I have time travelled. Twice."

＊ ＊ ＊

Although their meeting was about to end, Ashley wanted to hear the details about Seaman Jack's personal travels through time. This could be very important. Also, it was kind of nice to have this guy around.

Seaman Jack began his story.

"My first trip, so to speak, occurred on October 29, 1996 when I was a 17-year-old high school senior. I was walking to a fishing pond in an old deserted area we knew as the Old Golf Course, which is what it had been until about 50 years before then. I love to fish, and my friends told me it was a great spot. The place was an overgrown mess, nothing but weeds and wild vegetation. As I walked down a path toward the pond I noticed a step made of bricks off to my right. I thought it was strange because the steps were the only man-made structure that I saw, except for the crumbling foundation of the old club house, about 100 yards from where I stood. I have no idea why, but I walked onto the bricks and then stepped down. It was the most amazing experience of my young life. The overgrown mess was suddenly a manicured golf course, and I stood near the 15th tee. My watch said it was 11:30 a.m., the exact same time before I stepped off the bricks. A foursome of golfers headed my way. They wore classic old fashioned golf attire from the 1920s, including knickers. They looked like characters from the movie *The Great Gatsby*. I guess they thought it was odd to see a kid in blue jeans wearing a sweatshirt that said "South Central High Basketball Champs 1993" and carrying a fishing pole near the 15th tee. 'How's the fishing today?' asked one of the men. I asked where I could find the pond and they all looked at me like I was crazy, which I began to think I was. I was thirsty, so I walked to the clubhouse to get some water. As I walked I noticed more golfers dressed like the 1920s. I didn't see any women. I also saw no golf carts.

The clubhouse was a beautiful old place. All of the rooms had walnut paneling on the walls. I walked into an area that looked like a lounge. I wanted to catch the news on TV. There was no TV. A water pitcher sat on a table with glasses, so I helped myself. I then walked into the bar to buy a soda. I thought I had stumbled into a wake. I never saw a bunch of more depressed people in my life. One man sobbed. Another guy, sitting at the bar and obviously drunk, kept saying, 'This is it. It's all over.'

I looked down at a table near the window and saw a copy of *The New York Times*. It was dated October 29, 1929 and had just one huge banner headline: 'Stock Prices Slump $14,000,000,000 in Nationwide Stampede to Unload.' Something told me to get the hell out of there. I couldn't think of any other way to do that than to go back to where this started. So I went to the brick steps, this time stepping up not down. I felt dizzy and then noticed that I was on the Old Golf Course and the pond was right nearby. I bent over, threw up, and went home. I never set foot in the Old Golf Course again."

"Why did you go back to that spot with the brick steps?" Ashley asked.

"I can't explain it. It just seemed like a way to undo something that was very strange. I figured if that's the place where the weirdness started, maybe that's where it would end. All of the other time travelers I interviewed said the same thing."

"What about your second experience?"

"I was 22 years old on December 7, 2001, just about 12 years ago. I went on a family vacation to Hawaii with my parents and my younger brother Harry. My Dad, a former Navy man you'll be happy to know, always wanted to visit Pearl Harbor, and he planned the trip so we could be there on the 60th anniversary of the Japanese attack. I worked for *The New York Times* and I was writing an article on Pearl Harbor, which dovetailed nicely with my parents' vacation invitation. Because it was only three months after the 9/11 attacks, the comparison to Pearl Harbor was a natural for any journalist, including me. Sunday morning my parents and Harry all decided to sleep late. I'm an early riser, so I woke up at around six and decided to walk along the harbor. I always loved history, and I imagined what this harborfront looked like 60 years before. It was 7:40 in the morning and I wanted to get a good viewing spot by 7:48, the exact time of the attack. As I walked along the concrete pier I noticed that there was a wooden board sunk right into the middle of it. For no reason that I remember, I stepped on the board. It sank down about an inch from my weight, and I tripped, falling forward. I managed to break my fall and avoid breaking my nose. I looked up at a propeller driven airplane heading straight for me firing machine guns. I ran off the pier and dropped down behind a bulldozer. Another plane flew by, and I noticed a big red rising sun insignia painted on its side. Some sixth sense told me that I shouldn't hide behind anything that may look like a target. I found a concrete drainage pipe and crawled inside. The sounds of bombs, bullets, and anti aircraft fire is difficult to explain. If hell exists, I think I was there. I looked at the *USS Arizona*, tied up to her birth in the harbor and not far from my position. The day before I stood on the memorial bridge over the ship that enables you to look down into the water and see her sunken hulk. Now she was very much afloat. Not for long. When the bombs ripped into the ship, the explosion shook the pipe I was in like a tin can. Fear can blunt your thoughts. You react to what's going on around you, and you can't draw conclusions easily. During a temporary lull in the bombing, my heart stopped racing enough to enable my brain to slip into reporter mode. I then realized that I was present at the attack on Pearl Harbor. I knew all about the second wave of bombers, so I decided I would use the lull to try to get away and return to 2001. Remembering my Old Golf Course experience of a few years before, I ran for the board in the middle of the pier. That's when I thought I'd never return. The concrete pier with the wooden board in the middle was now nothing but wooden boards. I stood in the approximate location where I went through the time portal, but couldn't get my bearings. The harbor looked very different in 1941. I then remembered the bulldozer that I first hid behind. I ran to the dozer and then onto the pier, going purely from memory, trying to retrace my steps. I lay down and looked at the dozer to give me the perspective I had when I first saw it. After a few position changes, I thought I found the spot where I tripped and I walked across the boards. Suddenly, everything became quiet except for a Navy band in the distance playing memorial music. The pier was concrete. I was back in 2001."

"Did you think you were losing your mind?" Ashley asked.

"Captain, I was *sure* I was losing my mind. As I told you before, you're the only person I ever told about these stories. The article I wrote for *The New York Times* about Pearl Harbor was a non-memorable travel piece, with some statistical comparisons to 9/11 thrown in. With all of the books and articles I've written, my life, if you'll pardon the pun, is an open book. But I've never talked about my own experiences with time travel, even in my book, *Living History*."

"Jack, I want you to keep thinking about those experiences. Yes, I know that you can't explain what happened, but you're the only person on this ship who has been through the portal, as you call it. You're the only guide we've got."

The meeting with Seaman Jack was over, and Ashley tried to sort through the astonishing things she had just heard.

She also realized that she loved the smell of Jack's after shave lotion.

# Chapter 10

It was April 11, 1861, one day before the start of the Civil War. As Ashley prepared her list for the next day, a thought struck her. That morning she had met with an over educated, highly accomplished man who held the second lowest rank in the Navy. He was the only one on the ship who could be described as a time travel expert. Because of his experience and his vast knowledge of the subject, Seaman Jack Thurber was one of the most important people on the *California*. But he was a seaman.

Ashley concluded that military necessity required that Seaman Jack Thurber become an officer. It's that simple. He's key to deciphering this strange mess, and that requires a managerial position. He's the only one on this ship who knows what time travel is all about. He needs to confer with senior staff, to attend meetings in the wardroom, and take on more responsibility than that of pay grade E-3. Because the ship would be at war the following morning at 0430, Ashley would have the legal ability to make what is often called a "battlefield promotion."

He also needs to spend more time in my office, a lot more, Ashley thought. Promoting Thurber to commissioned officer status had nothing to do with the Navy's prohibition against fraternizing with enlisted people. That's completely beside the point, Ashley told herself. She needed to make a command decision.

She rang her Marine aide Corporal Nesbitt. "Arnold, tell Seaman Thurber to report to my office immediately."

Thurber walked in and came to attention. "Good afternoon, Captain."

"Good afternoon Seaman Thurber, at ease." Ashley said with a crisp command voice.

"Seaman, that book that you're writing, the one about the Navy from a sailor's perspective — tell me if I'm wrong, but don't you think that recent events have made it irrelevant, at least for the time being?"

"I have to concur, Captain. I think I have a more interesting book in mind."

"I thought you'd agree."

"Then there's no reason why you should be an enlisted man rather than an officer."

Jack pointed out what he thought was an obvious problem with the idea that she floated. "Captain, there's no OCS for me to attend, no officer's training of any kind in our present circumstances."

"Seaman Thurber, tomorrow morning at 0430 Fort Sumter will be fired on. We will be at war. In time of war, Navy regulations authorize a commanding officer to make a battlefield promotion for the good of the service. At 0900 tomorrow we will have a special ceremony in the wardroom during which you will be appointed to the rank of Lieutenant Junior Grade. You will skip over the rank of Ensign. I'm going to do this because I need your knowledge and insights on a managerial level." *And I'll get to see a lot more of you. Stop it girl!*

"But Captain, all I know about the Navy is what I learned in boot camp, which is not exactly Annapolis. I don't see how I'm qualified."

"Let me ask you a few questions, Seaman Thurber."

"How do you distinguish bow from stern?"

"The bow is the pointy end."

"Excellent answer."

"What's the difference between port and starboard?"

"Starboard's right, port is left."

"Perfect."

"A staircase is called?"

"A ladder."

"Correct."

"When you walk to the stern, you walk?"

"Aft."

"Correct again."

"When you have to pee you go to the?"

"Head."

"Another correct answer."

"Seaman Thurber, you have achieved a score of 100. Tomorrow morning you will be Lieutenant Junior Grade Thurber. That is all. Dismissed."

\* \* \*

At dinner in the wardroom Captain Patterson discussed her meeting with Seaman Jack and announced her plan to appoint him a commissioned officer the next day. She discussed his credentials including his education and publishing achievements as well as his executive experience. She also talked about his knowledge of the phenomenon of time travel. She didn't mention his blue eyes. Or his after shave lotion.

What happened next shocked not only Captain Patterson but every officer in the room as well. Executive Officer Bradley said, "Captain I cannot agree with your promotion of Seaman Thurber. It will send a very bad message to the crew, especially the sailors who are in the Navy for a career. If they see a guy who they stood next to in the chow line one day who they would have to salute the next, I'm afraid morale could take a big hit. I think this is a reckless course of action."

The tension in the wardroom was almost painful. All eyes were glued to the table in front of them, as if to avoid looking at the scene of a car accident. Bradley had just crossed a bright line and violated a rule, both written and unwritten: never confront a commanding officer in public.

Navy regulations are written partially based on common sense. An executive officer is expected to voice any disagreement in strict privacy. In public he is expected to observe his role as second in command, not first. His job is to assist the captain in accomplishing the mission, and that includes showing physical and emotional deference to his commanding officer. Military people not only expect the process to work this way, they respect it. It's the way the system works. Military life is based on a chain of command. If one link in that chain is broken, as the analogy goes, the chain is weakened. When a chain is weakened, a ship can go adrift.

Captain Patterson had to think fast and act decisively. She couldn't ignore what Bradley said, nor could she ignore the negative dynamic that he created. There was a disturbance in the force and she had to undo it. Bradley had violated a cardinal military rule, and she knew that every officer in the room was on her side, for now.

"Commander," the Captain said, "we've all been under a tremendous amount of stress over the last day, and I'm sure that's includes you. I'm going to overlook your confrontational statement and scratch it off as an unintended response to the strange situation we're in." She then went in for the scoring shot. "Tomorrow at 0900 we will have a ceremony here in the wardroom, and Seaman John Thurber will be sworn in as Lieutenant Junior Grade Thurber. You, Commander Bradley, will perform the ceremony."

Bradley realized that he was boxed into a corner. He had just been given a direct order. Cross *that* line, and he may as well pack his bags. He simply said, "Aye aye, Captain."

One thought passed through the minds of every officer present, except for Bradley, "Go girl!" They realized that Captain Patterson had just righted a major wrong, and they were behind her. Even if Bradley had a good point, and a few thought he did, he violated a sacred military code to make it.

The next morning at 0430 the Battle of Fort Sumter would begin, and the Civil War would be on.

Ashley Patterson realized, as did the other officers in the wardroom, that another battle had just begun.

# *Chapter 11*

*G*eneral P.G.T. Beauregard had taken over command of the Confederate forces of South Carolina in March, 1861, making him the first general officer of the new Confederacy. Three months earlier, in December, 1860, South Carolina had issued an ordinance of secession, and was followed by six more Southern states in February, 1861. Beauregard would soon order a siege of the Union garrison at Fort Sumter, the plans for which were well underway.

Beauregard had a concern. He heard reports over the day about a gigantic *Gray Ship* plying the waters off Charleston. He called for his assistant, Major Ezekiel Townsend, and asked for a full report about the sightings.

Townsend went to the harborfront to find as much as he could about sightings of the *Gray Ship*. What he heard amazed him. He learned of no fewer than 15 sightings of the strange vessel. One man, the captain of a gun ship, told Townsend that he tried to follow the *Gray Ship*, but it was too fast. He described an array of odd shaped objects (guided missiles) as well as large deck guns. His gun boat was 45 feet in length. He estimated the *Gray Ship*'s length at least 15 times longer. He also noted that there were no visible smoke stacks and that the ship didn't let out any smoke at all. On the rear deck was a large machine of some sort that had long planks attached to its top (an Apache attack helicopter). He couldn't make out the name on the vessel's stern, but it had large painted numbers on the bow which was easily read as "36." Tall poles of some sort (antennae) were positioned all over the ship.

Townsend reported back to General Beauregard with his findings, especially the details provided by the gunship captain. "Fifteen times the length of a gunship?" Beauregard said. "Did this ship show any hostile intent to anyone sighting it?"

"No, General, but we just don't have enough information to determine her armament. All we know is that she's big, fast, and is covered with strange looking machines."

Beauregard wrote a message to Jefferson Davis, President of the Confederacy. He wanted Davis to know that the Yankees seem to have come up with an amazing new warship.

The bombardment of Fort Sumter would begin early the next morning. Beauregard decided not to wait for a reply from Davis, but resolved to go ahead with the plans and ignore the *Gray Ship*. He wondered how long the ship could be ignored.

# Chapter 12

W ars often begin with a great battle. The Japanese attack on Pearl Harbor, with over 3,000 lives lost, is a perfect example. Fort Sumter was not a great battle in a military sense, but its impact on history was profound.

In December 1860, five months before the bombardment, a Union Major, Robert Anderson, moved his command from nearby Fort Moultrie to Fort Sumter, a well fortified structure. General Beauregard, the Confederate commanding officer, systematically beefed up his gun batteries aimed at Fort Sumter. The SEAL recon team had seen evidence of this with large artillery caissons being wheeled toward the harborfront.

Abraham Lincoln, the new President of the United States, sent a message to the Governor of South Carolina, advising him that a ship would be dispatched to replenish the dwindling supplies at Fort Sumter. The result was an ultimatum from the Confederacy to abandon the fort. Major Anderson refused. The resupply ship was blocked, and Fort Sumter never got its replenishment.

At 0430 on the morning of April 12, 1861 Beauregard's guns opened fire on Fort Sumter.

\* \* \*

On the *USS California,* Captain Ashley Patterson checked her watch. At exactly 0430 she heard the first cannon volley. This isn't *Gone with the Wind* she thought. This is happening. She observed the action through a powerful telescope equipped with a night vision lens. She glanced at Ivan Campbell, the ship's navigator, who stood next to her. Neither officer spoke. People often feel a sense of elation when a prediction comes true. The two officers didn't feel elated. They were watching a grim confirmation of their strange new reality.

The bombardment lasted 34 hours until April 14, when Major Anderson, outmanned, outgunned, and short on supplies, agreed to abandon the fort. There were no casualties on either side as a direct result of the engagement. Two Union troops were killed when a gun exploded, ironically, during the surrender ceremony.

The Civil War had begun.

Ashley Patterson had a simple disturbing thought. Now what?

# Chapter 13

After breakfast in the wardroom, promptly at 0900, Captain Patterson called everyone to stand. Seaman John Thurber entered the room. As ordered, he wore an officer's khaki uniform, without any insignia on his lapels. Ashley turned to the Bradley and said: "Commander Bradley, please conduct the commissioning ceremony."

In a dry, desultory voice, Bradley read the oath of a commissioned officer in the United States Armed Forces. Ashley pinned Thurber's new bars on his uniform. Lieutenant Thurber saluted Ashley and she returned the salute. There was polite applause.

"Would you like to say a couple of words, Lieutenant?" said Captain Patterson.

Lieutenant Jack said, "Thank you ladies and gentlemen, and thank you Captain Patterson for acknowledging my vast military experience with this promotion." That brought a hearty laugh from all present, except Bradley.

"Lieutenant Thurber you will be assigned to the Communications Department. You will answer directly to Lt. Commander John White."

"Aye aye, Captain," said the ship's newest officer.

Bradley raged in silence. With this guy's background, he thought, he should be assigned to me. As XO, I'm the ship's chief administrative officer. The Navy's darling gets her way again.

\* \* \*

Ashley changed the subject. "We're going to head north. Because we're now at war, as strange as that may sound, we need to make contact with the Union government. The history books tell us that a man named Gideon Wells is the Secretary of the Navy, which was a cabinet position in 1861. He's the man we need to see. After all, he's our boss. Father Rick, our Civil War expert, tells me that Wells was a friend and confidant of Abraham Lincoln."

"How will we arrange a meeting, Captain?" asked Ivan Campbell.

Ashley said, "I'm going to send a delegation to simply walk into the Navy department and ask to see Wells. The leader of our delegation will introduce the group as representatives of the *Gray Ship*. That should open doors."

"Ivan, you'll lead the delegation," Ashley said. "Take Father Rick and Lt. Thurber with you. We need to show Secretary Wells that we know something about history, not to mention time travel. Your objective will be to invite the secretary to visit the *California*."

Bradley seethed. I should lead that delegation, he thought.

# *Chapter 4*

*T*he Executive Officer sat alone in his office sipping coffee. Things are starting to look clear, he thought. We're going to make contact with the Union high command and we'll be thrown into battle against the South. Like many on the ship, he had been reading up on the Civil War, and he knew what was coming. In July, about three months from now, we're going to throw our weight behind the Union forces at the Battle of Bull Run and turn a Confederate victory into a Confederate rout. It may even force a surrender and a quick end to the war. *Dashing Ashley* (the new nickname he used for Captain Patterson in his thoughts) will have another chapter in her story and another resume stuffer for her admiral's bars, bars that I should wear.

He never liked Ashley Patterson, and since she embarrassed him in the wardroom incident about Seaman Thurber's promotion, his dislike was turning to hatred. When she named Ivan Campbell to lead the delegation to the Navy Department, that cemented it. I'm second in command of this goddamn ship, he thought. I should be the one to make contact with the Secretary of the Navy.

Bradley realized that his career would soon be over, in 1861 or 2013. He was 45 years old and had been passed over twice for captain. Even though he had licked his drinking problem long ago, there were still black marks on his record. Because the captain is responsible for his annual fitness report, that wardroom incident probably tolled the end of his days in the Navy. I've been an officer since that bitch was in elementary school, he thought. Now she's a media darling, outranks me, and will probably be the final nail in my career coffin. I may as well be in the Confederate Navy.

Bradley sat bolt upright, spilling coffee all over his desk.

The Confederate Navy? As a Southerner and as a history buff, he always felt that the Civil War was a big mistake. But now that there's a war, is he on the right side?

The Confederate Navy, he kept thinking. If he were a Confederate officer he'd no sooner be a traitor to his country than Robert E. Lee or anyone who fought for the South. Not only would he become a captain, he thought, he could see a clear path to admiral. If Dashing Ashley and her new friend Lt. Thurber can figure out a way back to 2013, he would be perfectly content to finish out his career in the nineteenth-century. He has no wife, no kids, and very little that he wants to return to. Eighteen sixty-one sounds like a good year to me, he thought.

Bradley knows something that the Confederate command doesn't.

He knows the secrets of *The Gray Ship*.

# Chapter 15

The ship slowed to a position 10 miles southeast of the mouth of Chesapeake Bay, after a journey of 14 hours. The navigator was able to get a good fix with three church steeples that still existed on his 2013 charts. It was April 13, the day after the Battle of Fort Sumter.

The *California* carried a 40-foot motor launch with ample room to accommodate Secretary Wells and his delegation.

Captain Patterson ordered the boat lowered at 0400, well before sunrise. She had given up on the idea of total secrecy, knowing that there had been many sightings of the *Gray Ship*. The launch would find a place to tie up around dawn. The Marine corporal and the petty officer who was the boat captain were both armed and would provide security. If they were questioned, they would say they were from the *Gray Ship*.

Ivan Campbell, Father Rick and Lt. Jack Thurber boarded the launch at 0410. It was pitch dark, but the temperature was mild and the winds calm. Marine Corporal Robert Falanga tossed off the lines to a sailor on the ship. Petty Officer Michael Donizzio, the captain of the motor launch, maneuvered the boat away from the base of the ladder. Donizzio pulled the launch away from the *California* and steered toward the mouth of the Potomac River.

Campbell turned to Father Rick and Lt. Thurber and said, "I think this is a boat ride we'll never forget."

Father Rick looked at him and said, "Is that because we're motoring up the Potomac River in 1861 to visit the Secretary of the Navy and invite him to take a look at 2013?"

"Yeah, something like that Father," said Campbell.

Donizzio stayed in the center of the river because he did not have accurate charts for 1861. Although the boat was equipped with a depth meter, Donizzio knew, as did any experienced boater, that relying solely on a depth meter was poor seamanship. Water depth, especially in a busy river, can go from feet to inches in an instant, and many a boater has learned that a depth sounding device often lets you know that you're about to go aground in a couple of seconds. The launch was also equipped with radar, so piloting the boat up the Potomac wasn't difficult. They arrived at a pier that had a view of the not-quite finished Capital Dome. The time was 0545. Sunrise would be at 0630. Donizzio expertly guided the boat next to the pier, reversing her big diesel engines to bring it to a stop. Before he joined the Navy, Donizzio worked in his father's boatyard. Small boat handling came second nature to him.

Because it was still early, Donizzio put on a pot of coffee for his guests. As captain of the motor launch, he considered anyone aboard to be his guest.

"You'd make a great tour guide with your own boat, Mike," said Father Rick.

"Planning on it, Padre," said Donizzio. At 0800, Campbell said they should head for the Navy Department. Donizzio stepped onto the pier and walked up to a small building on the roadway that appeared to be a general store. He asked the proprietor where he could call for a carriage. The store owner called up to his son, who came bounding down the stairs.

"This young man will be happy to assist you," said the store owner. The kid, maybe 17 years old, ran behind the store and a couple of minutes later brought the horse drawn carriage to the front of the store. Donizzio hopped in and they rode down to the pier.

The carriage pulled up to the Navy Department at 0900. All three officers were wearing the period clothing that the SEALs had stolen from Morton's Dry Goods Store in Charleston.

The building that housed the Navy Department was a two-story structure with plain but elegant stone carving around its entrance, which was four steps above the street.

As they strode through the front door they all had the same thought: "No metal detector?"

The lobby of the building had no windows and was dimly lit by gas lamps. An officer sat at a desk off to the right about 25 feet from the entrance. On the other side of the room, opposite from the officer's desk, was a couch and a couple of chairs. Campbell walked up to the officer and got right to the point.

"Good morning, Lieutenant. We're officers from the *USS California*, which you may know as the *Gray Ship*. We've been sent by our captain to contact Secretary Wells."

Looking at their Morton's Dry Goods best the officer asked, "Are these your normal uniforms?"

"The Captain ordered the uniform of the day to be civilian clothes for the purpose of our visit," Campbell said.

"Please wait, gentlemen. I'll ask if Secretary Wells can see you." The officer walked through a large doorway opening.

Lt. Jack observed, "I guess they haven't invented an intercom system yet." They expected to be kept waiting awhile so they sat on the large sofa in the lobby. The union officer burst into the room in less than a minute.

"Secretary Wells will see you immediately," he said, trying to catch his breath. "Please follow me."

I guess the Secretary is anxious to see us, Campbell thought. They walked down a long hallway with quaint opaque windows on the doors, each imprinted with the purpose of the office. The officer opened the door and led them into Wells' office. The room was 20 feet by 20 feet, tastefully decorated with dark wood paneling. Each wall boasted paintings of famous naval battles.

Gideon Wells, age 59, with the largest white beard any of them had ever seen, sprang to his feet and almost sprinted around his desk to greet his visitors.

"So you're from the *Gray Ship* I've been hearing so much about," Wells said. "It is fortuitous indeed that you should seek me out." Charmingly stuffy language, thought Fr. Rick. "Gentlemen, my staff and I have been struggling for days to devise a plan to contact *you*. Please be seated." Campbell introduced his colleagues and himself.

A sailor appeared carrying a large tray with coffee, tea, and baked snacks. Wells asked, "Do you mind if I ask my aide, Commander Roebling, to join us?"

"Mr. Secretary, we're officers of the United States Navy," Campbell said. "That makes you our boss, sir. Please ask anyone you wish to join us." Commander David Roebling appeared and Wells introduced him.

Secretary Wells began the meeting. "I have heard many reports of *Gray Ship* sightings, most of which sound fanciful and not quite believable. Commander Campbell, please enlighten us."

Campbell began with the *Daylight Event*, and all of the strange things that happened over the last three days. He discussed Fort Sumter and how he witnessed the bombardment along with the captain. Campbell decided that he should get right to the major point and backfill the details. Gideon Wells was amazed. He didn't know that his mind was about to be blown, even though he wouldn't describe it that way.

"Our ship and all of its crew have somehow managed to stumble into an opening in time itself," Campbell said. "We've been calling it a time portal. Moments before the *Daylight Event* that I mentioned, the date was April 10, 2013, 152 years from now. We can't explain it, but one thing is certain: We have travelled through time; we are from the future."

Gideon Wells' eyes were riveted on Campbell. He then looked into the eyes of Fr. Rick and Lt. Jack. His aide Commander Roebling sat motionless, letting the Secretary deliver the response. "Gentlemen," said Wells, "do you expect us to believe this nonsense?"

"No sir, we don't," said Campbell. "That's why I'm here to extend the invitation of our captain to visit the *USS California*, the *Gray Ship*. We're inviting you to visit the future and see it with your own eyes."

# Chapter 16

Gideon Wells didn't want to waste any time, and he told Campbell that he would prepare to visit the *California* the next day. He told his aide, Roebling, to cancel all of his appointments for the next two days. He also told Roebling to find Admiral David Farragut and order him to join them. Farragut was an experienced admiral in the Union Navy, and Wells wanted an officer with a lot of sea knowledge to look at the *Gray Ship*.

Roebling arranged for sleeping quarters for the *Gray Ship* officers.

A coach took them to the waterfront at 8 a.m. the next day, April 14. As they approached the launch, Wells, Roebling, and Farragut exchanged glances. This elegant vessel was only a tender for the *Gray Ship*, Wells thought. Donizzio had tightened the lines to make it easier for his new guests to board the launch.

When they were all aboard, Campbell invited them into the pilot house. He introduced Donizzio, the boat captain, and asked him to explain the workings of the motor launch. Donizzio showed them the radar and depth meter, and described all of the switches on the large console. He pointed to the GPS plotter and explained that they had no satellite navigation. "Global Positioning System?" asked Farragut. Campbell, deciding that their education on twenty-first-century technology would begin now, answered his question. He described the rocket technology used to put satellites into orbit. He tried to explain how a metal object can orbit the earth.

"How many of these satellites are in the sky, Commander?" asked Wells.

"Over 1,000, sir, about half owned by the United States. But, of course, I'm talking about the year 2013. Now, presumably, there are none," said Campbell.

Donizzio asked Corporal Falanga to cast off the lines. When Donizzio turned on the twin Cummings diesel engines, each with 320 horsepower, the rumble was something that his new guests had never heard, or felt, before.

\* \* \*

Within a half hour, the *California* came into view. As they approached the ship, all that Wells, Farragut, and Roebling could do was stare. Neither they, nor anyone else in 1861, had ever seen a vessel so large. Farragut asked what about her top speed. When Campbell told him it was over 30 knots, he just shook his head. Campbell also explained the armaments that they were looking at. It was difficult to explain a guided missile to a man who fired cannon balls.

When they pulled next to the *California*, the ladder awaited them. Donizzio guided the boat so the exit gate lined up exactly next to the ladder threshold. As Wells stepped aboard, the shrill sound of the boatswain's pipe sounded across the ship, followed by, "United States Navy, arriving." It was the traditional way of announcing that a dignitary has just boarded the ship and what office the dignitary held. When Captain Patterson came aboard, the announcement would always be "*California*, arriving."

When the group reached the quarterdeck, the ship's ceremonial entry area, a phalanx of sailors in dress blues came to attention and saluted. Campbell escorted his guests to the captain's office. Wells and his colleagues would meet with the captain alone. The name Ashley can be male or female, and they were expecting to see a man. When Wells, Farragut, and Roebling were escorted into her office, Ashley almost felt sorry for them. As they looked at her they were more than confused, they were visibly flummoxed. In 1861 the very idea of a woman on a Navy ship was an anathema, but a woman captain was unbelievable. And a *colored* woman captain was unthinkable. Ashley approached each man individually and gave him a warm, firm handshake.

"Gentlemen, please be seated." They sat around a conference table. Ashley didn't want to sit behind her desk, in deference to the Secretary of the Navy. Ashley got right to the point.

"I realize that you're surprised that the *California's* commanding officer is not only a woman but a black woman, or 'colored' to use the language of your day." She gave them a brief synopsis of the advancement of African Americans over the past 152 years. She told them that two Secretaries of State in a row were black, and that the President of the United States in 2013 is a black man.

Gideon Wells, a staunch abolitionist, hated the institution of slavery and the treatment of "colored people." He even had changed parties from Democrat to Republican in no small part to support Abraham Lincoln in his White House run because he was so enthusiastic about Lincoln's desire to abolish slavery.

Wells looked at Ashley and said, "Madam Captain, I can only praise God that I have seen this day, and have seen with my own eyes the vindication of what President Lincoln stands for." He couldn't wait to report to Lincoln.

"Gentlemen, I fully appreciate how you must feel," Ashley said. "You're on a ship that you probably could not have imagined, meeting people who claim that they come from another time, and you're no doubt thinking that we all must be insane. I know that you would like an explanation of how this occurred. I'm afraid that I can't give you one because we're all as mystified as you. But the reality is that a few days ago this ship and all its crew were in the year 2013, and here we are in 1861. For lack of a better phrase, we've travelled in time. I believe you met Lieutenant John Thurber. Before he entered the Navy he was an well-known author and had written a famous book on the phenomenon of time travel. In a few minutes I'm going to ask Lt. Thurber to join us for lunch to answer all of your questions. I'm also going to invite Father Rick Sampson, our ship's chaplain, who you also met. Father Sampson, besides his religious vocation and Navy commission, is an expert on the Civil War. The war for us is history, but we now find that it has only just begun."

Father Rick and Lt. Jack were escorted into the captain's office where lunch was served. After lunch and a futile attempt at small talk, Ashley asked Lt. Jack to give their guests a synopsis of his book, *Living History,* as well as his personal experiences in crossing the time portal.

After Jack finished his report, Wells asked, "Lieutenant, in your two previous experiences going back in time, did you do anything that may have changed the future?"

"No sir," said Jack. "Although both of my experiences prior to this one were short, something just told me not to change anything. I guess it's a philosophical point Mr. Secretary. If you change the past, you won't know what the future may hold."

"Mr. Secretary, I think you have raised the most important question," Ashley said. "This ship can have a dramatic impact on the Civil War. Dare we do that?" Wells didn't reply. He just stroked his beard.

\* \* \*

Ashley asked Father Rick to discuss the Civil War, and what would happen over the next four years.

"Madam Captain," Wells shouted, "did you say *four years?*"

"Yes, sir. I'll let Father Rick fill in the details."

"Gentlemen," Father Rick said, "I'm going to review what I've studied in the history books, *our* history books, and from that history, what is going to happen in the next few years. The books told us that the Battle of Fort Sumter would happen at 0430 on the morning of April 12, 1861. Captain Patterson personally witnessed the first volley and checked her time piece. It was exactly at the time the history books said it would be." He looked at Ashley, who nodded.

"Over the next two months there will be battles, but they will amount to no more than skirmishes. In about three months, on July 21, the first major engagement of the war will occur near Manassas, Virginia by a creek called Bull Run. There was a great deal of speculation, especially on the Union side, that this battle would be decisive and would convince Jefferson Davis that it would be futile to continue the war. Two inexperienced armies clashed, ours led by General Irwin McDowell, the South led by General P.G.T Beauregard. Most expected the battle to be a Union victory. Instead it was a defeat. The battle saw 2,896 Union casualties, including 460 killed. The South had 1,982 casualties with 387 killed. Bull Run, or Manassas as the South called it, was the largest and the bloodiest battle in our nation's history up to that point."

Admiral Farragut spoke. "Father Sampson, those numbers are startling. Are you sure they're correct?"

"Yes, sir," said Father Rick. "It will get worse, much worse. For example, next year, on September 17, 1862 the Battle of Antietam will be fought. The South called it the Battle of Sharpsburg. It will be the bloodiest single day in American history, even up to 2013. All told 22,717 were killed, missing or wounded on both sides." Wells, Farragut and Roebling just looked at each other. Wells took a sip of water.

"Despite the massive casualties," Father Rick said, "there was no clear tactical victory at Antietam. There are going to be many other major battles in the next four years. The names are familiar to any school child from our time who studies history." Father Rick looked at his notes.

"I'm going to read to you, by order of date, the costliest battles of the next four years. These aren't the only battles but the costliest. The casualty numbers include dead, wounded, missing, or captured." Father Rick then read from his list. He spoke with a calculated monotony, as if reading a list of the dead at Sunday Mass:

*Fort Donelson* - February 1862 - 19,455 casualties.
*Shilo* - April 1862 - 23,741
*Manassas,* Second Battle - August 1862 - 25,251
*Antietam* - September 1862 - 26,134
*Stone's River* - December 1862 - 24,645
*Chancellorsville* - May 1863 - 30,099
*Gettysburg* - July 1863 - 51,112
*Chickamauga* - September 1863 - 34,624
*Spotsylvania* - May 1864 - 27,399
*Wilderness* - May 1864 - 25,416

He looked up from his notes. "Gentlemen, now I'm going to read the total casualties of the Civil War: All told, there were approximately 620,000 total casualties on both sides. Recent studies indicate that the total may be closer to 800,000. The next four years are going to be Hell on earth."

Wells, Farragut, and Roebling sat, ashen faced. They said nothing.

Gideon Wells then put his face in his hands and wept.

# Chapter 17

 radley seethed. *Why wasn't I invited to meet with the Union lead-
ers in the Captain's office? I'm second in command, and who does
she invite but a chaplain and a brand new officer. Did I spend 24 years in
this Navy to be treated like shit? Dashing Ashley is in over her head as usual.
I know every inch of this goddam ship and she brings in the rookies.*

Bradley was heading to his office when he saw Chief Petty Officer
Albert Ray walking toward him. Ray, the Chief Gunnery Mate, worked
directly under the command of Lt. Cmdr. Andrea Rubin, the Weapons
Officer. Bradley had known Chief Ray for years, going back to his drinking days. They had closed many a bar together. He was happy that Ray
was on the *California*. The two men had a natural feel for each other. They
both considered themselves "old South," Bradley from Louisiana and Ray
from Alabama. They both shared views on various subjects, especially
race, that were anachronisms in 2013 America. Bradley didn't like black
people but kept his views to himself, although he couldn't recall what he
may have said during long evenings on a barstool. Chief Ray's feelings for
black people were more direct: he hated blacks with a deep, brooding contempt. He hated black people generally and Captain Ashley Patterson in
particular. Like Bradley, he saw this young woman's rise to the command
of a Navy ship as a politically correct bow from the top brass because she
was a darling of the media.

"Good morning, Chief," Bradley said to his old friend.

"Good morning, sir, and how are you doing?" Ray asked. Word gets around fast on a ship, and Ray had heard that the visitors from the Union were being entertained without the presence of the XO. "I guess our fine captain figures she can do without your knowledge and experience, Commander," said Ray.

"Let's have a cup of coffee in my office," said Bradley. He escorted Ray in, and closed the door behind him.

Bradley knew that he couldn't pull off his idea of defecting to the Confederacy without help. The man sitting across from him just may be that help.

Chief Albert Ray, 43 years-old, balding and overweight, had once been a member of a Ku Klux Klan klavern in his hometown in Alabama. He had even risen to the exalted position of Grand Cyclops, the leader of his group. He had been in the Navy for 21 years. His job, as Chief Gunners Mate, was to oversee the condition and readiness of all weapons on the ship. He answered to Lt. Commander Andrea Rubin, the ship's weapons officer. He hated reporting to a woman although he hid his contempt.

"What bothers me, my old friend, is that it's easy to figure out what's going to happen," said Bradley. "Captain Patterson, or *Dashing Ashley* as I call her, is meeting with Lincoln's Navy Secretary at this very moment."

"It's obvious that she's going to offer this ship to fight against the South," Bradley said. "Even if she doesn't, the Secretary of the Navy has the power to simply order it so. Let's face it, since we find ourselves in 1861, the *California* is a Union ship. With the *California* thrown into the fight, the South won't have a prayer. The fire power on this one ship can turn the tide of any engagement. They'll probably surrender after the first battle, and the Confederacy will come to an end almost as soon as it began. Slavery will be abolished within months, without time for

Southern plantation owners to make a transition away from it. Slavery's an institution that can't be undone overnight. Besides, slave owners paid fair and square, and the slaves are their private property." Bradley looked intently at Ray, trying to judge his reaction.

"I hear you loud 'n clear Commander," said Ray. "Abe Lincoln shoved his foot up Ole Dixie's ass. The South just wanted to be left alone. Fuck'n Yankees just couldn't let all be well. They had to tell us what to do and how to do it. Makes you wish you could do sumpin about it."

Bradley sensed the beginning of an alliance.

"You know, Chief," said Bradley, "the people who fought for the South were called rebels. The ones who once served in the Northern military were even called traitors. But some people, like you and me, know that they were patriots fighting for their homeland. They were willing to fight and die for a just cause. Best example is Robert E. Lee himself."

"So now that we're here," said Chief Ray, "the South gets fucked all over again."

"Well, let's think about that," said Bradley. "When the SEALs were snooping around in Charleston they heard a lot of talk about a mysterious *Gray Ship*. Obviously that's us, the *California*. I imagine the Confederate command, both Army and Navy, must be very nervous. They're probably thinking the North has come up with a big new secret invention. Wouldn't it be interesting if the Confederacy had some inside information about the *California*, including her vulnerabilities? Wouldn't it also be interesting if they had some modern weapons to level the playing field? Wouldn't it be interesting if the South had, oh, I don't know, some rocket propelled grenades, night vision goggles, automatic carbines, surface to air, and anti-ship missiles? Wouldn't it be interesting?"

Chief Ray moved closer, lowered his voice and said, "That would be very interesting indeed, Commander."

# Chapter 18

aptain Patterson called SEAL Petty Officer Pete Campo to the bridge. "Petty Officer Campo, I understand that a Seaman Planck has signed up for your class."

"Yes ma'am. I saw his name on the roster this morning. I start a new beginner's class tomorrow and he'll be there."

"Let me tell you a few things about Planck. You'll see that he's tall, gangly, probably best described as gawky. And he's got a problem."

"What's that Captain?"

"A lot of his shipmates are making his life miserable, picking on him constantly and generally bullying him, all because of his appearance. He's what I call a 'bully magnet.' He needs confidence training and physical conditioning. I'm not looking for you to turn him into a SEAL, just a confident human being." She focused her eyes directly into Campo's and said, "Pete, I want you to pay special attention to this kid. He's a good crewmember, and I want him to be a better person. Can I count on you?"

"Captain, give me a month and you won't recognize this sailor."

# *Chapter 19*

Secretary Wells was still thinking about the horrible casualty statistics that Father Rick had described. Like everyone in command in the North, he had expected a short war. With the industrial strength, transportation, and communications of the Northern states, the Confederate administration would soon see that continued secession, not to mention war, would be futile. When the Erie Canal opened in New York State in 1825, it created a vast commercial network from Lake Erie to the Atlantic Ocean, building an industrial infrastructure the South could only envy. But, Wells thought, if the people on this ship are correct and they can tell him what the future holds, he would have to rethink everything about the Civil War, and so would Abraham Lincoln.

\* \* \*

Captain Patterson ordered Ivan Campbell to give their distinguished guests a tour of the *California*, further infuriating Bradley.

"Gentlemen, let me be candid with you, and tell you that we're no smarter than you are," Campbell said. "We came here with 152 years of scientific and technological advancement. On this tour I'm going to concentrate on our present capabilities. I've asked Father Rick, our ship's unofficial historian, to join us."

The tour began with a lecture delivered by Father Rick condensing 152 years of technological history into a few minutes. Father Rick had found a two page listing of the major technological discoveries in a book from the ship's library entitled: *Technology from the Civil War to the Manned Space Station*. He photocopied the pages and handed copies to their guests. As they were reading he snapped a photo of them with his IPad and handed it around to the men.

Admiral Farragut, an experienced military man, knowledgeable in science and technical matters, saw the significance of the IPad.

"This photograph that you just showed us which you took moments ago, can have a major impact on surveillance and reconnaissance."

"Yes, sir," said Campbell. "Wait until you see our drones and attack helicopter. Combine them with photography, and battlefield reconnaissance takes on a whole new dimension." They didn't ask what a drone or helicopter was. They knew they'd find out soon enough.

They read the pages and listened to Father Rick and Ivan Campbell. There, on a nuclear warship in Chesapeake Bay in 1861, they heard about wireless communication, the telephone, the light bulb, the transistor, photocopy machines, vacuum cleaners, washers and dryers, dishwashers, rocketry, missile guidance, automatic firing weapons, hand grenades, battle tanks, submarines, self propelled torpedoes, radar, sonar, radio, two-way radios, television, the personal computer, smart phones, IPads, IPods, space travel, and nuclear power.

To wrap a little history around the technology, Father Rick then discussed the Spanish American War, World War I, the Great Depression, World War II, the Korean War, the Cold War, the Kennedy assassination, Ed Sullivan, the Beatles, the Rolling Stones, the moon landing, Vietnam, the Gulf War, 9/11, Iraq and Afghanistan, and the election of Barack Obama as the first black President of the United States.

They began their tour on the bridge and ended up in the Combat Information Center (CIC). They headed to the Captain's office for a wrap-up and review. Campbell handed Secretary Wells a folder full of photographs so he could review this day at his desk. Wells' head spun with the strategic implications of what they had seen, Admiral Farragut's with the tactical possibilities.

"Captain Patterson, we shall take our leave now," Wells said. "The human mind can only comprehend a finite amount of information."

Ashley then said with a smile, "One hundred and fifty two years is a lot to ponder in a few hours, Mr. Secretary."

"We shall meet again soon," said Wells. "How do you recommend that we communicate?"

She told Campbell to give Wells a two-way radio. Campbell took one from his belt and showed them how to use it. He also gave them a supply of batteries.

"Captain Patterson," said Wells, "a private word with you Madam?" They walked over to a corner of the room. Wells leaned close to Ashley and said, "I want you to meet with President Lincoln as soon as possible."

Ashley came close to blowing her command presence. Every nerve ending in her body ordered her to jump up and down and squeal like a school girl. Instead, she said, with studied calmness, "Whatever you and the President deem appropriate, sir." *Abraham Lincoln — Yesssss!*

Wells, Farragut, and Roebling were lost in thought from their day on the *California*. But one thing they all knew without even verbalizing it.

In the last few hours, the Civil War had changed.

# *Chapter 20*

Secretary of Defense Robert Gates was on the phone with President Obama. "Mr. President, I have a simple but troublesome thing to tell you."

"Shoot Bob," said the President. Gates came right to the point. "We seem to have lost the *USS California*, a nuclear cruiser, off the coast of South Carolina." The president peppered him with questions about what steps were being taken. Both men knew that the situation was out of their hands for the time being. "Keep me in the loop, Bob. Whatever I'm doing, tell them to put you through."

"Yes, sir."

\* \* \*

The *USS Ticonderoga* steamed full speed to the last known location of the *California*. It would be on site within a half hour. Her forward sonar pinging freaked out every whale and dolphin in the Western Atlantic.

Three H-65 Coast Guard rescue helicopters from Coast Guard Station Charleston were speeding toward the coordinates of the last fix. The Coast Guard Cutter *Gallatin* steamed toward the site as well. The *Gallatin* had a rescue submersible aboard. By protocol, the local Coast Guard Sector Commander, Captain Eric Buehler, had operational command of the rescue effort, but because this involved a US Navy warship, he would take orders directly from the Chief of Naval Operations.

The lives of 630 American servicemen and women were at stake. Every man and woman on the rescue effort had that thought locked in their minds.

The *California* has been missing for twelve minutes.

# Chapter 21

A t 0930 on the morning of April 17, Bradley met Chief Ray in the weapons department. As Bradley suggested, Ray told Andrea Rubin that the XO wanted to do a routine check of the department's weapons so he could prepare a report for the captain. Rubin didn't think much about it, although normal protocol would have been for Bradley to contact her, the head of the weapons department, directly.

"Why don't you show me the portable rockets, rocket propelled grenades, hand held surface to air missiles, and the other small armaments," said Bradley.

Bradley noticed that the ordnance was not only stacked neatly but was also wrapped in small bundles for easy moving. "Looks like a couple of guys could move this stuff with ease, Chief."

The chief got into details. "This entire bulkhead (he pointed to a wall area five feet deep, six feet high and three feet wide) can fit into one Zodiac. That's why they pack the ammo like this, so that it can be moved ashore easily."

Bradley lowered his voice. "How often is inventory taken?"

"Once a day Commander," the chief leaned closer to Bradley, "by yours truly," he whispered. Bradley's eyes widened.

"I wonder how long it would take a couple of men to load that wall of ammo into a Zodiac," Bradley said in a low voice.

"Exactly 17 minutes. Add 10 if it's a couple of older guys (Ray winked). We train our men in loading Zodiacs as a drill."

Bradley asked, "Is the other bulkhead, the one on the starboard side, a mirror image of the one to port?"

"Exactly the same, sir." He anticipated Bradley's next question. "Yup, Two Zodiacs, double the bang for the ride."

"Will that leave any room for carbines?"

"Yes, sir. 50 carbines per Zodiac on top of the other items. But it means only one man per Zodiac if that's the amount of cargo they'll carry. But that's no big deal. A Zodiac is easier to drive than a tricycle."

The chief warmed to his weapons moving skills. "There's a way you can increase the capacity of weapons storage by 100 percent." This was better than Bradley had expected.

"How do you do that?" asked Bradley. The chief pointed to a survival raft capable of holding hold six people.

"Each of those babies can hold the same as a Zodiac without a man on board." said the chief.

"All together Chief, what do we have?"

Chief Ray took his inventory sheet from his pocket. "Here's the list sir: 50 M4A1 automatic carbine rifles; 100 rocket propelled grenades, 25 Colt 45s; 20 surface-to-air missiles including shoulder held launchers. We also have a total of 2,000 rounds of ammo for the carbines, and 750 rounds for the 45s."

"Looks like you could start your own gun company, Chief."

"Commander, you're lookin' at one ass whuppin', ammo movin', game changin', efficient redneck."

The only thought that plagued Bradley was how they would off load the weapons without being seen.

# Chapter 22

General Robert E. Lee commanded the Army of Northern Virginia, the largest army in the Confederacy. He wanted to see firsthand the result of the opening hostilities of the war. The entire Confederate military looked upon Lee as the leader. Lee also wanted to talk to General Beauregard about this mysterious *Gray Ship* that seemed to be the talk of the South.

After he toured Fort Sumter he could see that the result of the battle was a lot of masonry rubble. The walls were pockmarked from cannon fire, but the structure itself was still sound, a valuable new addition to the Confederacy's defenses.

General Beauregard invited Lee into his quarters in Charleston. He occupied a large office that had once housed an investment company. The space was 30 by 40 feet, equipped with leather furniture and a Persian rug. In the middle hung a crystal chandelier. This man doesn't look ready for battle, thought Lee.

"First, General, let me congratulate you on your successful siege of Fort Sumter," Lee said. "I understand that our Navy was also of great assistance in preventing the Yankees from being resupplied."

"Yes General, I would say that the Navy was crucial to the outcome. If they had been successful in restocking food and ammunition, the Yankees could have held on for a much longer time." Lee appreciated it when a commander gave credit to forces not under his command.

"I'm concerned, General, about all of the reports I've been getting about some strange *Gray Ship*," Lee said.

"I too am concerned about the *Gray Ship*, sir. I haven't seen it myself, but from the descriptions I've received, it sounds like it could be 600 feet long, although some reports have it as long as 2,000 feet. Its deck, according to reports, is covered with strange looking weapons. It has incredible speed and maneuvering ability, according to one of our captains who saw the ship up close."

"And we only know her as The *Gray Ship*?" asked Lee.

"I almost forgot to tell you, sir. She is the *USS California*. She bears the number '36' prominently on either side of her bow. One of our boats got close enough to read the lettering on her stern."

"Since we have a name and a number, do we not know anything about her?" asked Lee.

"That's the most puzzling thing of all, General. I contacted the local office of our Navy Department. They keep a list of all ships of the Union Navy. Neither the name *USS California* nor the number 36 appears on the list. We have a very effective spy in the Union Navy Department who keeps the list up to date."

"Has anyone seen any evidence of hostile intent from the *California*?" asked Lee.

"No sir, but she flies the Union flag, and we're at war. Hostile actions from that monstrous ship cannot be a long way off. We can't identify many of the weapons that have been described, but we can assume they're armaments because of their projectile shapes."

"From what you've heard, General, do you think one or more of our new ironclad ships could stand a chance against the *California*?" Lee asked.

"From what I have heard, sir, I'm not sure our entire Navy could stand up against her."

"General," said Lee, "I recommend posting lookouts at shore batteries along the coast. Have them make drawings of the ship. The ship probably moves too fast for a photograph. Once we have enough we can distribute the information to all of our naval forces."

"I shall see to that at once, General Lee."

So the North has a secret weapon, thought Lee.

# Chapter 23

After his 45-minute morning workout, Jack Thurber holed himself up in the ship's library with his laptop and portable hard drive. Like most writers, he was a pack rat. Technology makes it easy to be a packrat, and even encourages it. His portable hard drive holds two terabytes of data and set him back less than a hundred bucks. All of the research for every book he wrote is on that hard drive, with a backup on his office computer back home. His good friend, a techie, poked fun at Jack about his habit of carrying all his data on a portable drive.

"The cloud," his friend said "is the only way to go." All of his information could be carried on some remote server farm, backed up by dedicated computer dweebs.

Jack pondered that, on April 10, 2013 (or was it 1861?), the cloud disappeared. He patted his portable hard drive.

On orders from Captain Patterson he was reviewing all of the information he ever jotted down about time travel, specifically information on how to go back to the time you travelled from. In other words, how to get back to the wormhole.

Jack enjoyed himself. Work, whether mental or physical is what drives him. It's his life, a life that he had considered ending a few short years ago.

Jack's personnel file mentions that his wife Nancy had died in a car accident. What the file doesn't say is that Jack witnessed the accident.

Nor does it mention how much he loved her, cherished his every moment with her, and hated to be away from her. Nancy had taken her car to run an errand a half hour before Jack left the house to drive to a book interview. As he drove down the highway his eyes caught something in the air in front of him. In the opposite lane of travel, approximately 300 feet ahead, he saw a silver Lexus sedan, twisting and spinning crazily in the air. The car struck pavement and became airborne again, propelled by its momentum. After three bounces it came to a rest on its roof. He had one thought. It was more than a thought, more like a vice that gripped every square inch of his body and squeezed. That looks like Nancy's car.

The traffic came to a standstill. He flung open his door and ran to the scene of the wreck. He ran with abandon, not watching what was in front of his feet. He tripped over some debris on the shoulder of the road, pitching him forward. He broke his fall with his forearms. When he lifted his face and looked forward, he saw what would consume his life for years. Yes, it was Nancy's car. And there was Nancy, lying in the roadway, her body in two pieces.

That scene became the focus of his every waking hour. What he had seen was unthinkable. God how he hated that word. If any manuscript came across his editorial desk he would take it out with a vicious stroke of his red pencil. Unthinkable. How do you *unthink* an image, an image as stark as any that the human eye can behold. Yes, the image of Nancy's torn body was unthinkable, but how could he stop thinking about it endlessly. He not only contemplated suicide, he started to jot down plans for how he would do it. He considered finding the wormhole at Pearl Harbor and launching himself into war, an easy way to get killed.

His friend and book collaborator, the psychiatrist Benny Weinberg, took Jack on as if he were his most important case, because he was. As a psychiatrist for the New York City Police Department, Benny was no stranger to traumatic depression. Jack, normally an outgoing man at ease in any company, had become withdrawn and sullen.

Benny Weinberg and Jack had become close friends over the years. After Nancy's death Benny tried to reach out to him, but his efforts got nowhere. Jack didn't return phone calls. One day, after finally reaching him, Benny invited Jack over for lunch.

"Talk to me, Jack. You look like shit. What's going on?"

"The image Ben. That image of Nancy has become my life. I've tried everything to get it out of my face, but it's always there. Always. It's there right now as we're sitting here."

"Asshole."

Jack couldn't help laughing. Benny could go from psychiatrist to tough cop in an instant.

"It may be true, Benny, but why do you call me an asshole?"

"You're an asshole because you think your brilliant mind can reverse everything we know about the human psychology. You think you can take a horrible image and force it out of your mind. Remember the old parlor game where the game master would tell everybody not to think about green elephants. Of course that's the point of the game, the joke. The people playing the game couldn't think about anything *but* green elephants. The psychology is simple. The more we resist something the more it persists. Okay, so let me ask you a question. What are you thinking about right now."

"Green elephants."

"That's because you were trying not to think about it, just like you try not to think about Nancy's torn lifeless body. Jack, work with me on something. I want you to close your eyes and imagine yourself sitting in your car right after you saw Nancy's car crash to a stop."

"Benny, are you trying to fuck with my brain?"

"You've been doing a great job of fucking with your own brain, so how about giving me a crack at it. Okay, now I want you to reach into your glove compartment and take out a tape measure. Now I want you to open the door and walk slowly, don't run, walk slowly toward Nancy's body. Be careful, the road is slick with blood, gas, and oil. Now I want you to take the tape and measure the exact distance between Nancy's upper torso and her lower body."

"Ben, you've got to be joking."

"What the fuck do I look like, a standup comedian? Just follow my instructions. Now tell me exactly how far Nancy's upper torso is from her lower body." Jack said nothing.

"This isn't rocket science, shithead, what's the distance?"

"Six feet."

"Exactly six feet?"

"Well, six feet, four and a half inches."

Jack began to sob. "I'm sorry Benny, I'm sorry." He kept on sobbing.

Benny waited for the tears to stop. "Only an asshole like you could apologize for acting like a human being." Benny softened his voice and looked into Jack's eyes. "Jack, when I heard about Nancy's death and how you actually witnessed it, you know what I did? I cried. I cried like a baby. I cried for that beautiful woman who's young life was snuffed out, but mainly I cried for my friend. That would be you, Jack. You've experienced a trauma like few other human beings will ever face. But you've been handling it by trying to force it out of your mind. That won't work, Jack. That's a green fucking elephant. That's what the tape measure is all about. I want you to intentionally recreate that scene and allow it into your head. I want you to smell the smells, remember the sounds, listen to the sirens, hear the cops shouting. If you want me to be with you or on the phone when you do this, just let me know. That's the only way you're going to rob it of its power over you."

Now, five years after he lost Nancy, Jack was emerging from his cave of despair, thanks in no small part to his friend Benny. He seldom thought of women, only a woman, Nancy. But he recognized that he was having a strange feeling, not an unpleasant one. Here, on a warship at sea in a strange time, he was becoming interested in a beautiful woman, his commanding officer. It was more than an interest, more like an infatuation. He liked the feeling.

Okay, thought Jack. Time to get back to work.

\* \* \*

He began examining his two prior time journeys. Jack noted that, in his prior travels, one to the defunct golf course in 1929 and the other to Pearl Harbor in 1941, he was able to go back by finding the exact spot he came through. In the golf course trip, he walked in the opposite direction, but over the same spot. In the Pearl Harbor incident, he stepped on the same wooden plank in the same direction. These observations checked out with the other time travelers he had interviewed for his book. The key, obviously, is to find the spot, no matter how you cross it.

But the *California* had a problem. He talked extensively with Ivan Campbell, the ship's navigator, as well as the quartermaster of the watch and the OOD at the time of the *Daylight Event*. Because their last navigational fix was done by dead reckoning, simply plotting course and speed and making an educated guess of your position, they could have been anywhere within miles of where they hit the time portal. To get back to it the ship would have to steam in a dizzying monotonous back and forth pattern for God know how long. His new found navigational knowledge told him that wind, current and sea conditions could have a big impact on how straight they travelled.

He also had another concern, a big one. All of the people he interviewed had crossed a land based portal. This was his own experience as well. His extensive research revealed nothing about time travel through a portal in the ocean, nor had he ever heard anything about a large ship with 630 people slipping through the same portal.

But they were stuck with that fact.

There are no signs that say, "Time Portal – Please Enter Here."

# Chapter 29

After lunch in the wardroom Father Rick asked Ashley if he could speak with her in her office. "Of course," said Ashley. If there is one person on the ship her door is always open to it's Father Rick.

"What's up Father? I hope you're going to tell me somebody slipped us all one big mickey, and we've all had the same strange dream."

"I wish I could, Captain."

"I want to talk to you about the crew. I'm worried that morale is starting to stretch thin. It's been a few days since we crossed the time portal. At first it was an interesting diversion for everyone on the ship. Some may have even enjoyed the excitement of it. But I've been getting vibrations that people want out of this, or at least they want you to try to get the ship back home. As you decided, very few secrets about time travel have been kept from the crew. Jack Thurber has made us all amateur experts in travelling through time. Every crew member knows one thing. They've heard about the idea of getting back to the time we came from by finding the exact location of the portal. Captain, if I've heard it once I've heard it a hundred times in the last two days, 'When are we going to start looking for the portal?'"

# *Chapter 25*

After Father Rick left, Ashley was alone with her thoughts. With all of the feverish activity of the last few days, she seldom had time to just think. Or was it that she kept busy because she didn't want to think? A thought kept intruding, not a fully formed thought, not fully formed perhaps because it was so difficult to deal with. It was like a dark weather front on the horizon. You can't ignore it, you know it means trouble; you just wish it would go away.

Pretty soon my crew is going to expect me to commit treason, Ashley thought. Word was out, as Father Rick just reminded her, that the way to go back was to find the place you came in. She never asked Jack Thurber to keep it secret. Under their strange circumstances secrecy can be a morale killer. Every person on the ship had the same question, "When are we going to try to go back?"

Before the *Daylight Event*, everyone aboard knew that they would return home after their deployment to the Persian Gulf. Return home to husbands and wives, mothers and fathers, sons and daughters, friends and lovers. As Father Rick reminded Ashley, people can only operate for a short time with no hope for a future. He had just told her that the crew was getting obsessed with the idea of going back.

This is the storm cloud she worried about, and she knew the storm could be rough. Ashley decided to stop forcing the trouble out of her head.

So here's my problem, Ashley thought. This is an American warship, the property of the United States Government. We take our orders from the government, ultimately from the Commander in Chief, Abraham Lincoln. After he speaks to Gideon Wells, Lincoln will want the *California* to join the fight, either in direct battle support or as the lead ship in the blockade of the South. But my crew wants to go back to where we came from. They want to go home. I can't fight the Civil War *and* go back to where we came from. It's one or the other."

I risk mutiny or commit treason. Nice choice.

# Chapter 26

It was 1850 hours and the mess hall was crowded. The crew's mess was open 24 hours a day to accommodate sailors coming off watch. For those who had a regular workday, the mess hall followed the traffic pattern of any food service facility.

Suddenly there was a loud sound in the corner of the hall, a sound of plates crashing to the deck. This sound is not uncommon at sea, where a sudden wave can reduce a well-stacked rack of dinnerware to a pile of rubble. But the sea was calm, which made the sound that much more startling. First Class Petty Officer William Jordan was lying face down in the smashup of plates. Petty Officer Emilio Lopez, a hospital corpsman, was eating nearby. Instinctively Lopez rushed to the man's aid and immediately saw that Jordan showed symptoms of a heart attack.

Lopez yelled for people to clear the area while he administered CPR using a defibrillator that he grabbed from a nearby bulkhead. The medical department had been called, and Lt. John Ambrose, one of the ship's two physicians, was on the scene within two minutes. Lopez's CPR had stabilized the man, who was immediately carried to the medical department on a gurney. Jordan took fast breaths and sweated profusely. Commander Joseph Perino, the ship's medical officer, arrived within moments. Jordan's pulse rate was extremely high and his breathing became shallow. Perino ordered an emergency tracheotomy and a breathing tube. He also injected nitroglycerin to help with the man's pain. Perino could see that this was more than a mild heart attack.

People in the medical department often joked that the most important medical equipment on the ship was the helicopter pad on the stern. In normal circumstances Perino would have ordered a helicopter Medivac to a shore hospital, or, if at sea, to the nearest aircraft carrier, which is equipped with a larger hospital unit. But these weren't normal times. The last place Perino wanted to send this man was a hospital ashore.

All physicians are familiar with the history of medical progress. Perino didn't have to do research to know that the state of medical technology in 1861 was primitive by modern standards. He knew the statistics. Of the 620,000 casualties in the Civil War, over half were from disease. Most of the disease was spread by unknowing battlefield doctors and nurses, spreading infection from patient to patient. A doctor would amputate a leg, then go to the next victim and treat the man's wounds without even washing his hands.

The accepted theory of disease propagation in the mid-nineteenth century was the miasma theory, the belief that disease spread through the air by vapors released by rotting matter or fetid water. A person would breathe in a bad vapor and disease would result.

It would be many years before germ theory, the idea that infection can be spread by microorganisms, was accepted by the medical profession. In the decade after the Civil War, an English surgeon named Joseph Lister, working from the microbiological theories of Louis Pasteur, would develop the concept of a sterile operating environment. Until then, hospitals were not much better than battlefield medical tents. Civil societies created hospitals as places where people would go to get better, to have their wounds treated or their diseases cured. The sad irony was that, in mid-nineteenth-century America, a hospital was the most dangerous place to be if you needed medical help. No, thought Perino, the best place for this poor guy is this warship.

Perino then had a disturbing thought. That goes for the rest of us, too.

# Chapter 27

"Captain I'd like to talk about the Butterfly Effect," Father Rick said. Ashley, Father Rick and Lt. Jack Thurber were in the captain's office for a scheduled meeting. Ashley thought of these two men as her Time Travel Brain Trust, friends and guides to help her cope with their new reality.

"The Butterfly Effect," said Ashley, "yes, I've heard of it. It's a theory that a butterfly flapping its wings can cause a disturbance in the atmosphere, and even though it's a tiny disturbance, it can result in a hurricane in another part of the world."

"You summarize it perfectly Captain. Would you agree Jack?"

"Yes," Jack said. "I once wrote an article about the Butterfly Effect for the *Washington Post*." *Is there anything this guy hasn't written about?* Ashley thought. "While doing time travel research for my book, I figured I'd derive an article from a chapter. The Butterfly Effect is a scientific theory hatched by an American mathematician and meteorologist named Edward Lorenz. He was an expert on chaos theory. Captain Patterson summarized it well: a little flap of the wings here, a big storm over there. It's become a metaphor for small actions having huge results."

"Let's talk about the Butterfly Effect and the *USS California*," said Father Rick. "We all saw the reaction of Gideon Wells when I summarized the history of the Civil War. The man was very upset about the casualty numbers I gave him. When I said that the war would last four years I thought the poor guy would faint. I think it's pretty safe to say that he wants the *California* as part of his arsenal. He wants to use our modern weapons to intercede in the war and bring it to a fast conclusion. My guess is that we'll be part of the naval blockade of the South, or the Battle of Bull Run about three months from now. So tell me if I'm wrong. Gideon Wells wants to use this ship to change history."

"I totally agree, Father," said Ashley. "From the bits of conversation I picked up between him and Admiral Farragut, they were all but picking out targets. Yes, Wells didn't like the history that he heard, and he wants to change it. And the *California* is a big part of his plan."

Father Rick didn't want to put words in the mouth of his good friend and commanding officer. He asked her simply, "Is that okay with you?" Jack listened intently to this conversation.

"Yes, it's okay for two reasons," said Ashley. "First, from my perspective as a military officer, I follow orders. The *California* is a US Navy ship, and Wells is the Secretary of the Navy. That's the easy part. But second, I have to say this. Gideon Wells wasn't the only one in the room who felt emotional after you read those horrifying casualty numbers. I kept wondering, how we can we prevent this."

"Captain, may I offer a contrarian view?" asked Rick.

"Father, I may be your commanding officer, but you're my pastor and my friend. Please tell us what's on your mind."

"Well," Father Rick said, "I want to talk about Iowa."

"Iowa?" said Ashley and Jack simultaneously.

"Yes, Iowa. As I may have mentioned, I have a distant ancestor, Randolph Sampson, who fought in the Civil War on the Union side. He called Pennsylvania his home. I've tracked down my ancestral history and discovered that he had befriended a man from Iowa who was a wealthy landowner. They met at Appomattox, shortly after the South surrendered.

According to correspondence between the two, the man had fallen from a carriage and sprained his ankle badly. Grandpa Randolph, according to the letter of thanks, carried the man on his shoulder to a doctor's office some distance away. A few months later, as their friendship grew, the man offered Grandpa Randolph 100 acres of land for a cheap price. Grandpa Randolph was a farmer by trade, and he jumped at it. That was the beginning of many generations of Sampsons in Iowa, but most particularly, Peter and Margaret Sampson, my parents."

"I can never forget the story of how they met. It was May 19, 1963, a rainy day in Dubuque. My mother, a schoolteacher, was driving home when she had a flat tire. It happened right in front of Sampson's Automotive Supplies. As she stood there looking at the flat tire, a young man came running out with a jack, followed by a clerk carrying a tire. 'Do you get a lot of business this way?' said my mother. She and the young proprietor of Sampson's Automotive Supplies had a good laugh. He refused to accept payment, in exchange for her buying him a cup of coffee at the corner luncheonette. So they met, fell in love, got married and three years later brought into the world a future priest named Richard Sampson."

"There's a butterfly in this story somewhere, yes?" Ashley chided the chaplain.

"There certainly is Captain. A guy falls off a carriage in 1865, and in so doing sets up a series of events. Ninety eight years later, those events lead directly to my parents meeting on May 19, 1963, and on November 9, 1967, to the birth of your humble priest. Compare that guy falling off his cart to a butterfly flapping its wings."

Father Rick continued. "Now suppose we slipped through a wormhole and wound up at Appomattox in 1865. Suppose a strong young sailor named Jack Thurber was there at the scene. He sees the horse rear, runs up to the carriage, and prevents the man from falling and spraining his ankle. Grandpa Randolph would be a bystander, looking on. He would later return to his small farm in western Pennsylvania, and would never even visit Iowa. In 1963, there would be no Peter Sampson to save the damsel with the flat tire. And of all the things that happened in Dubuque, Iowa on November 9, 1967, the birth of Richard Sampson would not be one of them."

Oh shit, thought Ashley, I can see where this is going.

"That," said Father Rick "is why I wanted to talk about butterflies today."

"Lieutenant Jack," said Ashley, "any thoughts on this?"

Jack looked at Ashley and said, "The uncomfortable thing about logic, Captain, is that you can't resist it. You don't have to understand the Butterfly Effect to get the point that Father Rick makes. When I had those two incidents of slipping through a time portal, I did nothing to change what was going on when I got there. I just slipped into the past and slipped back. But Father Rick paints a picture that's pretty clear. A small change in the past can revoke history as we know it."

"Here's my serious concern," said Father Rick. "In the story I just told, I changed everything by just inserting a hypothetical correction – the guy never sprained his ankle. What we're talking about in our present circumstances goes much further than changing a fact or two. We intervene in the Civil War, and in so doing we change history. If everyone on this ship tracked their ancestry like I did, would they be able to predict with certainty that they are really here. Each of the little serendipities of life point us in different directions as well as our ancestors. Can we say that the lineage of everyone on this ship will remain exactly the same, even though we change the entire course of history?"

Father Rick continued. "So we intercede in the Civil War, after which we try to find our way back to 2013 by locating the wormhole. It's been six generations from 1861 to 2013. Every generation begins with the same simple story: boy meets girl. We'll feel the bumping and the night will turn to day. Will any of us exist after it happens?"

Ashley stood up and walked over to a port hole. She loved the ocean and never tired of looking at it. The ocean was her home, and when she looked at her home, it calmed her. She didn't have to think or analyze anything. The sea gave her answers. If ever she needed some answers it was now.

"I'm not a philosopher or a theologian," Ashley said, "I'm just a grunt line officer serving her country. But I do have faith in God." She looked at her friend Father Rick, who just closed his eyes and nodded in agreement. "I've heard more Rick Sampson sermons than I can remember when you talked about God's plan for us, how the joy of life comes from surrendering to His loving grace. Something inside me, and I can't explain it, says that God's plan goes beyond a sprained ankle or a flat tire. Something inside me says that our existence isn't as haphazard as a butterfly flapping its wings. I believe that God put us here. It's our job not to blow it."

Ashley continued, her voice rising slightly. "We're going to intervene in the Civil War, probably at the Battle of Bull Run. We're going to kick ass, scare the living shit out of the Confederacy, bring an early end to the horror, and save a few hundred thousand lives. Then we're going to find a way home, and we'll all be there when it happens. If I'm wrong, Father, you won't be around to say 'I told you so.' "

"The meeting's over gentlemen. Thank you both for your thoughtful input. God bless you."

God bless all of us, she thought.

# *Chapter 28*

*G*ideon Wells' carriage rattled along the oval drive to the front entrance of the White House, as the President's residence was commonly known. It would be decades before the White House became the official name of the building. The circular drive leading up to the front entrance provided little security. As the years went by, presidential safety concerns would rearrange the entrance, replacing the long drive with a large and defensible lawn. There had been heavy rain recently and the path to the front door was its usual mess of potholes and ruts. One of the White House staff ran to the carriage and opened the door for Wells. His assistant climbed out the opposite door. Wells strode through the entrance, his shoes making a loud clapping sound on the stone floor. His assistant carried two large suitcases laden with items that Wells had been given on the *California.*

An aide escorted Wells into the President's office. He had suggested that Admiral Farragut be part of the meeting, but Lincoln let it be known that he wanted to meet with Wells alone. Lincoln stood to greet his old friend. Lincoln, as many a biographer would later note, did not try to be imposing, preferring instead to let a man be his own and speak freely. But at 6 feet 4 inches tall, Abraham Lincoln simply was imposing, whether he intended to be or not.

"So Mr. Secretary, people have been telling me that you've taken to strong drink," Lincoln joked.

Wells laughed. "Mr. President, after I tell you my story you may want to indulge yourself as well." Lincoln was intensely curious about the contents of the large suitcases, but he decided to let Wells tell the story in his own fashion.

"Mr. President," said Wells, "I hate to ruin a good story by telling the ending first, but that's exactly what I'm going to do. The people on the *USS California*, which we've been calling the *Gray Ship*, are of fine character and intelligence. Farragut and my aide Commander Roebling both agree. The officers and crew that I met makes one proud to have them in our Navy. During our tour of the vessel we saw or heard nothing that would even hint at prevarication of any sort."

"My dear Gideon," said Lincoln, "I thought you were getting to the end first."

"Mr. President, the people on the *USS California* are convinced that they came here through some strange portal from another time, April 2013, to be exact, 152 years into the future."

Lincoln said nothing. He sat down and stared out the window. He looked at Wells and massaged his tall forehead. He then scratched his beard and the back of his head. He folded his arms, unfolded them and stood up again. He then spread his arms to each side of his desk and stared at Wells.

Lincoln said, "Gideon, did you or Farragut or Roebling think that those people may be insane, suffering from delusional thoughts?"

"Sir," said Wells, "if they are insane then I am too, and I know I speak for Farragut and Roebling as well. I am convinced, Mr. President, that the *USS California* and her entire crew have come here from the year 2013. They have travelled through time. Of that I am certain."

From his days as a country lawyer and his many years as a politician, Lincoln always prided himself on staying ahead of a conversation. He had a skill for listening to a person and then thinking five sentences ahead. He could draw conclusions from what a man said, and then question the man on his conclusions, as well as those of the man speaking. But Abraham Lincoln did not feel he was ahead in this conversation. Lincoln was baffled, and he told Wells as much. "Please go on Mr. Secretary," said Lincoln, "Please convince me that you, or I, have not lost our minds."

He handed Lincoln a copy of the 35-page report that Campbell had prepared, one for Wells and one for Lincoln. "This report, Mr. President, has perfectly clear lettering as you can see. They prepared the report for us on a machine called a computer. A sailor sat before the instrument and tapped with his fingers on buttons. The letters appeared on the machine right in front of him. When he finished, he pressed another button and these pages that you see came out of yet a second machine called a printer."

Wells told Lincoln in detail about every aspect of their tour, including the weapons and propulsion devices. He explained, as best he could, this amazing thing called nuclear energy. "They said they can sail for over ten years without refueling. The technology and science is amazing." He told Lincoln about the guided missiles, the rocket propelled grenades, the fully automatic rifles, and the startling instrument called an IPad. "They communicate long distances without laying cable," Wells said. "They call it wireless. May I demonstrate, sir?"

"Please go ahead, Gideon."

Wells picked a two-way radio out of the suitcase and told Lincoln he was going to call the *California* by her code name, *Lima Juliette*. Wells was giddy with excitement, his great white beard swinging in the air with his movements. He pressed a button and said: "*Lima Juliette, Lima Juliette,* this is *Alpha Foxtrot,* radio check over." Within a couple of seconds a voice came out of the instrument. It said, "This is *Lima Juliette*, read you loud and clear *Alpha Foxtrot*."

"Alpha Foxtrot?" Lincoln asked. Wells beamed. "Sir, that is my new radio code name."

"Well," said Lincoln, "I believe congratulations are in order Mr. Foxtrot, or may I call you Alpha?" Lincoln sat down again.

Wells then told Lincoln that for all of the marvels that they saw aboard the *California*, the most shocking part of the tour was a talk prepared by a Commander Richard Sampson, the ship's chaplain and historian.

"Because they come from the future, Mr. President, they know the past, and their past is our future." At that, Lincoln held up his right hand, palm out. He stared at the ceiling, making sure he understood what he just heard.

"Please continue, Gideon."

Wells then told Lincoln about the casualty figures of the four years to come, summing them up with the most shocking number of all: 620,000 casualties or more, a number that's easy to write on a page, but almost impossible to hold in one's mind. Lincoln stared at Wells. Wells stared at the floor.

"Dear God," said Lincoln, "Dear God Almighty."

Wells opened one of the suitcases and withdrew folder after folder of crisp color photographs. The pictures were not just of the *California* but were a photographic montage of the United States Navy in the year 2013. He first showed Lincoln the *California* itself and her amazing machines. He then laid out pictures of some of the Navy's other ships, including aircraft carriers and nuclear ballistic missile submarines. Lincoln stared at the picture of an aircraft carrier, a photo of the *USS Ronald Reagan*. One photo showed an F-14 Tomcat fighter jet being launched off the deck by catapult.

"How many of these flying machines did you say the *California* has?" Lincoln asked.

"Just three Mr. President. One is a machine called a helicopter. Here it is in this picture. It lands and flies straight up and down. They call this machine an Apache Attack Helicopter. It can remain in the air in one position while it fires rockets, bullets, and bombs at an enemy. They also have these strange things they call helicopter drones that are flown without men aboard using that wireless business I mentioned a few minutes ago. They can use the drones to spy on the enemy, to fire rockets, and also to take photographs." Lincoln's eyes fixed on the drones.

"These drones, Gideon," said Lincoln, "can they take photographs while flying fast over an area?"

"Yes, Mr. President. The drones can take photographs or even a moving image that they call a video. The person on the ship who operates the drone can see the images in what they call 'real time,' as if you were looking at the object while it was being photographed. Until they went through that amazing *Daylight Event,* they used things they call satellites, metallic objects in the sky that actually circle the earth. They could somehow send a wireless message from the drone to the satellite or from the ship to the satellite and then to the drone. Until they lost the satellites they could operate a drone from, say, the State of Oregon while operating the machine here in Washington. They also used these satellites to navigate. They call it a Global Positioning System. Since they went through the time portal, they no longer have that ability. But the drones can still take photographs and send them back to the ship using radio waves, just as I did when I called the *California* on my radio." Lincoln just massaged his temples. Wells understood the confusion Lincoln experienced, just as he had two days before.

"So these drones can fly over an area and photograph troop movements and artillery positions?"

"Yes, Mr. President, these machines can have an enormous military impact. And the drone machine itself can also fire rockets. They have a way for troops on the ground to point a thing they call a laser, which is a device of some sort that I simply don't understand. A soldier would point this laser machine at a target such as an artillery battery, and the drone would fire its rocket directly at the battery. It's amazing, Mr. President."

"That it is my friend, that it is."

\* \* \*

"How many ships like the *California* are sailing the oceans, Mr. Secretary?" Lincoln asked.

Lincoln's question confused Wells. He thought he had made it clear that the *California* took a solitary trip through time. "Only one, Mr. President. The *California* took her strange journey all alone."

"So you're certain that there are no other ships like the *California* at sea at this very moment, Gideon?"

"Yes, sir, there are no others."

"And do you base your conclusion on personal observation?"

Wells realized that he was being cross examined by an expert lawyer. "No sir. I did not personally look for any other ships."

"Did you ask the officers on the *California* if they knew of any others?"

"No sir, I did not," said Wells.

"Now, Gideon, these gigantic ships in the photos that are called aircraft carriers, have you determined that there are none at sea?"

"No sir, I have not personally determined that."

"It seems to me," said Lincoln, "that in the vastness of the oceans it is impossible to say with certainty that there are no other *Gray Ships* afloat. Do you not agree, Gideon?"

Wells had to admit, "Well, no, Mr. President, I cannot say so with certainty."

Lincoln walked over to a window and stood silently, looking out at the grounds. The flowers were starting to bloom as spring opened its wings. Lincoln always saw spring as a time of new beginnings, a time of renewal.

He then turned to Wells and said, "Let me ask you a question, my friend. If you were Jefferson Davis, the President of the Confederacy, would you not be concerned about a whole fleet of these amazing vessels, maneuvering and ready to strike at your forces? And would not this worrisome possibility, if you were Davis, consume your thoughts and guide your decisions?"

Wells paused and stroked his beard. "If you put it that way Mr. President, I suppose Jeff Davis would be concerned. But, sir, he has no reason for worry, except for the one ship that he knows about, the *USS California*."

Lincoln walked over to his Navy Secretary and sat in a chair across from him, his long legs jutting forward as if pinning Wells to his chair. He peered into Wells' eyes and said, "Gideon, what if we give Davis something to worry about?" Wells eyes grew wide. He suddenly slapped his knee and laughed uproariously.

"Of course," said Wells. "We'll make them think that there's a fleet of *Gray Ships!*"

Lincoln smiled broadly. He then stood and walked over to the table that was covered with the photographs of ships.

"You have told me about the fearsome weapons aboard the *California*, Gideon. But these," Lincoln waved his hands over the array of photos, "these are our most potent weapons."

The phrase PsyOps or psychological operations did not exist in 1861, but the idea of using tricks to fool an enemy has been around since ancient times. Lincoln realized that they had an opportunity to prevent the slaughter that Wells told him about.

The *Gray Ship* fleet would soon put to sea.

# Chapter 29

The Coast Guard Cutter *Gallatin* arrived in the vicinity of the *California*'s last known position. It was 0327 and still pitch dark. Fortunately the sea was calm, always a good condition for an ocean search and rescue operation.

Commander Donald Hester, the CO of the *Gallatin*, contacted the Office of Naval Operations at the Pentagon to advise them that he had arrived on station and was commencing search and rescue operations.

The *Gallatin* was equipped with the US Navy's latest in underwater rescue technology. Known by the catchy phrase Submarine Rescue Diving and Recompression System's (SRDRS), it was designed for rescuing submarine crews. This SRDRS was nicknamed *"Bubbles."* It is a manned submersible and can dive to a depth of 2,000 feet.

The depth below the *Gallatin* was only 300 feet, making *Bubbles'* mission relatively easy. There was one problem. As the *Gallatin* approached the area, it had been pinging with its forward directional sonar to pick up a "target." The sonar waves returned no hits, meaning the *California* had not yet been located.

Hester decided to wait before he launched *Bubbles*. First they would try to locate the *California* by dragging a sonar array just beneath the surface in a plotted grid pattern.

Combined with sonar buoys dropped from the helicopters, they should be able to locate something as large as the *California* in a short time.

All sonar operators peered at their screens and listened for the telltale return sound of a metallic "hit." They heard silence.

The *California* has been missing for 18 minutes.

# Chapter 30

radley called Chief Ray to his office. He was careful to keep their meetings to a minimum and to communicate in short conversations at prearranged locations throughout the ship. Bradley knew that they needed more people to make their Confederacy plans work, but for now he kept it between himself and Chief Ray. At this point, the more people involved the greater the chance of a leak or slip up.

"What about the big weapons, Chief? The guided missiles, the five-inch guns, and even the ASROCS (anti submarine missile system) can do a hell of a lot of damage. We can't get them off the ship. Any way to disable them?"

"I've been thinking about just that, Commander. The first way is easy. I just remove the printed circuit boards for all of the big weapons systems. Every one of them, including the five inch guns, have a printed circuit board. I just take 'em out and toss 'em overboard. But the timing is tricky. All these systems, except for the ASROCs, are manned by crews around the clock. The boards would have to be yanked before anybody notices a problem."

"What about the five-inch guns?" asked Bradley. "Can't they be operated manually?"

"Excellent question, Commander. Yes they can be operated manually without a circuit board. For the guns I suggest we use thermite grenades.

Those little babies are designed to melt metal. They can burn at a temperature as high as 4,000 degrees. We have 100 of them aboard. Pop one of them down the barrel of a gun and it's time to buy a new gun. The grenades that we don't use we can put in the Zodiacs."

"So," said Bradley, "we can turn this cruiser into an unarmed cruise ship in a few minutes."

"Yes, sir. A cruise ship without a swimming pool."

Also, thought Bradley, a ship that can't defend herself can be sunk, especially if you use her own weapons against her.

# Chapter 31

EAL Petty Officer First Class Peter Campo is a master in the martial arts. He began as a freshman in high school, and by his second year in junior college he had become a black belt in both karate and the Korean skill of Taekwondo. He's also an expert in the Japanese "Gentle Way" or judo. He had taught martial arts at the Navy SEAL training school as well as the Naval Academy. When he reported aboard the *California* he asked Lieutenant Conroy if he could teach classes on the ship. Conroy ran the idea up the chain of command and Campo got the job.

Campo was about to start a beginner's class, his favorite. People new to the martial arts have no preconceived notions, and the classes are easier to teach and more fun. This class would include Simon Planck, the sailor who Captain Patterson ordered him to pay close attention to. Easy job, thought Campo. Give me an order and I follow it. He also relished the idea of helping this scrawny kid. Planck was one of 10 people in the class of seven men and three women.

"My name is Peter Campo, but you will call me Pete. You come to this class maybe not knowing how to swat a fly. I make you one promise: When you finish this class, flies will fear you." That cracked everybody up, as Pete intended. His style was not to lord his martial prowess over his students, but to respect them and show them how to get the respect of other people. Contrary to normal rules, he addressed each person beginning with their rank, such as Seaman or Petty Officer, not simply their last name. It took a bit longer, but it also showed respect.

Campo also knew the importance of early success for his students, and he intentionally placed himself in a position to be thrown around so a student could get the feel of executing a correct move.

The class began with judo, the "gentle way." But first, he ordered each of the students to bow in respect for each of the other students. He explained the simple idea behind judo, to use the force of an opponent against him. He asked Planck to come forward.

"Seaman Planck, I have a question," said Pete. "Have you ever tripped and fallen?"

"Yes, Pete," said Planck, thinking the question was dumb.

"Now Seaman Planck, did you notice that after you tripped, that the falling part was easy? You just went forward and hit the ground. It was easy because gravity did it for you. Judo is a lot like that. Now Seaman Planck, I want you to punch me in the nose. Don't worry, I'm not wearing a sidearm. Go ahead, punch me."

Seaman Planck threw the punch. Pete stepped slightly backward and to the right and grabbed Planck's fist as if it were a thrown ball, simultaneously putting his right arm around Planck's waist and gently throwing him to the matt.

"Gravity," said Pete, "just threw our friend Seaman Planck to the mat with only a minor assist from me. I used his forward momentum and just helped it to keep going forward." He did this five more times with Seaman Planck, asking everybody to watch carefully. "Now," said Pete, "I'm going to throw a punch at our friend Seaman Planck." Planck stiffened.

"Okay, Seaman Planck, here it comes." Pete threw an arcing punch, aiming it in such a way that if he did connect it would be with the fleshy part of his forearm. Just as he had learned from watching Campo, Planck "caught" Campo's fist and pulled his opponent toward him, flipping him to the mat (aided by Campo himself).

"Outstanding, Seaman Planck. Let's hear it for this guy." Everyone applauded. Planck bowed, as Pete slapped him on the shoulder. "Way to go, guy. Excellent job."

Planck couldn't remember the last time he felt proud. He didn't have many opportunities.

# *Chapter 32*

The day after Lincoln met with Navy Secretary Wells, he held a scheduled meeting of his eight cabinet members. The meeting began promptly at 8:30 a.m. Lincoln's spacious office also served as the cabinet meeting room, with its large conference table around which each of the cabinet members sat.

The day was overcast with heavy low clouds, which cut down on the natural light from the windows. A staff member lit the gas lamps hanging on the walls. Two staff waiters walked around the table pouring coffee and circulating plates of buns. At 45 degrees, it was cold for mid-April, and everyone welcomed the hot coffee. The staff left the room after they completed their chores just before the meeting began.

Lincoln, seated at the head of the conference table, placed his elbows on the table and touched his fingers together creating a cathedral-like arch, a familiar pose to the men present. It showed neither aggressiveness nor reticence. The pose didn't say I'm your friend or your enemy. The pose simply announced that it was time to get down to business.

"Gentlemen," said Lincoln, "you are about to experience the strangest meeting that you will ever attend." Lincoln sipped slowly from a cup of coffee to let his words sink in. The cabinet members glanced around the room at each other to see if someone understood why Lincoln said this.

They noticed that Gideon Wells smiled broadly behind his huge white beard.

"Yesterday I had a long meeting with Secretary Wells over here," said Lincoln, nodding in Wells' direction. "That, gentlemen, was the strangest meeting I ever attended, and now Secretary Wells and I are going to let you join in the fun." That brought a nervous chuckle from everyone.

As arranged, Wells reached into a large briefcase and withdrew a stack of documents, copies of the report summary that Campbell had given him. He passed them around. "Amazingly clear typeface," noted the Postmaster General.

"Please take a few moments to read this report, and I'll then ask Gideon to summarize his recent experience."

Wells gave his report, summarizing his day on the *USS California* with Admiral Farragut and Commander Roebling. He also passed around the Navy photographs of other amazing vessels. Wells then got to the most salient point, the point that he, Farragut, Roebling, and now President Lincoln had reached.

"Gentlemen," said Wells, "the *Gray Ship*, the *USS California*, does exist. It's real, and it came here from the year 2013."

Looks of shock and skepticism took over the room, the same shock and skepticism that recently hit Wells and Lincoln.

Wells then summarized the "history" of the Civil War that Chaplain Sampson provided, a history that would unfold over the next four years and would result in 620,000 casualties.

No one spoke for at least three minutes, each man hoping that someone else would ask a question or make a point that would dash this nonsense and bring them all back to reality.

Secretary of State Seward spoke. "Can we know for certain that the *California* is the only such ship afloat?" Secretary of War Cameron chimed in. "Exactly," said Cameron, "from a military point of view that is the most important question."

"I'll ask President Lincoln to answer that question," said Wells.

Lincoln stood and spoke. "The truth is, gentlemen, we don't know. Gideon tells me that the captain and officers on the *California* are unaware of any other vessels."

Lincoln raised his voice a bit. "But to say that there are no other American ships like the *California* plying the seas would be a lie. It would be as much a lie if I told you that I was certain there isn't a herd of buffalo behind that wall. There may be a herd, there may not be a herd, but the truth is I don't know." Gideon Wells concealed a smile with his hand. This was the Abe Lincoln, the skilled lawyer, that he heard yesterday.

Lincoln continued, "And, gentlemen, we don't want to lie and say that there are no more *California*s, because we don't have actual knowledge that there are not. And we certainly don't want to lie to Jefferson Davis and his rebel government do we?"

Everyone laughed, because everyone just got it. Cameron, the Secretary of War, said, "If I were in the Southern command, I would be frightened by the *California*. If I thought there may be dozens or hundreds more like her, I would be looking for a white flag to wave."

Lincoln was about to bring the meeting to a close. "Gentlemen, we have in the *USS California* a potent weapon, the most significant military advantage we could ever imagine. But the very thought that there may be more is the most potent weapon of all. The word will spread forth, in ways to be determined, that we don't know how many *Gray Ships* are out there. We just need to keep speaking the truth."

\* \* \*

Two days later, on April 19, 1861, President Lincoln would formally announce the beginning of the *Anaconda Plan*. Devised by Union General

Winfield Scott, the *Anaconda Plan* called for the blockade of Southern ports, to prevent the import of supplies and weaponry as well as to block the export of goods, especially cotton, to Europe. The name *Anaconda* came from the idea of a snake wrapping its coils around its prey to suffocate it.

# *Chapter* 33

*N*avy policy requires at least one officer to eat in the crew's mess every day. The idea behind the rule is to ensure that enlisted personnel receive good treatment. The officers on the *California* loved this duty because the food in the mess hall is far superior to wardroom fare.

Chaplain Sampson had another reason to eat in the crew's mess: he wanted to keep his finger on the elusive pulse called morale. He asked and received permission to eat in the crew's mess five times a week.

On his first breakfast visit, he walked down the chow line when he spotted a large sign hung over the buffet. "For Your Dining Pleasure, Today's Special – Chipped Beef on Toast Points (S.O.S.) Bon Appétit!" As every sailor knows, "S.O.S." refers to "Shit on a Shingle." Although it was an old Navy joke, the simple dish is very tasty. Father Rick enjoyed Valente's sense of humor. Dominic Valente, the ship's supply officer, personally wrote the special menu copy every day.

His tray full, Father Rick walked over to a table and said, "You guys mind if I join you?" Nobody minded. Everybody loved having Father Rick around. "Anyone wish to join me in grace?" The chaplain made the sign of the cross and intoned, "Heavenly Father guide us through these troubled seas, and save us from peril. In Your Holy Name, Amen."

"You guys look pretty good for being 152 years younger." Everyone cracked up. The *Daylight Event* had developed its own genre of humor. The chaplain then asked of no one in particular, "How's everybody putting up with this crazy time?"

Petty Officer Bill Martin replied. "At first, Padre, it was kind of exciting. I mean the idea of finding ourselves in 1861 was almost fun. But it's getting to be a drag, a real drag."

"How so Bill?" asked Father Rick. He always made it a point to refer to enlisted sailors by their first name, contrary to Navy rules and tradition. Because the only identifier on a sailor's uniform was a surname, people were amazed how the chaplain could remember so many first names. Father Rick would often tell his religious colleagues, "If a shepherd doesn't know his flock, he'll lose a lot of lambs."

Martin replied. "A few days ago we knew we were headed to the Persian Gulf. We knew we'd be there for six months, and then home. Now we just don't know the future, or when we'll see our families again. If you pardon the language, Padre, it sucks."

Father Rick looked into Martin's eyes and said, "If I recall Bill, your wife just had a baby girl a few days before we shipped out. I bet you miss them both."

"It's not just a case of missing them, Father. It's not knowing when, or if, I'll ever see them again." His eyes teared up.

"I bet it's not easy, Bill," said Father Rick. Martin just looked at his tray.

"Anybody else feel like Bill does?" asked the chaplain. Heads nodded in unison.

Petty Officer Jim Dayton, sitting a few seats down the table, said, "I know exactly how Martin feels. I was engaged to be married after we got back from the Gulf." He took out a photo of his pretty fiancée and passed it around. "Now I don't know when I'll see her again. I can't even talk to her or email her. It's a bad feeling, Father, real bad."

Petty Officer Andrea Dunne told the story about how she was texting her mother, who has severe liver cancer. "Mom's reply got cut off in the middle of a sentence. She was about to tell me something that her doctor said." Dunne put her face in her hands, wiped her eyes and said, her voice breaking up, "She may be dead for all I know."

Father Rick looked at her. "That must be very painful Andrea."

"It is, Padre, it's real painful. The worst part is not knowing, and not knowing when I'll know anything."

"Not having the Internet is the worst part," Seaman Gail Robinson said. All heads nodded vigorously. "We've gotten so used to instant communication that it feels like, I don't know, like I'm in the middle of a forest somewhere. What really hurts is that I know my folks, my brother and sister, not to mention my boyfriend, are all emailing, texting me and posting me on Facebook. They must think I'm dead."

"That's absolutely right," said Martin. "Not being able to send a message is bad enough, but the empty inbox is the worst."

"My father was a submarine sailor on a nuke," Said Petty Officer Juan Portillo. "When they went on patrol they'd be submerged for 90 days at a time. The sub could communicate by raising a buoy, and they could receive messages called 'family grams.' But the messages were censored, and if there was any bad news, it wouldn't get to a sailor until they returned to port. At least they knew that they'd be able to talk to their family eventually. We don't even know that."

A religious leader, whether a pastor, a priest, a rabbi, or a military chaplain, is part psychologist. He's expected to not only listen to problems, but to offer guidance. Father Rick knew that the first part of healing is recognizing that you have pain. This conversation, Sampson knew, was only the first part, acknowledging the pain. He also knew that this was just one small group of sailors and that there was a lot more pain on this ship.

"In the years I've been on earth," said the chaplain, "I've experienced a lot of pain, and listening to you folks reminds me of it. I remember when my mom had terminal cancer." He looked at Andrea Dunne, who bit her lip as he spoke. "As mom was dying, I came down with a terrible case of pneumonia. I felt like I was going to die, too. It's the closest I ever got to feeling real despair." He let his words linger, looking for a response.

"What did you do, Father?" asked Andrea Dunne.

"I decided to let it go, Andrea. I decided to put the problems in God's hands. I prayed. He saved me."

The chaplain looked around the table and looked into everyone's eyes. "You can't email or text me, but you all know where my office is. Come by at any time."

# Chapter 34

ather Rick rang Ashley's office. "A word with you Captain?"

"Sure, Father, come on up."

"My dining with the crew is turning out to be a good idea, Captain. The idea is good, but the experience is difficult. To be blunt, the crew is feeling the effects of living day-to-day not knowing if they have a future. I heard some pretty heart-wrenching stories from a lot of sailors, and I'm sure we'll hear them in the wardroom as well. People need to know there's something to look forward to, that there's a future you can plan for. Most of the stories are about families. They know their families, friends, and lovers are trying to contact them, and they can't reply. Frankly, Captain, I don't feel too great about the situation either."

"Nor do I, Rick. Nor do I."

"As a naval officer, Father, how much do you think these issues will affect our mission, whatever that may be?"

"All I can say, my friend, is that the mission can't be too long." He then asked, "When you meet with Lincoln, can you tell him about this growing problem?"

"I will. I have to."

# *Chapter 35*

*A*shley buzzed Jack's number. She worried about the crew's growing morale problem and wanted an update on Jack's plans for locating the worm hole for the trip back to 2013. It would also be nice just to see Jack.

"Lt. Thurber, please come to my office."

Jack appeared in the Captain's office within two minutes. "Yes, Captain?"

"I'm concerned about the crew, Jack. Are we telling them enough?"

"Is there a problem, if I may ask?" said Jack. Ashley told Jack about Father Rick's experience in the crew's mess, how morale was starting to get dicey because people didn't have a sense of their future.

"I may have something that will make things better, or at least make people feel better. I'm working on a spreadsheet to map the incidents of time away versus elapsed time in the present. It's trickier than it sounds because I never dug too deeply into that issue in my book. But I do have all of my interview notes, so I should have something for you by tomorrow."

"When I'm done with this spreadsheet, Captain, I think we'll have some good news for the crew. Today is April 17. We've been in the past for seven days. What the crew will be happy to know is that we've been gone for only a few minutes, maybe hours, in 2013 time. It's impossible to calculate exactly because we'll only know how long we've been gone in retrospect. Remember the guy from World War I. He was gone for eight months in the past but only five minutes in the present."

"Thank God you're aboard, Jack," Ashley said as she looked into his eyes.

He held her gaze and said, in a soft voice, "I thank God I am, too."

# Chapter 36

President Lincoln told Navy Secretary Wells to arrange a meeting with the Captain of the *California*. He also wanted Secretary of State Seward and Secretary of War Cameron to be at the meeting. Commander Campbell would be there also.

Wells loved his new toy, the two-way radio. "*Lima Juliette, Lima Juliette,* this is *Alpha Foxtrot,* over."

"*Alpha Foxtrot,* this is *Lima Juliette,* go ahead," said the officer of the deck.

"May I please speak to the Captain," said Wells. Ashley was on the bridge at the time and the OOD handed her the radio, telling her that Secretary Wells was on the radio.

"This is Captain Patterson. Good morning, Mr. Secretary."

"President Lincoln would like to meet with you and Commander Campbell at 11:30 this morning," said Wells.

"We shall be there, sir."

Ashley imagined coming home to her late husband Felix. "How was your day, Hon?" Felix would ask. "Oh, let's see," she imagined saying, "Got up early, showered, had breakfast and met with Abraham Lincoln. Just a routine day."

The *California* was still anchored in Chesapeake Bay. At 0900 two sailors swung the boat davits over the side of the ship and secured cables to the bow and stern of the motor launch. One of them hit a toggle switch, lowering the boat to the water. The day was mild, with a bright sun and temperatures in the lower 60s. As Ashley stepped onto the ladder, the boatswain's pipe sounded throughout the ship, followed by the announcement, "*California*, departing."

Ashley and Campbell were wearing their service dress blue uniforms. Ashley felt it was no longer necessary to disguise themselves in period civilian dress.

They looked at each other. They didn't speak. They knew they were about to make history, or maybe even change it.

The launch motored its way along the Potomac, drawing stares from anyone ashore or on nearby boats. Petty Officer Donizzio, the boat's captain, felt like a hero in a yacht club showing off his new boat. Donizzio eased the boat next to the pier, its twin diesel engines growling as he put it in reverse to stop the boat's forward motion.

A carriage awaited them. The driver opened the door and Ashley and Campbell climbed in. As their carriage rumbled up the cobblestone path to the White House entrance, Ashley glanced toward an area where the West Wing would eventually be, and noticed that the Rose Garden wasn't there yet either. She said, "I've been to the White House a few times. It looks much better in 2013."

Although she didn't like small talk, she would do anything, short of reciting nursery rhymes, to calm her growling stomach. An aide ran to open the carriage door for them. As Ashley stepped down her foot caught on a rung and she fell forward. The aide grabbed her arm and kept her from falling face first onto the cobblestones. Calm down, she said to herself.

Ashley and Campbell were escorted to the President's office, which was rectangular, not oval. An aide opened the door and motioned for them to enter. The thought crossed Ashley's mind that the superintendant's office at Annapolis was more opulent. Lincoln stood behind his desk with Wells and Seward to the right and War Secretary Cameron to the left. All eyes were on Ashley.

Wells had purposely avoided telling Lincoln that Captain Ashley Patterson was a woman. Ashley is a common name for a man. He also neglected to tell him that she was colored. He wanted his President to have the wonderful shock that he had experienced a few days ago.

Ashley had an urge to take out her smart phone and snap a picture of the expression on the men's faces. If a dancing unicorn had galloped in instead of Ashley, their faces couldn't have been more shocked. Obviously, Wells kept my identity a secret, Ashley thought.

Navy Secretary Wells said, "Mr. President, Secretary Seward, Secretary Cameron, it is my honor to introduce Captain Ashley Patterson, Commanding Officer of the *USS California*. And this gentleman is Commander Ivan Campbell, the ship's navigator."

Ashley and Campbell snapped sharp salutes. Ashley then offered her hand to the President, something a lady of the 1800s did not do. Lincoln, a man accustomed to taking charge of situations, was dumbfounded. He wasn't sure if he should shake her hand or kiss it. He did both.

"Madam Captain," Lincoln said, "I must say that I'm surprised that you're not only a woman, but a colored woman." Ashley felt calmer, the ice broken. She also marveled at Lincoln's voice. Thinking of the great marble statue in the Lincoln Memorial, she expected to hear a voice like rolling thunder or like Charlton Heston in *The Ten Commandments*. Instead, the President's voice was slightly high pitched, and his manner of speaking almost soft in tone.

She smiled and said, "In the good old twenty-first-century, Mr. President, we are known as black or African American." She then told the men about Colin Powell, Condoleezza Rice, and Barack Obama, the nation's first black President.

Wells beamed. He saw that his friend Abe Lincoln, a man who shared his abolitionist views, was as pleased as he had been to see what human progress can mean.

"We've received a thorough report," Lincoln said, "thanks to Secretary Wells and the written document that Commander Campbell provided us." Lincoln drew a deep breath. "Once we accepted the incredible fact that you have travelled here through time, and that you are able to tell us what will happen in the next four years, we all came to the same conclusion. We must terminate this horrible war as quickly as possible. I shall not abide the prediction that the war will bring 620,000 casualties. As God is my witness, may He smite me dead if I don't do everything in my power to halt the slaughter."

\* \* \*

Lincoln had a well-earned reputation as a raconteur, a man who would introduce a point with a lengthy story and humorous side stories. But this morning he got right to the point.

"Captain," said Lincoln, "the *USS California* is our weapon for bringing this war to a swift close. Our objective is simple, but its execution will not be easy. We will convince President Jefferson Davis and the command structure of the Confederacy that a protracted war will mean not only the defeat of the South, but its destruction."

"We will accomplish this task in three ways," Lincoln continued. "First, the *California* will assist Navy Secretary Wells and his admiral staff in a naval blockade of the Southern states. Second, the *California* will actively engage the enemy at the Battle of Bull Run, the first major battle of the War, according to you folks. That will be three months from now. And third, but perhaps most important, we will fool the enemy into thinking that the *California* is but one of a vast fleet of *Gray Ships* about to devastate the rebel cause. Navy Secretary Wells and War Secretary Cameron will now tell us about the plan they have devised.

Gideon Wells began. "The detailed plans for the *California's* involvement at Bull Run will be worked on by your staff and one of our generals who will be stationed on the *California*. Now I will speak about the plan to confuse the South into thinking that the *California* is not alone."

"It will be called *Operation Gray Ships*. The plan will have two parts. The first part involves your ship itself. The *California* is very fast with a top speed over thirty knots, faster than any other vessel on the water. You will steam from location to location, bringing with you fear and confusion. But besides speed, we want the *California* to actually appear to be more than one ship. Our plan is to paint over the large number 36 on your hull, and also to change the name of the ship on her stern on a regular basis. We also want the appearance of the deck itself to change from time to time. When people report seeing the ship they will see that their reports do not match up to the same ship. As a dramatist may put it, this will be a one act play with multiple costume changes."

"Your objective," War Secretary Cameron said, "is to be seen, contrary to typical naval operations. Of course, if you're fired upon, you will fire back. Is there any concern about that, Captain?"

"It will be the Confederate ship's captain who will have cause for concern, sir."

"Captain," continued Wells, "do you have enough personnel on board to do this work?"

"I believe we do, sir. I know we have two excellent officers in our engineering department to make this plan successful. If we need additional workmen and carpenters, I will ask for your assistance."

"And you shall get it," said Wells.

"The second part of *Operation Gray Ships* will be more literary than military. We have contacts at all major newspapers, and we are going to see to it that articles about the *Gray Ships* are published regularly. We need not worry about putting them in Southern papers. Confederate spies will bring the papers south as soon as they are published. I understand, Captain, that the fellow I met, Lieutenant John Thurber, is a skilled writer and journalist. Please tell the lieutenant that he will write the articles."

Secretary of State Seward stood. He looked at Lincoln and said, "Mr. President, I believe it would be accurate to say that never in the history of warfare has one military unit borne such a grave responsibility. The *USS California* can end this war."

Lincoln rose from his seat at the end of the table. He leaned forward, supported by his long arms. "Captain Patterson, Secretary Seward is correct. The *California* is the key to a swift victory. God works in strange ways, and He has seen fit to bring you to us from another time. In His justice we will end this terrible war, and He will also aid me in ending human bondage. As you know, Madam Captain, vast thousands of people of your race are at this very moment enslaved. I thank God that He has brought us Captain Ashley Patterson to show us what freedom can become."

Everyone in the room stood, faced Ashley, and gave her a loud round of applause. She nodded her head, proud that she managed to fight back tears.

\* \* \*

Ashley sensed that the meeting was about to end. She had to have a private word with Lincoln, and it wouldn't happen unless she asked.

Ashley said, after the applause stopped, "I thank you, Mr. President, and I thank all of you gentlemen for the confidence you've placed in the *California*. May I have a private word with you, Mr. President?"

Ashley knew that her request may be inappropriate, even insubordinate, but she knew she had to speak to Lincoln. "Of course, Madam Captain," said Lincoln. Everyone filed out of the room except Ashley and Lincoln. He motioned her to a chair and he sat in the one next to it.

"Mr. President, I'm worried about the morale of my crew. It actually goes deeper than just a morale problem. Our chaplain, Father Sampson, has been dining with the enlisted personnel, trying to gauge how they are standing up under the strange times we find ourselves in. They've all left behind, in another time, families and friends. From day to day, actually from moment to moment, they're without a sense of a certain future. They're emotionally upset, frightened, and sad. We come from the year 2013. Our country has enemies, God knows, but the Civil War is a faint memory, something we read about in history books."

"I have been wondering about this very thing, Captain, and I'm glad that you raise the matter. Do you have something to request of me? Is there something I can do?"

"Yes, sir, there is. We have some strong evidence that the *California* may be able to return to 2013 by finding the exact location where we slipped through the time portal. What I'm asking you Mr. President is this: After the Battle of Bull Run, I would like your permission to say farewell and to bring my crew home."

Lincoln stood and walked over to the window. He had just heard a request so reasonable he couldn't see how he could deny it. But in his few months as President he had learned a great deal about military strategy and tactics. He learned that there is one thing predictable about war, that it is unpredictable.

He returned to his chair next to Ashley. "Captain I appreciate the problem your crew finds themselves in. The morale and enthusiasm of your crew is crucial to the success of our plans. I understand that they need some certainty in their lives. We fully expect that your participation in the blockade, the *Gray Ship*s deception, and the Battle of Bull Run will turn the tide and force the South to capitulate. But war is full of surprises. So I can promise you this. If our plans are successful, you will have my full permission to return home, and I shall move heaven and earth to help you to accomplish it. But as President and Commander in Chief, I must say to you that your taking leave must depend on a successful outcome. Do you find that acceptable, Captain?"

Ashley knew it was all she could hope for.

"Thank you, Mr. President. We will make it a success."

# *Chapter 37*

ieutenant Commander Nick Wartella, the ship's Chief Engineering Officer called Lt. Jeff DeLouker and Lt. Jg. Nancy Forsyth
to his office for a meeting. Wartella had been briefed by Captain Patterson
and Commander Campbell on *Operation Gray Ships*.

Wartella, an Annapolis graduate, had recently been promoted to Lt.
Commander. His job as Engineering Officer on the *California* was his first
department head post. His subordinates know him as a bright officer with
little patience for imperfection. Captain Patterson thought that Wartella
was the perfect officer to head up the *California's* part of *Operation Gray
Ships*.

Wartella explained *Operation Gray Ships*, and their role in it, to DeLouker
and Forsyth.

"Navy Secretary Wells, according to Captain Patterson, characterized
our job as a one act play with multiple costume changes. The *California*
is the actor, and you two are in charge of changing costumes, as often as
once a day."

Lt. Jeff DeLouker was a mustang, an officer who rose through the
ranks as an enlisted man, and his salty language reflected it. He was in
charge of the "A" Division of the Engineering Department. The "A"
Division is charged with fixing what's broken, and even manufacturing
new equipment with available materials. Because a ship can't pull into a

service station at sea, the ability to make at-sea repairs is crucial. Everyone who ever worked with DeLouker knew him as a masterful organizer and leader. If he were a civilian he'd have been a wealthy contractor or real estate developer. But he loved the Navy and he loved making ships work.

Lt. Jg. Nancy Forsyth graduated from MIT with a degree in industrial design. Before joining the Navy, Forsythe worked for General Motors, designing sets and equipment for automobile shows. She had a reputation for designing spaces that were as imaginative as an opera set. As a consultant, she helped design the opening ceremony of the Winter Olympics at Salt Lake City, Utah. Her designs for that job were praised in *Architectural Digest*.

Forsyth and DeLouker were good friends. Before their assignments to the *California* they had worked together on a large remodeling project at the Naval War College in Newport, Rhode Island. DeLouker admired her design skills, and Forsyth was impressed with DeLouker's ability to manage complex projects. When Nancy Forsythe married her long-time girl friend, Jane Blake, Jeff and his wife Dianne attended the wedding. DeLouker had a non-stop sense of humor, earning him the nickname Taz, short for Tasmanian Devil. While at the War College project he would often introduce Forsyth as his wife, which usually resulted in a punch to his arm.

"So, Nance, we get to play in a costume drama together," said DeLouker as they sat down for their project planning meeting. Wartella had made DeLouker the project manager.

"This won't be easy, Taz," said Forsyth. "We've been assigned the job of making the *California* look like 20 different ships, and to make the changes once a day. I think we should be guided by three major principles. The stuff should be easy to put up, easy to take down, and easy to maintain."

"My troops will be happy to hear that, Nance."

"Okay, let's break the project down into parts," DeLouker said. "I'll start to list them and you just jump in with your ideas."

"First we need to look at the ship's name. We can't paint a new name on the stern every night, so we need to design large boards that can be bolted to the stern. The only problem is, boards are straight and the stern is curved."

"No problem, Jeff. I'll design a couple of triangular supports that can be easily bolted and unbolted."

"Perfect, Nance. We're going to need lumber from ashore. As soon as your designs are done I'll contact the Navy Department with a parts list. I figure in 1861 the Navy uses a lot of wood. I want the signs to be pulled up and lowered with four sailors, two on each end for stability in the wind and two to lower the sign itself. We'll need four steel grommets in the sign. We'll leave the shackles secured to the sign with the lines tied off on the ship to help with stability in rough weather. As I'm thinking about this, I'm sure we can do a name change in less than five minutes. What do you think, Nance?"

"I think it can be done," said Forsyth. "Good idea about using four people. A stiff wind can be a problem."

"Next we need the names for the signs," DeLouker said. "We'll make it simple and use the names of states. Northern states only, obviously, including Hawaii."

"Shithead," said Forsyth, "Hawaii didn't become a state until 1959."

"Hey, I got half a pay grade on you. Is that any way to talk to a superior officer?"

"Sorry, sir, I meant to say Lieutenant Shithead."

DeLouker laughed.

"I know Hawaii wasn't a state in 1861, my wise ass MIT graduate friend, but we need it as a name."

"Why?" asked Nancy.

"Simple. Our job is to fuck with their heads." Nancy held out the palm of her hand to give DeLouker a high five.

"Hawaii's in," she said.

"Next, we need to paint over the numbers on the bow," DeLouker said. "We can paint numbers on four by eight foot signs and bolt them onto the superstructure. Replacing two signs a night is another job that should take less than five minutes." Forsyth made a note.

"Now we need to come up with some new structures to lash to the deck," DeLouker continued. "Their photography can't capture moving objects, so they'll report sightings based on the ship's number, name and appearance. They'll probably make sketches, so we need the ship to look different every few days. We don't have to do this every night, because the rebels will just think they're looking at the same type of ship, just with a few structural changes from time to time."

"I've been thinking about just that, and I did some sketches." Forsyth said. "Look at these drawings, Jeff."

DeLouker took a few minutes to look at her renditions and jotted some questions. "You are fucking brilliant Nance, but you already know that. I can see where you're going with these. Just explain them to me."

She smiled at his salty compliment. "I see these as two basic structures each eight feet high that can be changed in a short time into six different shapes. The first one will be on the bow, but it can be moved a few feet aft to change its appearance. I've also included four panels that will be lashed to the basic structures but can be hoisted up to add another eight feet to each configuration. On the stern, we'll just have the walls of the structure lying on the helicopter pad. Assembly will simply mean hoisting the walls in place and securing them with bolts. The frames for the units need to be very firm, so I've designed in four inch square structural members. We have to worry about wind, Jeff. You're going to have to figure out the best way to secure these things to the deck."

"That shouldn't be a problem. There are tie downs already in place all over the deck."

"Jeff, we need to think about some interesting shaped objects that we may already have aboard."

"Holy shit," said DeLouker as he slammed his hands on the desk. "We have about 1,000 linear feet of 12 inch water pipe that we're supposed to deliver to the Gulf. They look just like..."

"Big guns?" Forsythe interjected.

"We can make this cruiser look like a battleship," DeLouker said. Another occasion for a high five.

"I love that idea, Jeff. I'll design a wooden frame to hold the 'guns.'"

"I just thought of something else," DeLouker said. "We have a dozen banquet tables aboard. They're used for in-port receptions for the Navy League and stuff like that. Each table is 10 feet in diameter. We can paint them white, lash them to the rails, six on each side of the ship. I haven't the foggiest fucking idea what they're supposed to be, but neither will the rebels."

"Great idea."

"Nancy, I want our costume drama to be ready for a curtain call by May 11. That's two weeks from now. Can we make that happen?"

"Taz, you got the crew, I got the plans. We can make this work." Another high five.

# Chapter 38

So we're going to go home, maybe, Ashley thought. She couldn't get her conversation with Lincoln out of her mind. Lincoln tied his permission for the *California's* return attempt to the success of *Operation Gray Ships* and the Battle of Bull Run. Ashley knew, as any military leader did, that war had its surprises, setbacks, and disappointments. She remembered German Field Marshal von Moltke's famous quote, "No battle plan ever survives the first contact with the enemy." What if something goes wrong, she thought over and over. She remembered *Operation Eagle Claw*, Jimmy Carter's daring attempt to free the Iranian hostages by a military insertion in 1980. Eight dead, four wounded, six helicopters and one transport plane destroyed.

What if something goes wrong? Ashley knew the answer to the question. If the South didn't surrender after the *California's* blockade duty and the Battle of Bull Run, Lincoln would want to keep her in the nineteenth century, at least for a while. How long? Thought Ashley. My crew couldn't care less about fighting an enemy from the history books. They want to go home, and so do I.

\* \* \*

Ashley walked onto deck to look at the ocean. The scared little girl, the girl who doubted her success, the girl who wanted to curl up in a fetal position, the little girl named Splashy — that little girl wanted to come out and play. Ashley remembered the role play exercise that Father Rick had recommended. "Talk to your demons," Father Rick advised, after she had told him about demon Splashy. "Reason with them and take away their power."

So Ashley stared at the sea and talked to Splashy. "Listen Splashy. I'm the captain of this ship, the commanding officer. Over 600 lives depend on me making the right decisions. Now please leave me alone, and I'll buy you something nice when this is over." She didn't think Splashy got the message.

Ashley continued talking, this time to herself, not Splashy. *Operation Gray Ships* and the Battle of Bull Run will be complete successes. I'm going to make it happen, and we'll be on our way home. She could hear little Splashy skipping rope and laughing in the distance.

# Chapter 39

shley called Jack Thurber to her office. Every time she met with this man she felt increasingly comfortable. Often, she would call for a short meeting just to see him and chat. After every meeting, she felt like she had an emotional massage. The tensions of leadership wafted away. Ashley had felt this way before, when she was dating Felix. She knew the feeling well.

Ashley was falling in love.

But today she was nervous. She was about to ask Jack to do something that would raise the journalistic hairs on the back of his neck. She was about to ask this Pulitzer Prize winner to become the biggest liar of the Civil War.

"Coffee, Jack?" asked Ashley.

"Love some. Please, I'll get it."

Ashley loved how Jack was always appropriately deferential to her position. But then he could walk in wearing a clown costume, red nose, honking horn and all, and Ashley would have found it charming.

Ashley explained *Operation Gray Ships*, as laid out by Navy Secretary Wells. She also told him in detail about Abraham Lincoln, his charisma, charm, and intelligence. Jack thought about how he would love to interview Lincoln for an article.

"*Operation Gray Ship*s has two parts," said Ashley. "The first part involves our Engineering and Deck Departments. They're going to give the *California* the appearance of being 20 different ships. In 2013, we would call this PsyOps or Psychological Operations. The idea is to weaken the enemy's resolve through deceit. The Doolittle Raid on Tokyo in the early days of World War II is a perfect example. It didn't do much damage, but it showed the Japanese government that they were dealing with a tough customer."

"Part two involves you, Jack, on specific recommendation from the Secretary of the Navy. You must have made quite an impression on him."

"It will be your mission, Jack, to write a series of newspaper articles describing the 20 ships of the *Gray Fleet*, where they were sighted, what they look like, and what they're capable of. These stories will be fed to all of the major Union newspapers. The Administration feels that it's not necessary to try to leak these articles to the Confederacy because Southern spies will take care of that. The whole idea is to strike fear into the hearts of the Confederate government. As one of our salty officers in Engineering puts it, our job is to 'fuck with their heads.' "

Jack put down his coffee. He rubbed his face with his hands. He then picked up the coffee and took another sip.

"Ashl...Captain, you're asking me to do something that rubs against every rule I've made for myself as a writer. At Columbia Journalism, if there is one thing they pounded into our heads, it's that you simply don't lie. If there's a story, interview the people involved, and get two back-up sources before you go to press. I've done the same in my books. Nothing went in until I made sure it was accurate. Now you're asking me to sit down and pound out lies."

"I thought you'd have a problem with this, Jack, because you're a man of integrity." *Which is one of the things I love about you. Stop, stop. Stay focused.*

"May I ask you to consider a few things?" said Ashley.

"Of course, Captain," said Jack, the recipient of a full Ashley Patterson Eye Job.

"First, you won't write the articles over your own byline. With all due respects, my celebrity friend, nobody in the nineteenth-century has the foggiest idea who you are. You will essentially be a ghost writer. Second, you've written a few novels, yes?"

"Yes, I've written three novels."

"Is fiction a lie, or is it just telling a story?" Ashley asked. Jack raised his coffee cup and nodded his head to Ashley as if to ask if she wanted another. Ashley shook her head, while Jack bought some time by going to the coffee pot. This woman would make a great lawyer, Jack thought. "Well, yes, Captain, fiction is storytelling, but fiction never disguises itself as truth."

Ashley then fired the broadside.

"Jack, my job is to kill the enemy. Your job is to confuse them. The more you confuse them, the fewer I have to kill. The fewer I have to kill, the quicker we can get the hell out of here and go back to where we came from. Is that really an ethical problem?"

"When do I start, Captain?"

# Chapter 40

"Captain, a moment of your time, ma'am?" Bradley said.

"Yes, please come up to my office, Commander."

Since the incident in the wardroom when he had confronted the captain in public, Bradley felt ostracized. His feeling was accurate. To any observer, and there were a lot of them, it was obvious that Captain Patterson had unofficially appointed the navigator, Ivan Campbell, as the executive officer. Campbell had led the first delegation to the Navy Department, conducted the tour of the ship, and accompanied the captain on her visit with Lincoln. The only thing that tempered Bradley's seething resentment was his plan to defect to the Confederacy. Don't get mad, get even, Bradley recalled the old saying. It's time to calm down, suck it up and get the job done, Bradley thought.

"What is it, Commander?" Ashley asked. She no longer called him by his first name, the common way a captain addresses her senior officers.

"Captain, I just wanted you to know that I've prepared a detailed project flow diagram with what I know about *Operation Gray Ships*. It occurred to me that there's a lot of moveable parts and I thought that a detailed timeline would be useful." He handed her the spreadsheet that he had prepared, with blanks representing the details he didn't know. He didn't know a lot because he was effectively left outside of the command loop.

"Thank you, Commander. This will be very useful."

Bradley then said, "Captain, I never formally apologized for making an ass of myself in the wardroom a few days ago, and I want you to know that I am sorry for getting totally out of line. I'll make this public in the wardroom if you wish, ma'am."

"Well, thank you, Commander. I accept your apology. A public apology won't be necessary."

Every synapse in Ashley's brain fired. Can I trust this guy, she thought, or does he have something up his sleeve? She hated not being able to trust a senior officer, especially one who is technically second in command. But *Operation Gray Ships* was an open secret, she thought, and Bradley does have excellent organizational skills.

"Please check with Nick Wartella in Engineering. He'll show you our plans for appearance changes. This is a project that needs careful tracking." Ashley knew that with Wartella and the two officers in charge of the project there was nothing to worry about, but another set of eyes wasn't a bad idea. But something in the part of Ashley's brain that controlled trust was not functioning properly with this guy.

"Aye aye, Captain," said Bradley.

Bradley thought Ashley was easy to manipulate.

Ashley thought Bradley was a snake.

# Chapter 41

Within moments of the *California's* disappearance, Frank Orzo, Duty Officer at NavOps, had addressed everyone in the room, reminding them that the *California's* disappearance was secret. It would be up to the Department of Defense or the White House when and if it would be announced to the press.

Petty Officer Third Class Toby Miller was on duty at NavOps. His job was to monitor one of the screens showing the position of ships and report to Orzo. He nonchalantly took out his IPhone, and, in complete violation of policy, texted his sister-in-law Janet Miller, who had just landed a job in the marketing department of *The New York Times:* "One of our ships, *USS California*, is missing. GFF (go fucking figure)." He thought this wasn't a problem because she wasn't a reporter. He just loved to impress her with his important job at the Pentagon.

\* \* \*

Captain Vera Esposito, aide to Chief of Naval Operations, answered the phone. Ray Cohen, a reporter with *The New York Times* was on the line. Admiral Roughead told her to stall while he called Secretary of Defense. Gates put him on hold while he patched through a conference call to the White House. Chief of Staff Bill Daley picked up and patched in Press Secretary Jay Carney. Everyone on the conference call knew one thing – if you try to put a cat back in the bag, you will get scratched and bitten. Bill Daley said to Gates, "I think Admiral Roughead should tell the *Times* what's going on." All agreed.

White House staffers, especially the Chief of Staff and the Press Secretary, hate to see breaking news of national security on TV. But you can't unleak a leak, they all knew. Daley ended the call by saying, "I want the name of the turd who leaked this."

Admiral Roughead picked up reporter Cohen's call and told him what they knew. The *California* was missing, and a massive sea rescue operation was underway. Within minutes of *The New York Times* exclusive being posted to its online edition, every major news outlet in the world had picked up on the story.

Janet Miller, marketing assistant at *The New York Times* and Petty Officer Miller's sister-in-law, was surprised when she got a major promotion to the newsroom within two days.

The *California* has been missing for 25 minutes

# Chapter 42

Commander Bradley walked through the compartment where the SEALs were just finishing their morning exercises. He approached Lieutenant Conroy and said good morning.

"Good morning, sir," said Conroy.

"I'd like a few minutes of your time in my office, Lieutenant."

After he showered and changed, Conroy reported to Bradley's office. "We have some concerns, Lieutenant, about our upcoming engagements." Conroy assumed the "we" meant the top brass on the ship, including Captain Patterson, although Bradley had not discussed what he was about to reveal with anyone. "As I'm sure you've been told, Lieutenant, the *California* is going to assist in the Battle of Bull Run in July. The SEALs' involvement hasn't been officially determined yet, but we know that you will have an important role in the operation."

"I've assumed that, sir. That's why I've ordered extra physical training and weapons readiness drills."

"Weapons readiness is a big concern, Lieutenant. When the engagement begins, the *California* will be at sea, many miles from the scene, and there's no way we can get a ship this large up Bull Run Creek. We need to come up with a plan to get a weapons cache ashore way in advance of the battle. I've checked with the weapons department and they showed me how many weapons and ammo can fit in a couple of Zodiacs and rafts.

We can set up a camouflaged weapons depot with a hardened perimeter and a small security force consisting of SEALs and some sailors to help with moving the weapons. We have no idea what sea conditions will be like on the eve of battle, so if we wait until then to load the Zodiacs, we'll risk compromising the mission. Besides, I'm sure that part of your objective will be to plant lasers to guide in the missiles and bombs. That will take advance preparation."

Conroy looked at the desk and scratched his head. "That sounds like a workable plan, sir. I'm just worried about setting up a large weapons cache in hostile territory. We have the better weapons, that's for sure, but if they send a cavalry brigade against us we could have a big problem."

"You will have support from the Apache attack helicopter as well as the helicopter drones. I wouldn't worry about it."

The idea had a lot going for it, Conroy had to admit. "I'll prepare a written plan and submit it to you, sir."

"Don't worry about the sailors who will accompany the SEAL squad, Lieutenant. I will hand pick them myself."

# Chapter 43

ather Rick stood in the chow line preparing for lunch with the crew. He looked up to see Supply Officer Valente's sign of the day. It read:

"If Any of Our Culinary Selections Don't Meet with Your Complete Approval, *JOIN THE ARMY!*"

As he walked across the mess hall he met Dominic Valente.

"Dom, I have to tell you how much I love your daily food announcements. This crew needs a few laughs."

"Yes, Padre, they do need laughs. What I'm hearing from the crew isn't good. These people want to go home. I can't say I blame them. Please keep coming to the mess hall. These sailors love to see you. I'll personally serve you an extra dessert."

Fr. Rick laughed. "Thanks for the input, Dom, and keep up with the great signs. How are we doing with supplies?"

"It's becoming a problem, Father. A Union supply ship pulled alongside the last time we were outside of Washington. What I have on my normal list of items doesn't square with what they have to offer. Come July I think my Selection of the Day sign will read, "Wormhole Road Kill."

Father Rick laughed. "I can't wait."

Sampson made it a rule to sit with a different group of sailors at each meal. He spotted a group he hadn't dined with before and walked toward the table. "Please have a seat, Padre," said Petty Officer Tyrone Jones. Jones introduced the chaplain to each of the eight sailors at the table, although Father Rick already knew their names. "So what's new, Padre?" asked Jones.

"Well, a horse walks into a bar and the bartender says 'Why the long face'?" The uproarious laughter told the chaplain that they had never heard the old joke before. "Haven't you guys ever heard of Henny Youngman?" asked Father Rick. Confused looks. Either I'm getting older or they're getting younger, thought Father Rick.

"So how's everything going with you guys?" Father Rick asked. He braced himself for another bunch of sad stories about sailors missing their loved ones. He expected tears, and readied himself to be the shoulder to cry on. What he heard startled him. It wasn't sadness that he heard but frustration, bordering on anger.

Tyrone Jones led off. "Well, Padre, you ask how everything is going. It's weird, sir. Here we are, a bunch of sailors from the twenty-first century, and we're fixing to pick a fight with people we whupped over 150 years ago. Hey, I'm a black man. If I lived in 1861 and my people were in chains, I'd be looking to do some ass kicking. But we're from 2013. Our president is a black guy, my brother just married a white girl, my next door neighbor is a Filipino, and my captain is a black woman. This war was over a long time ago. Why don't we just go home?"

The table appeared to be in total agreement, with "amens," "right-ons," and fist pumping. Seaman Bobby Curtis leaned over and looked down the table toward Father Rick. "Yes, Bobby?" said the chaplain.

"When I signed up," said Curtis, "we were fighting a bunch of people who wanted to kill us. These Southerners don't even know who we are."

Petty Officer Pete Mosely weighed in. "Padre, when the shooting starts, people are going to get hurt and killed, at sea or on land. If one of us gets popped in this stupid war, it will make no more sense than a drive-by in Detroit. We should bag ass out of here and get back to fighting real bad guys."

Petty Officer Ike Ivey had graduated from junior college before joining the Navy. He intended to get his bachelor's degree when his stint was up. A history buff, he hoped to become a high school history teacher some day. "Father, I've been reading a lot about the Civil War. In four years there were 620,000 casualties." Almost everyone at the table said the same thing, "What?"

Ivey continued. "These nineteenth-century people are out of their minds. They think it's a noble thing to march into cannon fire shoulder to shoulder. Now here we are, about to go shoulder to shoulder with these maniacs. We don't belong here, Padre."

Petty officer William Tyson spoke. "I'm from Mississippi, about as southern as southern gets. I'm a black guy and my neighbor's a white guy. We play softball together. Our kids go to school together. My father is the mayor of my town. He ran against a white man in a town where 80 percent of the voters are white. My dad won in a landslide. This fucking, excuse me, friggin' war was over a long time ago. It's like waking up dead guys and killing them all over again."

Father Rick realized it was time to talk, not just listen. "So I take it you guys are a bit angry." The head nodding was unanimous. "I'm going to ask you to consider something. Our involvement in this war is going to be very limited. The purpose, from what I understand, is to cut down on the killing by convincing the South that it's a terrible idea to continue. It's not top secret that this ship is going to go through some daily changes in appearance. The idea is to make the Confederacy think that there's more than one of us. If we do get into actual combat, the idea is the same, to convince the South to give it up, and save a few hundred thousand lives. Then, we steam for home."

Father Rick realized that it was important to shore up support for the captain, which is part of the chaplain's job. "I want you folks to know something, and I'm speaking from the bottom of my heart. Captain Ashley Patterson is the finest officer I have ever served with. I meet with her often. And get this: she cares about you and the entire crew — a lot. She wants to go back to where we came from as much as you and I do."

# *Chapter 44*

Chief Ray knocked on Bradley's office door. "Enter," Bradley said. Ray walked into the office, closing the door behind him. He hadn't noticed how small the office was before, about nine feet by twelve. This was another thing that preyed on Bradley's nerves. *Dashing Ashley* had an expansive office while his couldn't be a quarter the size of hers. "Have a seat, Chief," said Bradley, "if you can find the room."

"The Captain sure has given you some cozy quarters, Commander." Bradley just waved his hand dismissively.

"Chief, I've come up with an idea to make our weapons moving plan a lot easier. Not only easier, but it will kill two birds with one stone. The SEALs are going to move the weapons for us." Ray's eyes widened. He couldn't believe what he just heard.

"I don't get it, Commander."

"Here's the idea Chief. I've already spoken to Conroy, the SEAL honcho, and he agrees. I told him that I worried about the riskiness of moving two Zodiacs and two rafts full of weapons on the eve of battle. I said that we don't know what sea conditions will be like and the danger of losing the cache of weapons is too great. I convinced him that we should move the weapons way in advance of the battle, and set up a defensive perimeter around them."

"But if the SEALs are in charge of the weapons what happens to the big plan, the plan to join the Confederacy?"

Bradley stared into Ray's eyes. "The SEALs will only look like they're in charge. We need to have at least six of our people with them."

The Chief smiled. "Our people, Commander?"

"Yes, our people. Chief, we have to expand our strength to accomplish our mission. We need bunch of sailors who will want to join us in the Confederacy."

"Commander, you'll be happy to know your old friend has been thinking down the road. There's a group of good ole' boys aboard, rebels to the soles of their feet. There are twelve of them, four first class and eight second class petty officers. These are tough dudes, Commander. They even have a name they call themselves, although they keep it quiet: the Confederate Navy. Maybe they'd like to make that name official."

"You haven't said anything to them have you?" asked Bradley, concerned about the security of their plan.

"Of course not, sir. I've just asked a simple question of each of them. I wanted to see where their minds are on our upcoming operations." Ray leaned closer and said, "I just asked each of 'em how they felt about our upcoming war against the South?"

"And what were their responses?"

"Commander, these ole' boys are spittin' mad. I got the clear impression that they're fixing on doing something. What it is I don't know, but it's something. I guess you're thinking, like I am, that we can give these boys something to do, something for Ole Dixie."

"Tell me a little more about these guys, Chief."

"Well sir, six of them are gunners mates and work directly for me. Two are boatswains mates, tough guys. One is a boilerman, and the other is an electronics technician."

"I want a list of their names. I'll check the personnel file on each of them. Do they know how to use small arms?"

"Yes, sir. All of them are checked out with weapons. It's mandatory for my guys, but the others do it because they're good 'ole boys, and shooting comes natural."

"But I'm still a little confused about one thing Commander. What about the SEALs?"

Bradley sat up straight. In his mind, he climbed to the high road.

"When Robert E. Lee joined the Confederacy, he knew that it would mean taking up arms against people he knew well. He didn't like the idea, but he knew it was his sacred patriotic duty. The SEALs will become collateral damage in our mission. Once ashore, they will have to be killed."

"We'll meet again soon, Chief."

"Aye aye, sir."

# Chapter 45

Jeff DeLouker and Nancy Forsyth were in the ship's maintenance and repair shop discussing the design of the *California*'s upcoming "costume changes." They were going over Forsyth's drawings for the large shed structures that would serve as bogus gun turrets. Both the fore and aft sheds would be eight feet high, and would grow by another eight feet by hoisting four additional walls that would lay collapsed on the roof of the sheds until needed.

"We're going to need another member on our committee, Nance."

"Who and why?"

"Father Rick, the chaplain, is the who. Weather is the why. We are going to need a lot of prayer, Nance. If we hit a big storm with all this crap we're adding to the decks we're fucked."

DeLouker and Forsyth went to Nick Wartella's office. Wartella invited them in. "How's our costume change operation going?"

"That's what we wanted to see you about Commander. My sidekick here designs stuff that can take a beating, and my team knows how to batten down for heavy weather, but if we hit a major storm we could have a big problem."

"Hurricane season is coming," added Forsyth. "Jeff is right. If we hit a bad storm our costume may get washed out to sea. We can take some heavy weather, no problem. But we don't have the ability to outrun a hurricane if we don't know it's coming."

"We all know that our weather forecasting took a hit when we lost our satellites and long range communications," DeLouker said. "Nancy and I just wanted to give you a heads up, in case you didn't have anything else to worry about."

"You're both right. Thanks for thinking this through. I'll talk to the captain."

\* \* \*

After Wartella told her about the concerns of his design team, Ashley called a meeting with Ivan Campbell, the navigator, and Lt. Kathy Cooney, the ship's meteorologist, who is part of the navigation division.

Campbell and Cooney entered the Captain's office. "I just got a very savvy heads up from our engineering department," Ashley said. "They're concerned that a big storm could compromise *Operation Gray Ships* by blowing all of their work out to sea. Weather is something we haven't been thinking a lot about lately, but it's time to think about it now."

"I'll turn it over to Lt. Stormy here, Captain." The Captain smiled at his nickname for Cooney.

"I wish I could give you good news, but I can't," said Cooney. "After I graduated from OCS I went to Navy meteorology school because I found it interesting. But without the right tools, it isn't interesting, it's scary. My job as the ship's meteorologist had been one of tracking, monitoring, and reporting. I would constantly check the satellite weather reports and the weather faxes. I would also watch CNN and the Weather Channel on our TV hookup, I'm embarrassed to admit. That's why the job of a modern ship's meteorologist is part-time. I have other responsibilities in the navigation department. The only thing I have to monitor now is the condition of the sky and the ship's two barometers. We do have radar, but the range isn't good enough to keep us out of big trouble."

"How good are you at reading the sky, Lieutenant?" asked Ashley.

"As good as anybody, Captain, which also means as bad as anybody. We've all heard, 'Red sky at night, sailor's delight, red sky in morning, sailor take warning.' But for serious weather forecasting, that's pure nonsense. A fast moving front, and fronts can move very fast, will blow away any silly saying. Yes, the clouds can tell us a lot, but the situation can change very fast, as many a captain who went down with a ship in a storm found out."

"As you see it Kathy, what's the major problem we have to worry about?" Campbell asked.

"Here's what keeps me up at night. Today is May 3. In less than a month from now, on June 1, the Atlantic Hurricane Season begins, or at least it did in 2013. Both of you have been in the Navy a lot longer than I have, so you know the drill when it comes to hurricanes. You head the other way and outrun them. That's the only way to deal with a hurricane. Even in the early part of the twentieth-century, after ship-to-ship wireless telegraphs came into use, mariners were in a better spot than we find ourselves in. Ships could send warnings to other ships. We don't even have that capability. Even the hindsight of history isn't much good. I know we have plenty of historical data on CD-ROMs in our library, but there have been ferocious storms at sea that never made the newspapers. The only way people knew of them was when a lot of ships never returned to port."

"I assume that you think the weather stations ashore will not be of much help," Ashley said.

"That's right captain. They're primitive at best, lacking the same technology that we're missing. For example, the Galveston Hurricane of 1900, 39 years from now, was (will be?) the worst hurricane in American history, with over 6,000 lives lost. The technology of weather stations at the time wasn't close to satellite imagery. Simply stated, the people in Galveston didn't know it was coming. That same problem can apply to the *California*."

"What steps do you recommend, Kathy?" Campbell asked.

"Sir, I'm making copies of photos of every known cloud formation, and I will be posting them around the ship. We have a lot of old salts on this ship, and maybe one of them may see something that I've missed. But even if they do, reading the sky is no substitute for accurate forecasting. It's the only thing we have. Radar is good, but it will only show us that we're about to get hit. It won't allow us enough time to outrun a storm."

"Ivan," said Ashley, "I want you to come up with a list of safe harbors up and down the coast. It may give us a shot at ducking for cover if we realize some big weather is on us. We have to deal with the hand we've been dealt. Losing our fancy new *Gray Ship* costuming may be the least of our problems."

# Chapter 96

*T*he *Boston Globe*
  "Sighting of Amazing Gray Vessel off Coast of Maine –
Four Fishermen Report a Very Large and Fast Ship"
By Lucas McPherson, May 4, 1861

A ship the likes of which has never been seen has been reported by a fishing vessel off the coast of Deer Isle, Maine. According to the Angus Monahan, captain of the Ariana B., a fishing boat out of Gloucester, Massachusetts, he saw a very large *Gray Ship* approximately a quarter-mile from his boat. "I have never seen anything like it before. It's the biggest ship of any kind that I've seen before, and I've been fishing these waters for over 20 years." He looked at the ship through his spyglass and was able to see structures on her deck that he couldn't identify, other than two objects that appeared to be large cannons. Three other crewmembers of the Ariana B. were interviewed and they confirmed captain Monahan's statement. Although they weren't close enough to determine the exact lettering on her stern, two of the men insisted that it read *"USS California."* Large numbers on each side of her bow read "36."

The ship is also extremely fast, according to the fisherman. She was headed in the same direction as their fishing boat and was miles ahead of them within a few minutes.

There have been at least a dozen other reports of a *Gray Ship* steaming off the New England Coast in recent weeks, but Monahan and his crew were close enough to give a detailed description of the craft. All four of the men insisted that it must be a ship of war because of the objects that appeared to be cannons on her deck. The Navy Department was contacted but had no comment.

# Chapter 47

S imon Planck, recently promoted to Petty Officer, was in his 15th session of Pete Campo's martial arts class.

"Today," said Campo, "we begin the ancient art of karate."

He called Simon Planck to the front of the class.

"Petty Officer Planck, look at me, and do exactly as I do."

Campo held his left arm tucked against his side, and then thrust his right fist forward, turning his fist inward as he did. He then repeated the maneuver with his other arm. He did this ten times with each arm. Each time he did the thrust of his fist, he let out a shout, "*Kia.*"

Planck then went through the series of thrusts imitating Campo's movements. Campo bowed toward Planck, and then gave him a swat to his left arm, saying, "Great job, Petty Officer Planck." Campo meant it. In each session, he noticed that Planck honed his new skills with a passion. Planck executed the opening thrusts flawlessly.

Campo then lined up the class in rows with enough space between each student to avoid injury.

Planck was exhausted from the series of punching thrusts. Campo surprised him when he told him to stay in the front of the class.

"People, do exactly what Petty Officer Planck does."

He just stood to the side as Planck led the class. When he saw that a move needed adjusting, he walked up to Planck, raised a hand and went through the move himself, without speaking a word.

Although dead tired, Planck continued leading the exercise, blanking his mind to his exhaustion and the heavy feeling in his arms, concentrating only on the task.

When the class came to an end, Planck wanted to continue. His body didn't, but his spirit did.

Campo pulled Planck over to the side after the class.

"You're a leader, Petty Officer Planck. I hope you understand that."

# Chapter 48

"Captain, may I have a word with you?" said Karen Sobel, the Personnel Officer.

"Come on up, Karen."

"You asked me to keep you up to date on something, and it's been a few weeks. It's about Simon Planck."

Oh shit, thought Ashley, he's being bullied again. Ashley lowered her head and voice. "Tell me about it, Karen."

"It's great news, Captain," Sobel said, sensing that Ashley expected bad news. "He's completed about fifteen of those martial arts classes, and the difference is dramatic. I swear the kid's voice is deeper, he moves with a kind of pride, and he smiles a lot. He actually smiles. His work is perfect. His uniforms even seem to fit better."

Campo had told Ashley that Planck would be a different sailor in a matter of weeks, and he was right. The discipline of martial arts is a perfect tonic for this bully magnet.

"If I may, Captain, in all my years in the Navy I've never seen a commanding officer take such an interest in a sailor in need. A month ago he was a sad sack. Now he's got confidence, and it shows."

"Thanks, Karen. You have no idea how good that makes me feel."

Ashley told Sobel that she discovered something about herself in high school: she hated bullying. She had nothing but contempt for the *Mean*

*Girls*, the in-crowd that rules the hallways by intimidating the girls who didn't make the cut. One day after soccer practice, she noticed a teammate fixing a note on another girl's locker. She looked at the note. It read, "Is ugliness and stupidity catching? If so, please stay away. Better yet, why not quit the team?" The girl whose locker the note was taped to was one of life's wounded birds. Physically unattractive with a terrible case of teen-age acne, the girl was a natural "bully magnet." Ashley, the team captain, pulled the note off the door and ran after the girl who put it there. She considered saying, "Barbara, this really isn't nice," or "I really wish you wouldn't do this." Instead, Ashley focused her large brown eyes on Barbara the bully and said, "Precisely what the hell is this all about?" After that incident, Ashley took the wounded bird, Maureen O'Day, under her wing. She spent time helping her with her soccer plays and singled her out for praise whenever she made a good kick or pass. She then spoke to each of the Mean Girls individually and let it be known that Maureen O'Day is not to be fucked with.

Ashley and Maureen remained friends over the years and correspond often. As Ashley's Navy career progressed, Maureen O'Day's career was also doing well. O'Day became a Senior Vice President at Microsoft. She also coaches girls' soccer at her daughter's high school.

"She was lucky you were her team captain," said Sobel, "and Simon Planck is lucky you're his commanding officer."

# *Chapter 49*

*I*t was 0800 on May 11, 1861. Lt. DeLouker addressed his team of 18 sailors who would be tasked to assemble the costume change for *Operation Gray Ships*. DeLouker dubbed them the *Gray Ship Gang*. Lt. Jg. Nancy Forsyth stood next to him. The ship was still anchored in Chesapeake Bay.

"You guys have been busting ass for the last couple of weeks, and you've done a great job. That's the good news," DeLouker said. "The bad news is that the work isn't over yet, but it will get easier. Lt. Forsyth here has done an amazing job of designing these structures, and part of that design makes for easy and fast assembly and break-down. Once we put together the two major fore and aft structures, the regular daily changes should be a snap. This morning we'll assemble the two major structures. This afternoon we will go through our first time-drill on assembling the rest. Any questions?"

The entire group of 18 began to assemble of the main "turret" towards the bow. DeLouker supervised, with Forsyth at his side for technical questions. Forsyth had labeled each piece of the structures in bright large lettering to make for quick assembly. By mid-morning the structure was complete and the water pipe "guns" were inserted into the holes provided. DeLouker was amazed at the precision that Forsyth had put into the design. The pipes slipped easily into the frame and were bolted down on the inside. The pipes were set at a 45-degree angle, mimicking the appearance of large guns. Each pipe section was 12 inches in diameter and 20 feet long. A 14-foot section of each pipe was visible beyond the structure.

Captain Ashley looked down from the bridge, and called Nick Wartella. "Your people have done a great job, Nick. Those set designs look like the real thing even up close."

By 1230, the gang had completed the aft structure, along with its "guns." DeLouker congratulated them and called a lunch break. He had prearranged with the mess hall that the *Gray Ship Gang* would go to the head of the line.

After lunch, the *Gray Ship Gang* broke up into smaller units to work on the ship's name plate, the changing number boards, and the banquet tables. Four sailors were assigned to the nameplate change on the stern, four to the number boards to be mounted on the superstructure, and eight were assigned to the banquet tables.

The nameplate board was the most important. The team hoisted the first name change board into place, *USS Hawaii*. With two sailors holding the board with ropes, two others bolted the board in place with pneumatic drills. DeLouker had insisted on large bolts and washers to make the job easier and faster. DeLouker couldn't believe his stop watch. The entire operation took only five minutes, and this was the first attempt.

The change in the ship's number took four minutes per board, including hoisting and bolting.

All eight bright white banquet tables were lashed to the ship's rails in six minutes.

DeLouker assembled the entire *Gray Ship Gang* on deck. The time was 1415, 45 minutes after they returned from lunch. "I'm not going to bullshit you people. You did one out-fucking-standing job. Knock off for the rest of the day. Read, relax, watch movies. Whoever coined the old Navy phrase *Can Do* had you people in mind. Dismissed."

The *USS Hawaii* was ready for action. The *Gray Ships Fleet* was on the move.

# *Chapter 50*

*A*t 1700 the *California* (*USS Hawaii* for the time being) weighed anchor and headed for Wilmington, North Carolina. Captain Patterson had decided to begin their blockade duty there because there had been so many sightings of the *Gray Ship*, and now she would give the rebels a real eye-full.

The *California* arrived in the waters off Wilmington at 0700 on May 12, 1861 shortly after sunrise. As if announced, they spotted a long fast-moving vessel headed toward Charleston Harbor, a classic blockade runner. The ship appeared to be unarmed or at least very light on offensive guns. She was about a half mile southeast of the *California's* position, on a course that would bring her within 300 yards of the *California's* bow.

Captain Patterson ordered General Quarters. The long shrill sound of the boatswain's pipe was followed by, "General quarters, general quarters, all hands man your battle stations." As the blockade runner was about 500 yards from the *California*, the Captain ordered a warning shot across her bow from one of the five-inch guns. The blockade runner slowed and began to turn. Seeing the *California* and hearing the sound of her guns must have been terrifying, Ashley thought. They could see her name, the *CSS Advance*.

The *California's* Rules of Engagement were to open fire on a vessel only when threatened. The objective, in the strange rules of *Operation Gray Ships*, was to be seen. Captain Patterson ordered the ship to steer a course that would take it within easy observation distance of the blockade runner. She passed within 100 yards of the vessel and then turned sharply to starboard so that her stern and the name, *USS Hawaii*, could be clearly visible. This maneuver would become known among the crew as the *Gray Ship Moon*.

Aboard the *Advance*, the captain ordered anyone not otherwise engaged to write down their observations. One of his crew was a skilled artist who sketched what he saw. He had a clear view of her name, her number "78," and her gigantic guns.

Captain Patterson ordered the *California* to head in the opposite direction, contrary to the instincts of any fighting captain, but entirely in keeping with the objective of *Operation Gray Ships*.

The *Advance* arrived in Charleston Harbor about an hour later. What her crew had seen became the talk of the waterfront.

✻ ✻ ✻

The headline of *The Anderson Intelligencer* from Anderson Court House, South Carolina shouted:

"New *Gray Ship* Sighted — *USS Hawaii*"

May 12, 1861, by John Fergus

Another gigantic *Gray Ship* was sighted yesterday while attacking the *CSS Advance*. The name of the ship is the *USS Hawaii*, bearing the number "78" on her superstructure. It is similar in appearance to the *USS California*, which was seen a few weeks ago, but it had massive guns and other structures that couldn't be identified. Large circular objects along the ship's rails could be seen, six on each side. Their use is unknown. The *Advance* did not suffer any damage and the *Hawaii* broke off the engagement. Robert Mason, the Captain of the *Advance* said, "I have never seen guns so large, nor have I ever seen a ship so fast."

# Chapter 51

T he *California*, under a different name every 24 hours, cruised the coast of North Carolina for the next month, punctuated by two trips back to Washington to communicate with the Union command and to take on supplies.

Depending on the day, the ship would be known as the *USS California, Connecticut, Delaware, Hawaii, Idaho, Illinois, Indiana, Iowa, Kansas, Maine, Massachusetts, Minnesota, Missouri, New Hampshire, New Jersey, New York, Ohio, Oregon, Pennsylvania* and *Wisconsin*.

The ship's actions were becoming almost routine. They would spot a Confederate vessel, fire a warning shot, and then pull a *Gray Ship Moon*, showing the crews of the rebel ships a new name every day. During any close encounter with a Southern ship, Captain Patterson ordered that General Quarters be sounded, and all hands would man their battle station. This was standard naval doctrine: if there is a possibility of hostile action, battle stations must be manned. It also served a practical purpose: to relieve monotony and keep morale up.

By June 1, the *California* had interdicted 36 blockade runners, forcing them to change course away from Wilmington. Not one vessel had fired on the *California*. Apparently the very sight of one of the *Gray Ships* was enough to convince a captain to retreat and wait for another day.

On June 2 the *California* set a course for the mouth of the Potomac for a visit to Washington. The Captain ordered Campbell and Jack Thurber to visit the Navy Department. She wanted Jack Thurber to assess the results, if any, of his leaked newspaper articles.

They arrived at the Navy Department at 1100. Campbell and Thurber didn't expect to meet with Secretary Wells, but he ushered them in as soon as they arrived. Wells thirsted for information and also was bursting to tell them some good news.

"Have a seat, gentlemen," said Wells. Campbell gave Wells a summary of their encounters in the waters off Wilmington – 36 ships interdicted, 36 turned around. No hostile fire from any Confederate ship. He also discussed the daily costume and name changes, and the ship's maneuvers to make sure the name was visible. He didn't mention that the maneuver had become known as the *Gray Ship Moon.*

"Here are the results from our intelligence reports," said Wells. "Ship visits to Wilmington have decreased 95 percent in the last two weeks, the two weeks that the *California,* under her various names, has been on duty. It seems that the very threat that the *Gray Ships* pose has dramatically altered commerce to that one city alone. As vessels divert to other ports they are attacked by our ships. In two weeks the *California* has proven to be the most important part of the blockade. *Operation Gray Ships* is performing splendidly."

"Sir, have you been able to assess whether my newspaper articles have had any impact?" asked Jack.

"Impact, my dear Lieutenant, does not accurately describe what your articles have accomplished."

Wells walked across the room and retrieved a bundle of newspapers from all over the South. He plopped them down on the table in front of Jack.

"Just look at a few of these headlines."

"*USS New Jersey* is the Latest *Gray Ship* to Attack Southern Shipping"
*The Macon Telegraph*

"*USS Pennsylvania* Seen Cruising Near Wilmington, North Carolina"
*The Weekly Raleigh Register*

"*USS Oregon* — The Latest Gray Ship to Join the Northern Fleet" *The Southern Illustrated News*

"*USS Maryland* Fires Guns at British Supply Ship" *The Daily Richmond Examiner*

"Read some of the details, gentlemen," Wells said. Jack read, in some cases word for word, what he had written for Northern newspapers. It seemed that he had become a one-man wire service for newspapers all over the South. "I don't know if I should be flattered or angry that they're stealing my words," said Jack with a laugh.

"Be neither flattered nor angry, Lieutenant. Be proud that your work is having an enormous impact on our war effort."

"I noticed one upsetting article from the *Macon Telegraph*," said Campbell. "It says here that we fired on a civilian picnic, killing dozens of people. That is simply not true. We've never fired on the shore. We haven't even fired directly at a ship."

"Commander, truth and war make strange bedfellows."

\* \* \*

"Sir," said Campbell, "we weren't' expecting to meet with you today. If we were, I'm sure Captain Patterson would have come along."

"Not a problem at all, Commander. I realize that I surprised you. I just wanted to hear the information myself first hand. Please convey to the Captain that the *California* should cruise off Norfolk, Virginia for the next two weeks. It's less than 200 miles from here, so it will be easy to return if need be."

"Before you leave we should discuss one more thing," said Wells. "Let me ask you a blunt question, Commander. Do you expect hostile fire?"

"Yes sir, I do. Captain Patterson has discussed this with all Department Heads as well. It's inevitable that some overly enthusiastic ship captain, we would call him 'trigger happy,' will open fire on us. Whenever we engage a vessel, we are at battle stations, and all gun and missile batteries are ready to respond."

"When I toured the California, "said Wells, "you told me about your Harpoon Anti Ship missiles."

This guy's got a great memory. Campbell thought.

"Yes sir. Our Harpoon batteries are ready to fire on command."

"Don't hesitate to use them, Commander."

# *Chapter 52*

When they returned aboard the *California*, Campbell and Thurber briefed the Captain on their meeting with Wells.

"I hope he wasn't insulted that I didn't join you," Ashley said.

"Not at all, Captain. His meeting with us was a surprise."

"Our Rules of Engagement have been changed," Campbell said. "Secretary Wells remembered our weapons from his tour. He said that if we're fired upon that we shouldn't hesitate to use our Harpoon anti-ship missiles."

\* \* \*

The *California* steamed off Norfolk on June 3, disguised for that day as the *USS Colorado*. At 1100 hours the Officer of the Deck reported to Captain Patterson that a large combatant vessel was three miles off the *California's* starboard side and closing on her position. Through his high powered binoculars the OOD could see that the ship carried eight large guns on each side. He estimated the ship's length to be 200 feet. She was under sail, but he could see that she was designed for steam as well as sail. Also, four merchant vessels were within sight.

The OOD contacted the Captain, who ordered him to sound General Quarters, sending the crew to their battle stations.

Ashley put on her helmet and flak jacket and went to the bridge, her battle station.

As the Confederate ship came within 500 yards of the *California*, it fired a volley of eight cannon shells. The shells hit the water 100 feet off the *California's* port bow.

Each of the *California's* missile and gun batteries had a number. Battery five was the Harpoon anti-ship missile battery.

Ashley pressed the talk button on her headset.

"This is Captain Patterson. Battery Five fire one." The Harpoon missile is 15 feet in length, weighs 1,140 pounds and carries a 490-pound warhead of penetrating explosives. It is guided to its target by active radar signal.

The missile struck the Confederate warship in the middle of her hull and exploded inside the ship, sending a fist of smoke and fire 100 feet into the air. The ship visibly cracked in half as the blast lifted it out of the water. The aft section sank immediately. The bow section bobbed at the surface for 15 seconds before it sank.

Captain Patterson ordered the *California/Colorado* to close on the ship's final position to look for survivors. They found two sailors clinging to wreckage. The Captain eased the ship next to them and a ladder was lowered over the side. Neither man was seriously hurt because they were fortunate enough to be standing behind an iron bulkhead when the Harpoon hit. When asked, they said that their ship was the *CSS Chattanooga*. They were brought to sick bay for a medical exam and given clean fatigues to wear. They were then escorted to the Captain's office.

Both men were still visibly frightened. They were also amazed that the Captain of the ship was not only a woman but a colored woman. Ashley ordered coffee and sandwiches and told them to have a seat.

"Do either of you have any idea why your captain chose to open fire on this ship?" Ashley asked. One of the men, Jubal Johnston, answered.

"Captain, ma'am, our Captain, Randolph Brown, has been looking for a fight with the *Gray Ship* ever since he first heard of it. It's like he couldn't get it out of his mind. The rest of us thought that we were picking a fight that we couldn't win. I guess we were right."

"You're on the *USS...*" Ashley had to think for a moment, "*Colorado*. How many other *Gray Ships* have you personally seen?" One man said he had seen five, the other ten.

After a few questions, Ashley realized that these men had no significant intelligence to give her. She then gave them a verbal tour of the *California's* (*Colorado's*) weapons, exaggerating their number and strength. The men had seen what a Harpoon missile can do first-hand, so they didn't doubt what she was telling them.

"Our orders are plain, sailors," said Ashley. "If any *Gray Ship* is fired upon, the attacking vessel will be sunk immediately."

The men assumed that they were prisoners of war, and, judging from the food, they weren't unhappy with the prospect. They were shocked when the Captain told them they would be put ashore under cover of darkness.

The Captain's final words to them, as they were boarding a Zodiac for their trip to land, was meant to be spread. "Whoever will listen to you, tell them to do all they can to end this war. You cannot win it."

The Zodiac shoved off with one man steering and a Marine guarding the two sailors.

The sinking of the Confederate ship was the first combat the *California* had encountered. Ashley hoped that the two released survivors would spread the word. Fighting a *Gray Ship* means death.

# Chapter 53

Jefferson Davis was the President of the Confederate States of America since its inception. Elected to a term of six years in 1861, he would serve through the entire Civil War. Davis wasn't well known for his ability to work with others, and he insisted on answers from subordinates even when there were no answers to be had.

On June 5, 1861, he met with Stephen Mallory, Secretary of Confederate Navy. Mallory was a former United States Senator and had long held the position of Chairman of the Committee on Naval Affairs for the United States. Mallory knew the United States Navy as well as any man alive. Jefferson Davis wanted to know everything Mallory knew about the *Gray Ships*.

"Have a seat, Mr. Secretary. We have a lot to talk about. If there is one subject that I hear about every day it is the *Gray Ships*. Just this morning I received a report that the *Chattanooga* was sunk two days ago with just one shot from the *USS Colorado*, one of the *Gray Ships*. Please tell me what you know, Mr. Secretary."

"Mr. President, I served as Chairman of the Committee on Naval Affairs for over 10 years, and I knew everything there was to know about the ships of the United States Navy. I was kept informed about any new ship building projects. A log in my office had details on every vessel in the

Navy. I never heard anything about any *Gray Ships,* an obvious secret that nobody wished to share with the Senate."

"You never heard any mention about any secret shipbuilding project?" asked Davis.

"No sir. If it was a secret I would be the first to know. Congress provided the funding for all naval matters."

"But here is what I now know about these strange ships," said Mallory. "There have been hundreds of sightings by hundreds of people, most of whom are of unimpeachable integrity. My office has put together all of the reports and organized the information. Twenty different ships have been sighted. Each ship is between 600 and 1,000 feet in length, although size estimates vary. All of the ships are extremely fast, over 30 knots. They are also highly maneuverable."

"They all bear a resemblance to the *USS California,* the first *Gray Ship* sighted, but there are many different variations. Some of the ships boast gigantic guns on their forward turrets. Some of the ships have round white objects about ten to twelve feet in diameter along the rails of the ship. There are six on each side. We have no idea what these objects are for. Many of the armaments aren't recognizable. Some of the weapons are not guns as we know them. In the incident where the *Chattanooga* was sunk two days ago, *The Gray Ship* only fired one shot. Witnesses described the shell as a long object, between 10 and 15 feet. It entered the *Chattanooga's* hull and exploded. When it hit the *Chattanooga,* the ship was blown up into two pieces and sunk in less than a half minute. Witnesses from nearby ships told of a tower of fire and smoke over 100 feet in the air."

"We have interviewed the only two surviving sailors who had been taken prisoner," Mallory continued. "They described sights that are hard to believe. They told of weapons so powerful, that the shell that sank the *Chattanooga* was only a small part of their arsenal. We don't know why the men were put ashore and not kept as prisoners of war. Neither do the men themselves. They described being treated fairly and even in a friendly manner. The most amazing thing that they reported was that the captain of the ship is a colored woman."

Davis stood up. If Mallory had told him that the *Gray Ship* was made out of cheese, he couldn't have been more shocked. "Are these men reliable?" asked Davis. "They went through a terrifying ordeal, and it may have affected their thinking."

"I met them myself, and I'm convinced of their truthfulness. They talked about meeting with the captain in her office and being given coffee and food. They each described her physical appearance so exactly I find it impossible to believe that they created the story."

"Mr. Secretary, you held the office of Chairman of the Committee on Naval Affairs until five months ago. Besides not knowing about the *Gray Ships*, you were also kept ignorant of a colored woman serving as a captain of a Union ship. How can that possibly be, sir?"

Mallory shook his head as if to clear it. "Mr. President, I was in regular communication with Isaac Toucey, Secretary of the Union Navy until he was replaced by Gideon Wells. Toucey and I had become friends, and we met at least once a month. He kept me informed about personnel matters as well as the fleet. I find it unbelievable that he would have kept from me the fact that a Negro woman was the commanding officer of a Navy ship."

"Secrecy," Davis said, "appears to be deeply imbedded in the Union government. I was in the United States Senate, and I served as Secretary of War under President Pierce. I never heard of these matters and neither did you. I wonder how much other information was kept from us."

"Mr. Secretary, keep me informed by cable dispatch whenever you hear of anything new involving the *Gray Ships* or the mysterious captain."

"I fear that there will be many more surprises for us in the future," said Davis.

# *Chapter 54*

The *California* steamed up and down the Southern coast for three weeks. Captain Patterson followed the procedure of firing across the bow of merchant ships and blockade runners, then executing *The Gray Ship Moon* to make sure the men on the Confederate vessel got a good look at her name.

On June 26, 1861, under the name *USS Massachusetts*, the *California* was cruising slowly to update her nautical charts. The officer of the deck received a sonar report that an underwater object was bearing down on the ship at a slow rate of speed. Based on research from Father Rick's Civil War library, the OOD identified the object as the *CSS Hunley*, a Confederate submarine. According to the history books, the Hunley was 40 feet long and travelled at a speed of four knots, propelled by a hand cranked shaft. The *Hunley* carried a crew of eight. It was armed with an explosive torpedo at the end of a long spar. Whoever commanded the vessel was unaware of sonar, and believed that he could sneak up on the *California*.

The OOD contacted Captain Patterson who immediately went to the bridge. The *Hunley* was 200 yards from the *California* and closing. "Whoever is driving this thing is crazier than the skipper of the *Chattanooga*," Ashley said to the OOD.

"Order all ahead two-thirds and steer course 090 Lieutenant." A course that would take the *California* away from the submarine.

"Aye Aye, Captain."

That thing can't possibly do us any harm, thought Ashley. Yes, it's an enemy vessel, and yes, it's aiming for us, and yes, we can blow it out of the water easily, she thought. But the idea of killing eight people who didn't stand a chance bothered her.

"Screw it," Ashley said the Bellamy. "We'll just leave the area and let them get their exercise with their hand-driven propeller. Do not engage."

"Aye Aye, Captain."

# Chapter 55

The *California* headed north to prepare for the Battle of Bull Run on July 21, 1861. Ashley knew that Bull Run was the second prong of the *California's* role in the war effort, the first being the blockade duty and *Operation Gray Ships*. Bull Run had to be a success.

In her previous communications with Lincoln's war staff, she suggested that a Union colonel or general come aboard the *California* to help plan for the battle. The Union high command could count on naval support from its existing Navy, but, because of her weapons, the *California* would bring an entirely new dimension to battle planning. Also, for the first time, the Union Army would have combat air support. Lincoln ordered Brigadier General Irwin McDowell, the Commander of the Army of Northeastern Virginia, to report aboard the *California*. McDowell would bring his aide, Colonel James Burns.

On June 27, the *California* dropped anchor near the mouth of the Potomac. It was 0800 hours, and the motor launch was lowered over the side. It was a hot humid day with a temperature of 82 degrees Fahrenheit, even though it was early morning. When boat captain Donizzio saw Gen. McDowell and Col. Burns waiting on the pier, he couldn't believe that they were wearing blue wool uniforms. They're going to love the air conditioning on the *California*, he thought. Donizzio saluted his new guests and helped them aboard.

As McDowell stepped onto the ladder platform of the *California*, the boatswain's pipe alerted the ship, "Army of Northeastern Virginia, arriving."

The plan called for McDowell and Burns to stay aboard the *California* for three days of battle planning. After they were shown to their state-rooms, they were escorted into Captain Patterson's office at 0915. Because the subject of the meeting would be ground operations, Ashley invited SEAL Lieutenant Conroy and Marine Colonel Matthew Bingham to the meeting. Bingham would conduct the meeting. Blow-up photocopies of maps of the area around Manassas, Virginia were spread out on the table, as well as history books.

"Gentlemen," said Colonel Bingham, "I'm sure that you have never been involved in a battle plan that included history books. But the simple fact is that we know what happened at Bull Run, and the books will help us to change the outcome."

Both McDowell and Burns had been thoroughly briefed on the *California's* technical abilities, so Col. Bingham got right down to details.

"The *California's* role in the battle will have three components," Bingham said. "We'll provide air surveillance and ground combat support by our attack helicopter and drone helicopters. There will also be heavy weapons support from the ship itself. We will also make available small arms, rocket propelled grenades, regular hand grenades, and, perhaps most important of all, two-way radios."

"Now I will show you our aerial capabilities, and to do that we'll go to our Combat Information Center."

The meeting moved to the CIC. Bingham introduced Lieutenants Andrew Cinque and Bob Nathan, the drone pilots. To save time, Nathan had already launched his drone and it flew over Bull Run Creek as they spoke. McDowell and Burns were amazed to see the real time video of what would soon be a battlefield.

"You can see, gentlemen," said Bingham, "what this can mean for your troop movements. You will see the enemy's moves as he makes them. The drone videos will remove the element of surprise from the battle, at least from the Union point of view. If the enemy begins a flanking maneuver, for example, we will see it, and the *California* can send in a missile to prevent it. We also have our Apache Attack Helicopter to provide gun and missile support."

The meeting went on for another hour. Both Gen. McDowell and Col. Burns peppered Bingham with questions. McDowell especially wanted to know the quantity of weapons that would be taken ashore. Bingham replied, "There will be 50 automatic rifles; 100 rocket propelled grenades, 25 Colt 45 pistols. We also have a total of 2,000 rounds of ammunition for the rifles, and 750 rounds for the 45s."

"It isn't a lot in terms of quantity," Conroy said, "but these weapons are deadly, especially the rocket propelled grenades."

"We will move the weapons ashore in five days to give us time to train your troops in their use," Bingham said. Neither Bingham nor Conroy were comfortable with sending such a large cache of weapons and ammunition into enemy territory, but it did make logistical sense.

"The major impact," said Captain Patterson, "will come from the missiles that we fire from the ship. We have aboard twelve Tomahawk cruise missiles with over 1,000 pounds of explosives in their warheads. Our Harpoon missiles are used primarily against ships, but they can also be fired at land targets. You may recall that we sank the Confederate warship *Chattanooga* with one Harpoon missile."

McDowell and Burns exchanged glances, both feeling like medieval warriors suddenly transported to the future.

# Chapter 56

The worldwide newswires crackled with reports of the missing *California*. Daytime TV news shows covered little else. A news anchor earns his or her money with a story like this. How many ways are there to say, "They haven't found the *California* yet."? Most of the reports were background stories about other ships that went missing.

Defense Secretary Robert Gates was on the phone with President Obama.

"I recommend that you hold a press conference, Mr. President. TV anchors are running out of things to say, and they're starting to speculate."

"Bob, can you tell me anything, anything at all beyond what you've already said?"

"No, sir." said Gates.

"Okay, I'm going to hit the airwaves in one hour," said the President. "That will give us a little more time to find something out."

The *California* has been missing for 38 minutes.

# Chapter 57

It was July 2, 1861, the date scheduled to move the large cache of weapons and ammunition ashore. Bradley was in charge of the operation. Four SEALs were assigned to the task, led by Petty Officer Giordano, as well as eight sailors who Bradley had personally picked for the job. All were dressed in the civilian clothes that the SEALs had obtained from Morton's Dry Goods Store in Charleston.

Two Zodiacs and two inflatable life rafts were lowered into the water. The day was clear, the temperature in the low 80s, and, most important, there was no wind and the seas were calm. The objective was to motor up the Potomac River to the Occoquan River, a tributary that linked up with Bull Run Creek near Manassas. Bradley calculated that the trip would take four hours to the point of unloading.

The time was 2300 hours, 11 p.m. They left in darkness to avoid possible detection by Confederate forces.

Because they had no GPS availability they navigated by shore landmarks.

When they arrived at the unloading location at 0400, Giordano went ashore first to see if there was adequate cover. The spot was perfect, surrounded by trees and brush. Giordano looked for openings where they could string wire for perimeter security. They began to unload the weapons.

Two of the SEALs used their knives to chop down vegetation to use as camouflage cover. By 0500 they were done. Two of the SEALs stood watch while the others grabbed some sleep.

At 0900, after a few hours of sleep and breakfast consisting of MREs, or Meals Ready to Eat, Bradley announced that he was going to look around. Bradley had done his research in the ship's library. He had discovered that General Beauregard's camp headquarters was three miles from their location, which was exactly why he chose the spot. Before he left the camp, Bradley called Captain Patterson on his two-way radio. He told her that the mission had gone off without incident and that he would report back later. He then turned his radio off.

* * *

Giordano had just finished washing his face over a basin. He reached for his towel to wipe himself dry. When he took the towel from his face he was looking at Seaman John Locklear pointing a 45 at his forehead. It was the last thing Giordano ever saw. Tony (Geo) Giordano, the SEAL hero of his Brooklyn neighborhood, was dead.

Bradley arrived at General Beauregard's headquarters within 45 minutes. Before approaching the house, he called Petty Officer Spencer, one of his handpicked sailors. Spencer said, "Apple blossom," a prearranged code that meant that the SEALs had been murdered.

Two guards stopped Bradley 200 feet from the General's house. Bradley simply said, "Please tell the General that my name is Commander Philip Bradley, and I'm a representative of the *Gray Ship*. One of the men remained to guard Bradley while the other entered the house to inform the General. The man came running out of the house and immediately escorted Bradley inside.

General Beauregard remained seated at his desk and asked Bradley to more fully identify himself. Bradley told him that he was the Executive

Officer of the *USS California*, better known as one of the *Gray Ships*. He explained that he wore civilian clothing because he was on a secret mission.

"Commander," said Beauregard, "how can you be on a secret mission and stand here telling your enemy about it?"

"Because, sir, I am not your enemy."

# Chapter 58

"If you're not my enemy, sir, then who are you?" Beauregard asked.

"I am a loyal son of the South, General, and I am here to help the Confederacy win the Civil War."

"I'm listening, Commander."

For the next half hour, Bradley told Beauregard the *California's* story of time travel that began on April 10. He did not discuss *Operation Gray Ships*, believing that he should keep that information to himself for the time being. Also, this stratagem portrayed Bradley as a man who stood against a fleet of enemy ships, sword drawn, ready to defend the South against 20 colossal vessels.

Bradley ended his story by telling Beauregard about the cache of amazing weapons located less than three miles away, weapons that were Bradley's contribution to the Confederate war effort.

General Beauregard thought this man was quite insane, but, because he offered a new supply of weapons, he felt that he should see what this character was talking about. Beauregard ordered a carriage for Bradley and himself.

They rode the short distance to the weapons cache. When they arrived Bradley jumped from the carriage and waved his arms expansively toward the weapons. They were piled six feet high, four feet deep and twenty feet in length.

Bradley first took an M4A1 carbine from a box and handed it to Seaman Dwight Harborrow, an expert marksman. Harborrow pointed the rifle at a tree 100 yards away and squeezed the trigger once. They could see the wood splinter from where they stood. He then squeezed the trigger three times in quick succession, resulting in more splintered wood. He then squeezed the trigger and held it. Beauregard and his men had never seen an automatic weapon fire. Seaman Harborrow then explained that the magazine could hold 30 rounds of bullets. Beauregard's military tactician brain was on alert. A squad of ten men with such weapons could devastate an oncoming force. Ten men could replace a hundred he thought.

Harborrow then demonstrated a rocket propelled grenade or RPG. Because the rocket has no guidance of any sort, he aimed at a tree that was closer. He fired the grenade at a tree 75 yards away. The tree exploded and toppled. "This weapon," said Bradley, "is especially useful against a vehicle of any type, such as a munitions cart or a caisson."

Bradley then ordered another sailor to stand up a two by four foot metal plank supported by logs to keep it upright. Seaman Harborrow fired a 45 caliber pistol at the plank from a distance of 25 yards. Because a 45 has a soft bullet, it is known for its stopping power, as the lead expands when it goes through a target. The bullet tore a five inch hole in the plank. "This pistol," said Bradley, "will stop a charging horse in its tracks."

Bradley then withdrew a two-way radio from a bag. He sent a sailor with another radio a distance of 100 yards. "Johnson, can you hear me?" said Bradley.

Beauregard heard the loud clear voice come out of the instrument saying, "Yes, sir."

Although he doubted Bradley's sanity, Beauregard could not doubt what he had seen with his own eyes.

The time was now 1130 hours. Beauregard decided that it would be best to take lunch with this man to learn more details of his plan.

"Captain, or is it Commander Bradley?" said Beauregard.

"I'm scheduled to be promoted to Captain shortly, General," Bradley lied. He knew that Beauregard wouldn't to be able to access his personnel file.

"We shall return to my headquarters and have lunch. We have a lot to talk about."

Beauregard ordered the all the soldiers he had brought along to stay with the weapons to provide additional security.

Beauregard and Bradley got into the General's carriage and rode back to his headquarters. As they rode in the carriage Beauregard stared at Bradley, trying to determine if he could trust this man.

# Chapter 59

She hadn't heard from Bradley in three hours. Ashley called him on the two-way radio. "Tango Tango, this is Lima Juliette, come in." There was no response after repeated attempts to get Bradley on the radio. Her alternate contact was Petty Officer Giordano, and she switched channels on the radio. "Zulu Xray, Zulu Xray, this is Lima Juliette, come in."

After three calls a voice answered, "This is Zulu Xray, go ahead Lima Juliette."

"This is Captain Patterson. Is that you Giordano?"

"Yes, ma'am, Giordano here," came the response in a distinctive Southern drawl. Ashley knew Giordano was from Brooklyn, and he had the accent to prove it. Ashley's nerves went into high alert.

"I'm just checking to make sure everything is okay."

"Everything is AOK here, Captain," drawled the voice.

"I expect reports hourly," said Ashley. "Lima Juliette, over and out."

"Get Lieutenant Conroy here NOW," Ashley screamed to the Junior Officer of the Deck. Within a minute Conroy was on the bridge.

"I have a concern Frank, a big one. Here, call Giordano to say hello," she said, handing Conroy the radio.

"Zulu Xray, Zulu Xray, this is Lima Juliette, come in," said Conroy.

"Yes, sir," came the drawled response.

"Geo, this is Lt. Conroy, I'm just following up on the Captain's call to see if you need anything from the ship."

"We're good, Lieutenant. If we need anything from y'all we'll give a holler," came the response. Ashley motioned a finger across her throat to break off the conversation.

"This is Lima Juliette, over and out."

Ashley stared at Conroy. There was no need to ask a question.

"If that's Giordano," said Conroy, "I'm Lady GaGa."

"Are you sure you had a good idea to send those weapons ashore, Lieutenant?" Ashley asked.

Conroy's jaw dropped. "Captain, it was Commander Bradley's idea." Ashley felt faint.

She called CIC and spoke to Lt. Bea Toliver, the Combat Systems Officer. "Lieutenant, launch a drone immediately and send it to the coordinates of the weapons camp ashore. How long to the site?"

"It'll be overhead in 15 minutes, Captain."

Ashley and Conroy went below to CIC.

# Chapter 60

The drone helicopters on the *California* are equipped with sound dampening technology, making it difficult to hear them when overhead. The drone sent to investigate the weapons camp arrived overhead at 1215 hours, flying at an altitude of a half mile. As the drone flew over the weapons site it transmitted real-time video to CIC on the *California*.

The Captain and Conroy watched as the video cam showed the camp. They could see the piles of weapons, surrounded by, "Holy shit, 12 Southern mounted cavalrymen," shouted Ashley. The soldiers appeared to be chatting with the eight sailors. They were inspecting the weapons. "Move the cursor up and to the right and zoom in," Ashley said to the drone pilot. She looked at Conroy and said, "What do those mounds look like to you, Frank?"

Conroy moved closer to the monitor and stared at the four mounds.

"Those are freshly dug graves, Captain. Someone was even thoughtful enough to plant a rifle with a SEAL cap on top." He looked at Ashley. "My guys have been killed, Captain."

"Increase altitude, Lieutenant." Ashley said to the drone pilot. "I want surveillance of the immediate area."

A farmhouse surrounded by hundreds of Southern infantry and cavalry soldiers came into view. That must be a headquarters of some sort, Ashley thought, probably Beauregard's.

General Beauregard and Commander Bradley were having lunch at a table on the lawn in front of headquarters to escape the heat of the cabin.

"Drop down for a better look," Ashley said. "Now zoom in on those two men at the table in front of the farm house."

"You scumbag!" shouted Conroy, with an immediate apology for his profanity.

There was Commander Philip Bradley, Executive Officer of the *USS California*, dining with a Confederate General. From photos that Father Rick had shown her, Ashley knew she was looking at General Beauregard. "Photo this," she said to drone pilot Nathan, who snapped a still photo of the scene for further identification.

Ashley yelled to a nearby officer, "Get me Personnel Officer Sobel and the Warrant Officer Ciano, the Master at Arms and get them here immediately. NOW!"

Within minutes, Sobel and Ciano were in CIC.

"We have evidence that XO Bradley has committed treason and is defecting to the Confederacy." I want you to break into his office, confiscate all paperwork, and impound it in the lockup."

As Sobel and Ciano were about to leave the room, Conroy said, "Excuse me Captain, a word with you please." Ashley was miffed that Conroy slowed down the action.

"Captain, are we sure that this conspiracy is only ashore?"

My God, thought Ashley. She gave Conroy an attaboy slap on the shoulder and said to Sobel and Ciano, "What you are about to do is absolutely Top Secret. No word to anyone but me." She wondered if there was anybody in CIC to worry about.

"Aye Aye, Captain," they both said as they left the room to go to the XO's office.

Chief Warrant Officer Dennis Ciano, as Master at Arms, was the ship's law enforcement boss, the Top Cop of the *California*. He easily broke the lock on the door and they entered. Sobel went to the first pile of papers, Bradley's out box. There, on the top of the pile, was a letter on Bradley's stationery that began: "Dear Captain Patterson." It was dated today. Sobel said to Ciano, "Dennis, collect all documents and bring them to impound as the captain ordered. I'm bringing this to her now."

\* \* \*

Sobel raced back to CIC. Not expecting her back so soon, Ashley said, "Karen, did you have a question?"

"Captain, I think you may want to read this immediately. It's addressed to you. I haven't read it."

Ashley looked at the letter.

Dear Captain Patterson:

I resign my commission in the United States Navy, effective immediately. As you read this I shall have already made contact with the Confederacy, and I am now a servant of the Confederate States of America.

Captain, you chose to intervene in history and to fight a war that was long ago over. My Southern heritage and my conscience force me to take up arms against the United States, along with eight of my fellow crewmen, whose names are attached.

In the spirit of Robert E. Lee and other brave patriots who fought on the Southern side, I make this decision.

Very truly yours,

Philip Bradley, former Commander, United States Navy

# Chapter 61

Ashley's head pounded, her heart raced, and she was perspiring. She heard the sound of a whining little girl jumping rope. "You blew it Ashley," said little Splashy. "You wanted to jump in and be a hero and now you've managed to fuck it all up. Why did you trust that asshole, just because he's a man and older than you?" *At ease, you little bitch, thought Ashley. I'm in command. Dismissed.*

Ashley didn't need a meeting. She didn't need to talk to Father Rick, Jack, or Ivan Campbell. She didn't need to talk to anyone. She had all the information she needed. Those weapons are now in enemy hands. They need to be destroyed. She has to act, now.

"Get me Battery 3 on the phone," she said to Toliver. Battery 3 was the Cruise Missile battery, the most destructive weapons on the ship.

"This is Battery 3, Captain, Lieutenant Jamal Jacob speaking."

"Arm one missile and aim for the target on the drone signal," Ashley said.

"Missile one armed and ready, Captain."

"Fire one," said Ashley.

The *California* shuddered from the blast of the Tomahawk missile as it rocketed away from the ship. In CIC they had a visual from the missile as it raced toward its target.

\* \* \*

The soldiers and sailors were chatting at the weapons camp. Bradley's hand-picked sailors were explaining each weapon and its proper use. They were sipping fresh coffee, a few pots having just been made.

Three miles away at General Beauregard's headquarters, the General and Bradley enjoyed a lunch of fresh chicken and collard greens while they discussed Bradley's future and his role in the war effort. Beauregard drilled Bradley on the big weapons aboard the *California*. Bradley was proud of his foresight at having left aboard his main conspirator, Chief Ray. Bradley explained how Ray would disable the main weapons. Two other trusted sailors were with Ray, Bradley noted.

The men at the weapons camp, as well as Beauregard and Bradley, heard a strange sound in the sky. Bradley knew the sound very well, having taken advanced weapons courses. The men at the camp had no idea what it was.

The Tomahawk struck in the middle of the weapons cache with a ground shaking explosion, flattening trees and pulverizing the weapons and anyone near them. A plume of smoke and fire shot up 200 feet into the air. It left a crater 12 feet deep and 20 feet wide. No one survived the attack. All of the horses perished as well.

At Beauregard's headquarters three miles away, the shock wave from the blast tore through the trees like a hurricane. Fifteen horses in a corral jumped the fence and stampeded. The dinnerware on the table bounced two inches into the air. Both men instinctively ducked under the table.

His ears still ringing, Beauregard looked at Bradley and said, "I believe, Commander, that you were just telling me about your colleague's plan to disarm the weapons aboard the ship."

# Chapter 62

Ashley turned to drone pilot Nathan and said, "Hover over the area until the smoke clears so we can get some BDA (battle damage assessment)."

"Aye aye, Captain." said Nathan, shaken by what he had seen on his monitor.

"I need to see Col. Bingham, NOW." Ashley said to her aide Corporal Nesbitt.

When Bingham walked into CIC, Ashley grabbed him by the arm, looked into his eyes and said, "Matt, I want your entire platoon guarding our weapons systems, absolutely fucking immediately." She quickly explained the Bradley defection and the possibility of more conspirators on the ship. Weapons guard duty was the Marines' battle stations so they were ready to go. "And, Matt," Ashley said, "safeties off. Shoot to kill anyone who approaches a weapon."

Within four minutes, at least three Marines guarded each weapon battery.

\* \* \*

The smoke had cleared from the sight of the blast at the weapons camp. What they saw wasn't pretty, but it did show that the Tomahawk did its job. "If any weapon survived that blast," Conroy said, "it will be useless."

The drone then circled Beauregard's headquarters. The site was one of chaos, with horses and men scattering across the monitor. Ashley hunched over the monitor next to the pilot. She was looking for Bradley and Beauregard, but they weren't in sight.

# Chapter 63

Ashley realized that she needed to communicate with her department heads as well as the crew. You don't fire a cruise missile and not explain it to people, Ashley thought.

When the officers assembled, Ashley got right to the point.

"Our Executive Officer, Commander Philip Bradley, has committed treason and murder. He has defected to the Confederacy, taking eight sailors with him." She read the letter from Bradley to dispel any doubts.

"A few minutes ago I fired a Tomahawk to destroy the weapons. There was no choice. They were already in the hands of Confederate forces. The SEALs have been murdered." She passed around a still shot of the four graves with the SEAL caps on top of them.

"We don't know if Bradley left any co-conspirators on the ship," said Ashley, "but it's likely that he did. Disabling our main weapon batteries would be an obvious part of his plan. I've ordered Colonel Bingham to assign marines to guard every battery, and they're doing so as I speak. I've also ordered Master-at-Arms Ciano to put on extra security in the engine room, the reactor room and CIC. From this point forward, I want every officer on this ship to carry a side arm."

Ashley then announced that the new Executive Officer of the *California* would be Lt. Cmdr. Ivan Campbell and that he would now have the rank of full commander. This surprised no one because it was obvious that Campbell was the *de facto* second in command for weeks. She also announced that Lt. Wayne Bellamy would be the new Navigator.

"Ivan Campbell has my full trust and support and I expect everyone to show him the same. He did a great job as navigator. Hey, he never got us lost," said Ashley, attempting to inject a bit of levity into the tense situation.

"Never got us lost?" said Nick Wartella. "Then what the hell are we doing in the nineteenth-century?" They all enjoyed the laugh, a welcome one.

The open secret in the room, as Ashley and everyone there knew, was that a co-conspirator could be at this very meeting.

# Chapter 64

Ashley's phone rang. "Captain, a word with you please?" said Father Rick.

"Come on up Father. Bring Scotch."

Father Rick walked into the Captain's office wearing his usual smile.

"Father, I hope what you have to say begins with, 'Two guys walk into a bar.'"

"I take it, my friend, that you have had a somewhat stressful day," said Father Rick.

"Well, let's see. My XO defects to the Confederacy, steals half the ship's weapons, commits treason and murder, causing me to fire a Tomahawk Cruise Missile, and I missed the bastard. Yes, it's been a trying day, Father."

Father Rick reached across the table and grabbed his friend's hands, saying, "Let's bow our heads in prayer, Ashley."

"Heavenly Father, please watch over and bless those in peril on the sea, and please bless and give strength to your daughter, our leader, Ashley Patterson."

That was it. Ashley lost it. She broke down, which is exactly what her friend hoped for. Her shoulders heaved as she sobbed. Father Rick didn't attempt to console her; he wanted her to let it out. When she stopped crying, she said, sniffling. "You know Father, you're the only one on this ship that I could do that in front of.

"I know," said the chaplain, "that's why I'm here."

"Tomorrow, with your permission, I'd like to have a memorial service at 0800 for our fallen SEALs as well as for the misguided kids who died in the blast. And I would like you to speak at the service."

"Of course. I'll be there."

"Anything else, my friend?" Ashley said as the chaplain got up to leave.

"Yes, one thing. How's little Splashy doing?"

"She's in the brig until further notice."

Father Rick smiled and made the sign of the cross, giving her his blessing.

# Chapter 65

Ashley called Jack Thurber's line. "Could you come to my office please, Lieutenant." said Ashley, trying to affect a command voice.

Jack sat down across the table from Ashley. Their eyes locked for a few moments before either of them spoke, something that was happening more frequently.

"How was your day, Captain?" asked Jack without any sense of irony or humor. He knew she had been through hell.

"Well, Jack," said Ashley," I just spent a few minutes with Father Rick. I'm feeling much better now. And thank you for asking."

"Jack, I don't have to review for you the last few hours. We have a defector who committed treason as well as murder, and I had to destroy half the ship's small weapons as a result. Our drone tells us that Bradley wasn't at the site of the blast but three miles away having a meal with Confederate General Beauregard. What we know is that a high ranking officer from this ship has gone over to the enemy, and is presumably spilling secrets all over Beauregard's headquarters. But we also must assume, and I'm not alone in this, that there may be other conspirators on the ship. I've ordered high security for all of our weapons batteries as well as critical spaces on the ship, but we're at risk. I've been combing my brain, imagining one of those actors from *CSI*, *NCIS* or *Criminal Minds*, and what they would do or think. Hell, they do it every week in less than an hour."

Jack laughed.

"Then the thought occurred to me that we have one of the best investigative journalists in the country right on this ship, actually sitting across the desk from me. You know how to get into a person's head and to think like a detective, as you've done in so many of your books and articles. You can pick up nuances in speech and behavior."

"Well, thank you for those kind words, Captain. I do admit that I have a sixth sense for picking up subconscious signals from people." *Good,* thought Ashley, *then let's run away and get married. Cut this out, NOW.*

"Tell me about Bradley, Jack. Psych this guy out for me."

Jack looked uncomfortable. "I've been thinking about this man constantly for weeks. But before I get into my thinking about him, Captain, I want to give you an apology."

"Apology? For what?"

"I saw trouble with this guy weeks ago, but I kept my mouth shut. I didn't think it was my place as a recent seaman to be giving you my opinions of a senior officer. I should have blown a whistle, loudly."

"Jack, you're a fellow officer and a confidant. I also think of you as a friend." *Not to mention, I think I'm in love with you,* she thought. *STOP!*

"Tell me about Bradley, including everything you noticed or heard about him."

"I always look for a person's incentives, something journalists share with micro-economists. What drives people in certain directions has as much to do with objective incentives as it has to do with subconscious thoughts. Although I haven't seen his personnel file, I've spoken to a lot of people who know him. Bradley is a man at the end of his career. He's had a drinking problem and has been passed over for promotion twice. If his career wasn't dying under its own weight, his confrontation with you in the wardroom probably nailed it. And the most significant part of that scenario is that he must have realized it as well. He's 10 years older than you and below you in rank. You have the job he thinks he deserved. He knows that you're on the track for admiral while he'll muster out on the pension of a three striper. I believe that he not only resents you, he hates you. Here is a guy, divorced with no immediate family, at the end of his chosen career. Here is a guy who believed that the twenty-first century wasn't treating him right. He's a man with no future. Except for the Confederacy that is. Looking at incentives, what could be more appealing to him: washing out of the US Navy or becoming a big shot in the Confederate Navy? Now let's pile on some more incentives, the incentives of the Confederate Navy. The *Gray Ships* have become a fixation in the South, judging from all of the newspaper reports."

"And thanks to your excellent articles that have been plagiarized all over Dixie."

"Well, thanks Captain, but they wouldn't print those articles if they didn't believe them."

"Let me ask you Captain, what are you worried about with Bradley?"

"The two obvious worries, or at least they're obvious to me, is that first, he blows the cover on the *Gray Ships* deception, and second, he convinces the South to avoid the Battle of Bull Run."

"I have a different view," said Jack. "Bradley is a man looking to trade things to get to his incentives. He wants to be a Confederate admiral, something that's beyond his grasp in the United States Navy, in 1861 or 2013. He wants to be the guy who can show them how to handle the *Gray Ships Fleet*, not just one *Gray Ship*. The South is very big on honor and chivalry, although somehow owning human slaves never worked its way into that thinking. They're probably looking at this guy as a simple turncoat, a traitor. Yes he can be useful, but he needs to have a lot to trade to convince them he's one of them. Also, Bradley wants Bull Run to happen because it will enable him to tell the Confederacy 'I told you those weapons were bad.' I would place bets on Bradley lying to the South as he's lied to you."

"Do you think we should try to capture him, Jack?"

"The man's a traitor and a murderer, Captain. The consequences of that are beyond my pay grade. But, yes, I would try, just in case I'm wrong, and he spills all of his knowledge."

"Let's change subjects, Jack. What about the possibility of conspirators who may have remained on this ship?"

"As I've been thinking about Bradley, I kept my reporter's antennae up. I've been looking at a few sailors who I think may be with Bradley. I base these observations on snippets of conversation and questions I've asked other people." He handed Ashley a list of 11 people he had doubts about.

Ashley perused the list. "Oh, my God," she yelled. "All eight of the sailors who went ashore with Bradley are on this list. So far, Jack, you're pitching a perfect game." She looked at the three who were still on the ship.

One name jumped off the page. "Holy shit. Chief Albert Ray. He's the ship's Chief Gunnery Mate, just below Andrea Rubin, the Weapons Officer. He knows every weapons system on this ship."

"We'll continue our talk in a minute, Jack."

\* \* \*

"Colonel Bingham please pick up a phone," Ashley almost screamed over the PA system.

"Yes, Captain," said Bingham.

"Matt, I have some strong evidence that Chief Gunner's Mate Ray may be a conspirator. He knows our weapons better than anyone on the ship."

"I'll track him down immediately, ma'am, and take him into custody for questioning." Each of the Marines wore ear buds for instant communication. Bingham said to all of them, "If you see Chief Gunners Mate Albert Ray, arrest him immediately and call me."

Bingham then went to the gun deck to visit with each of his Marines. As he walked around the wooden structure on the stern that had been erected for a costume change, he noticed a pool of blood spilling out across the deck coming from Battery 3, the Tomahawk missile battery. His training took over. He stepped behind the structure and cocked his Colt 45. Chief Ray jumped from behind the structure and fired a silencer equipped handgun directly at the Colonel's head. Bingham died immediately.

Petty Officer Simon Planck was walking along a weather deck two levels above when he saw Colonel Bingham fall. Planck had completed 20 classes in Pete Campo's Martial Arts training. Now feeling physically fit, he raced down the ladder to give assistance. As he stepped around a turret he startled Chief Ray, who was looking in the other direction. He saw that Ray had a gun in one hand and a printed circuit board in the other. As Ray raised the gun, Planck delivered a swirling karate kick to his face, knocking Ray to the deck. He then grabbed Bingham's gun from the deck and pointed it at Ray. He hoped that the safety wasn't on because he hadn't fired a weapon since boot camp. He trained the gun on Ray, making sure that he wasn't moving. He kicked Ray's gun from his hand and it went skidding across the deck. Planck had no idea what to do so he just screamed, "Marine down!" Four Marine guards came running. Planck raised the gun over his head and said, "That's the one," pointing to Chief Ray." As the Marines approached him, Ray suddenly spun and took another gun from a holster. He pointed it at Planck and fired, landing the shot in Planck's left shoulder. The Marines shot and killed Ray.

"Good work, Sailor," Sergeant Charlie Sorese said to Planck as he collapsed to the deck. "Corpsman!" shouted Sorese into his mouthpiece. "Corpsman to main deck aft. Man down, man down."

Ray had killed Marine Sergeant John Newfield as well as Colonel Bingham before the Marines shot him.

Sergeant Sorese called the officer of the deck on the bridge, who immediately dispatched Warrant Officer Ciano. The OOD then called Captain Patterson to report the event. Ashley called Sergeant Sorese to her office, telling Jack to stay there.

"What's going on?" asked Jack.

"Your perfect game is still running hot, Jack. Chief Ray just killed two marines and wounded a sailor. Ray is dead. That leaves two from your list."

Ashley announced over the PA. "Master at Arms, pick up a phone." She told Ciano the names of the two remaining suspects, and told him to turn the ship upside down and shake it if he had to.

Both sailors from Jack's list were located within minutes and were taken to the brig for interrogation.

"Congratulations, Jack, you pitched a perfect game."

"Perfect?" said Jack. "Two good guys dead, one wounded."

Ashley turned to Sorese. "Who's the sailor who was shot?"

"Petty Officer Simon Planck, ma'am. That kid deserves the Navy Cross. If it wasn't for him, Ray would have gone on killing."

Ashley swallowed hard. "What's his condition Sergeant, do you know?"

"Just a shoulder wound, Captain. It hit some bone and tissue but I'm sure he'll be okay."

# Chapter 66

The memorial service was held on the forward deck to accommodate a large crowd. Everyone on the ship, except for those on watch, attended the service. People stood on top of gun turrets, torpedo batteries and lined up along the entire rail. It wasn't an Episcopal mass but a short inter-denominational ceremony. After Father Rick read the formal parts of the service, he asked Captain Patterson to approach the microphone.

"Yesterday was a day that no one expected nor could have expected," Ashley said. "It was a day that saw treason, violence, murder, and amazing courage. It was a day that broke our hearts and made us proud. Chaplain Sampson has asked us to pray for our fallen brothers as well as for the misguided souls who turned their backs on us and our country. Like you, I bowed my head in prayer. Let us also pray for our wounded shipmate, Petty Officer Simon Planck, whose heroism and quick thinking saved countless lives." Ashley said, nodding in Planck's direction. Planck was sitting in a wheelchair off to the starboard side. The crew gave him a thunderous round of applause and cheers, a sound that Planck never expected to hear. He raised his good arm in thanks.

"Our mission continues. May God grant us the strength to carry on... so we can soon go home."

Another round of loud applause and cheers. Not the normal sounds of a memorial service, thought Father Rick, but then what is normal for a ship from 2013 stuck in 1861?

\* \* \*

After the memorial service, Ashley called Navy Secretary Wells on the radio. She had to consider radio security now because Bradley presumably had a radio and could monitor any messages to or from the *California.* There was a secure channel, but she was sure Bradley knew what it was.

She told Wells she would be there within the hour. When Wells asked why they couldn't just talk on the radio, Ashley told him that she would explain when she saw him.

At 0915 Ashley stepped onto the platform at the bottom of the ladder to board the motor launch. The boatswain's pipe sounded, followed by "*California,* departing." Lt. Frank Conroy accompanied her.

As they motored up the Potomac, Ashley said to Conroy, "The last time I was in Washington, we all discussed theoretical military possibilities. Here we are after one day of hellish combat. Our war has begun."

"Yes, it has, Captain," said Conroy, "and I've already lost 25 percent of my men."

"If I may, Captain, what about Bradley?"

"Do you mean to ask if we're going to try to capture him?"

"Yes, ma'am, that's exactly what I mean."

"The answer is yes, and we'll discuss the details later today. But for now Lieutenant, I want you to plant one thing in your brain. The mission to find Bradley will not be 'payback.' The mission will be to find and capture a traitor and murderer, and to bring him to justice."

\* \* \*

They arrived at the Navy Department at 1030 hours. Ashley told Wells about the events of July 2, and asked Conroy to give his observations. Wells was surprised but not shocked. In the strange situation of the *California*, it was inevitable that there may be some defections, he thought. Ashley also told him about the security precautions she had taken.

"The only change in plans, Mr. Secretary, will be our ability to train Union troops and supply small arms support. Over 50 percent of our small arms have been destroyed, including the rocket propelled grenades. My objective now is to make sure that we can provide support from our major weapons systems."

Wells asked about the impact of Bradley telling General Beauregard about the plans.

"That is a major concern, sir. But Lt. Thurber has convinced me that Bradley may withhold his knowledge of *Operation Gray Ships*, as well as his knowledge of the history of Bull Run, simply to enhance his credibility with the South. My thinking is that maybe he wants the South to believe that the *Gray Ships* really are a fleet."

"And there is another fact that we know for certain, one that gives us an insight into Bradley's plans."

"Please go on, Captain. Facts are always superior to speculation."

"The Chief Petty Officer that was killed, Bradley's accomplice, was found with an object in his hand that we call a printed circuit board. It controls the firing procedures of all of our missiles and big guns. There is one circuit board with each weapon platform. The obvious objective was to disable the *California's* ability to fire weapons."

"Thank God the man was intercepted," said Wells.

"Yes, but Bradley doesn't know that. He thinks that the Battle of Bull Run will start without the *California's* firepower. He wants Bull Run to happen, so he can be the hero who saved the day."

# Chapter 67

O n July 3 at 1300 hours, Ashley met with Lt. Conroy in her office, along with her new Executive Officer, Ivan Campbell and Jack Thurber.

"I've invited Lt. Thurber here because of his long career in investigative journalism. He's the closest we have to a detective on board." *And, frankly, I just like to be near him.*

"We're about to start a manhunt almost as serious as the search for Osama Bin Laden. In a way it's more serious, because Bradley can still do us a lot of harm. Lt. Thurber is of the opinion that Bradley may not divulge the *Gray Ships* secret or even the upcoming Battle of Bull Run. But we can't assume the best. We have to be prepared that Bradley will try to undermine the Union efforts."

"The big question, of course, is where to find him. The South is a gigantic area, and Bradley could be anywhere. Any thoughts?"

"He's between here and Richmond, Captain, and closer to Richmond than here," said Conroy.

Ashley, Campbell and Thurber stared at Conroy.

"How can you possibly know that, Frank?"

Conroy explained that the new two-way radios have powerful homing devices in them, and very few people know this. The device is a simple homing beacon, nothing as sophisticated as a GPS receiver in a cell phone, but it is a beacon. Conroy told them that he stood on deck and tried it.

He received a very faint signal from a location in a direct line between them and Richmond. "The closer you get to the radio, the stronger will be the sound. It will make the difference between finding a needle in a hay stack and finding a needle on a pool table. By the way, no signal came from the weapons camp that we destroyed, so the only radio that's in the wrong hands is Bradley's."

Ashley looked at a map. She pointed out that Richmond is about 90 miles by land from their current location. "It's quite a hike," she said.

"The plan, Captain, will look like this. We steal some rebel uniforms and horses and head to Richmond."

"Where will you get the uniforms, and who will teach your guys to ride horses?"

Conroy explained that clothing supply depots are usually located at an army's command headquarters, such as Beauregard's near the destroyed weapons camp. "All of my guys ride horses, Captain. We were trained on them for Afghanistan."

"So we sneak in, steal some uniforms, steal some horses, and be on our merry way. Piece of cake," said Conroy. "If you're a SEAL, that is."

# Chapter 68

The Coast Guard Cutter *Gallatin* was dragging a sonar array, trying to get an audible return from the presumably sunken *California*. At one point during the search, the *Gallatin* came within 25 yards of the wormhole through which the *California* slipped into 1861.

Coast Guard Sector Commander Eric Buehler had reconciled himself to receiving telephone calls every few minutes from the White House, the Office of Naval Operations at the Pentagon, and various Senators and Congressmen who had a *California* crewmember from their state or district. He gave the job of handling the press to his public relations staff.

The disappearance of the *California* dominated news programs and online news updates the world over. It was also the major topic in the wild world of unedited blogs, Twitter and Facebook posts, even though it was still early morning. A Google search of *USS California* showed more hits than any other searches combined.

Fox News veteran anchor Sheppard Smith was fast asleep. His phone rang at 3:30 a.m. After five rings, he awoke and looked at the alarm clock. His producer told him about the *California* and said to get to the studio as soon as possible.

Smith arrived on the set at 4:25 a.m. After a quick huddle with his producer they focused on three angles to the story. News outlets always look for an angle, otherwise news can just mean cold facts. The first angle would be possible terrorism, as it always is for a sudden event, especially one involving the military. The second angle would involve the sea rescue operation. They would need an expert on sonar. Smith's producer looked at his database and called a guy from Florida they had used before. The third angle was a sensitive one, the possibility of human error. The producer got a retired Navy captain on the phone.

The broadcast began. "We have received a report that the nuclear missile cruiser *USS California* is missing. Terrorism (angle one) can't be ruled out, of course, but the timing of this event, if someone caused it and wanted publicity from it, is very strange. The *California* went missing at 3:09 a.m. Eastern Time, hardly a busy part of a news cycle. We'll be tracking the possibility of terrorism throughout the morning. Sonar arrays are being dragged near the *California's* last known position by the Coast Guard Cutter *Gallatin*, and so far they haven't detected a metal object beneath the surface of the water. We have on the phone Fox News contributor Peter Welch, an engineer who is an expert in sonar technology." (angle two).

"Good morning Mr. Welch," said Smith, "and thank you for getting up so early to talk to us. Please give us your take on what's happening."

"Frankly, I'm surprised," said the sonar expert, "that there has been no audible return at all so far. I understand the sonar has been active for over a half hour and that they are near the last known location of the ship." The guy then went into technical jargon until Smith cut him off. "Mr. Welch," said Smith, "we have to take a break. We will be contacting you later for an update. I thank you again, sir."

After the commercial break, Smith spoke to retired US Navy cruiser Captain Fred Notter. (angle three).

"In your experience, sir, how could something like this happen?" asked Smith.

"At this point, Sheppard, I have to say I'm baffled," said Notter. "If a ship simply disappears off both the satellite and radar grids, it's usually an indication that the vessel has sunk. But from what I've been told, the water depth in her last known location was less than 300 feet, yet sonar shows nothing. I hate to say it but the loved ones of the *California*'s crew will have to wait until this mystery is solved."

"Thank you, Captain Notter," said Smith as he turned to the camera. "It goes without saying that we'll be tracking this story throughout the day and will bring you the latest news as soon as it breaks."

At the headquarters of Al Jazeera in Doha, Qatar, news editor Mohammed Al-Qudz was typing an article that speculated whether American stealth technology could be at play in the *California* incident. "If they can hide an airplane from radar, can they also hide a ship?" Al-Qudz wrote.

The *USS California* had now been missing for an hour and a half.

# Chapter 69

Lt. Conroy called a meeting of SEAL Squad Bravo in the ship's video theater.

The squad consists of Petty Officers Timothy Blake, Walter Cummings, Edward Jones, Stephen Jordan, Franco Lopez, John Tarback, and Joseph Tucker. The squad would be led by Conroy.

"This mission will have two parts," said Conroy, "First, we've been ordered to capture Phillip Bradley, a man formerly known as Commander Bradley. He is a traitor and a murderer. He killed four of our guys. But this mission is not about 'payback.' Our prime objective is to capture Bradley and bring him back to justice. He's a self-serving prick, and I don't expect him to choose death. I have a hunch that when he's confronted, he'll put his hands up and surrender."

"And what if he doesn't surrender, Lieutenant?" asked Tim Blake.

"Then we kill the bastard," said Conroy.

"Second, we're going to observe and report enemy troop strength, and call in aerial surveillance and strikes if appropriate. Any strikes, whether by drone or a missile from the ship, will be approved by the captain."

He then explained that they would land in a Zodiac near the weapons camp that was destroyed. "I figure that they won't be expecting any visits from the *California* there. From the camp we'll proceed about three miles to the Beauregard headquarters. We can expect it to be heavily defended, so we will infiltrate at night. All weapons will have silencers for us to take out guards. Once we break into the clothing bunker, we pick out a uniform for each of us. The horses are trained Army animals and shouldn't be too spooky. Petty Officer Tarback here has a way with horses, so he'll head up that part of the operation."

"Today is July 3. We will move out in three days on July 6, a Saturday, at 2200 hours, after dark. We'll arrive on Sunday morning. I've picked a Sunday because things always get a bit relaxed on the day of Sabbath. Remember Pear Harbor? It will also give us two days to study maps and make detailed plans. I expect to arrive on site at 0100 hours, which will give us plenty of darkness to do our job."

"It's a distance of about 90 miles from where we'll be to Richmond. We'll take a break every 30 miles, mainly to give the horses a rest."

"Any questions?"

He handed out a phonetic word pronunciation chart that Father Rick had prepared. Speaking with a Southern accent wasn't difficult. It just required adhering to a few principles. Drop the "g" sound, the sheet suggested, substituting "mornin" for "morning." Most of the squad had seen service in Afghanistan, so this looked a lot easier than trying to speak conversational Arabic.

"Okay," said Conroy, "grab a map and start studying."

# Chapter 70

At 2200 hours on July 6 the SEALs boarded the Zodiac for the trip to the weapons camp. The weather was oppressively hot and humid, even at night, the kind of weather SEALs train for. They arrived at the old weapons camp, as it has become known, at 0115 in the morning. They deflated the Zodiac, folded it over its engine and hid it under brush for future retrieval.

They began the hike to Beauregard's headquarters, a distance of about three miles. Each man was carrying 30 pounds of gear so they walked slowly both to conserve energy and to keep their ears open for hoof beats. They arrived at the headquarters at 0215 hours, and walked to a large shed, which they identified from drone surveillance as the probable supply depot. Cummings easily picked through the lock and they were inside. Tarback stayed outside as guard. Uniforms were stacked four feet high on a long bench. Using flashlights, they each picked out a uniform and tried it on. Because of the SEALs' obsession with preparation, they had drilled this maneuver on the ship for hours, reaching for clothing with their eyes closed, then shining a flashlight on the size, and then quickly putting the uniform on.

John Tarback had a reputation from his SEAL training as a "horse whisperer." He grew up on a ranch in Oklahoma and loved working with horses, as horses loved working with him.

Three horse corrals were located near headquarters, each guarded by two soldiers. Conroy picked the corral farthest from the building. It contained 15 horses. Petty Officers Jordan and Lopez were tasked to handle the guards. They each fired their silenced weapons at the guards, killing them instantly. Tarback entered the enclosure and gently coaxed eight horses to the opening, one horse at a time. Cummings and Tucker brought the saddles from the small barn nearby. The saddles they used in SEAL training camp were different from the ones they found, and it took a bit of figuring to strap them correctly on the horses. The darkness didn't help.

After saddling up, Conroy led the group in the opposite direction from the road they took to the camp. According to his map, there was another road about a half mile from their position. Petty Officer Tim Blake rode the point position in front of the group. He kept his automatic rifle at the ready as did the rest of the SEALs in case they encountered a rebel patrol.

Each of the men gave his new horse a name. Donnelly named his horse *Brooklyn*, in honor of his slain friend Tony Giordano.

Conroy looked at his watch. It was 0245 hours. Their uniform and horse acquisition job took only a half hour. They were 90 miles from Richmond, and they would ride for 30 miles before taking a break. Conroy didn't want to risk a horse injury, so they moved along the road at a moderate pace. He estimated they would be half way to Richmond by 0730 hours. They would rest for an hour and move out at 0900 after a breakfast of MREs and a brief nap.

"We'll take one more break between here and Richmond," said Conroy, "and then we'll remain on the outskirts of the city until darkness. Then we'll tie the horses up and proceed on foot. The signal from Bradley's radio is getting stronger, so I know we're on the right track."

"Okay, move out," said Conroy.

# Chapter 71

According to the plan, a drone would fly over an area north of Richmond on the afternoon of July 7. The *California* would be too far away from Richmond for effective radio speech transmissions. The drone radio frequency, on the other hand, enables an effective flying range of over 125 miles. The drone would locate the SEALs by a laser transmitter.

SEAL Squad Bravo continued along the road to Richmond. It was a warm day, but not oppressive, with temperatures in the low 80s.

At 1030 hours they came upon a small cavalry unit of about 25 mounted soldiers. Conroy gave a hand signal indicating to his men to enter a wooded area. Although they were wearing Confederate uniforms, Conroy wanted to avoid contact. Apparently they had not been seen, and the cavalry unit passed by without incident. Peering through the trees, Conroy took note of the pennant the lead rider carried. It was the flag of the Army of Northern Virginia, the Army of Robert E. Lee. He would transmit that information by code to the drone when it flew overhead.

A half hour later, the squad came upon a group of women walking along the road. As they passed, each of the SEALs doffed his hat and said "Mornin, ma'am." One of the women yelled, "When is Ole' Bobby Lee going to march on Washington?"

"Soon enough, ma'am," said Conroy. "Ya'll seen our camp have ye? We're trying to locate the General's headquarters, and we seem to have gotten lost."

The woman, assuming they were just a group of soldiers trying to hook up with the main Army, said, "It's just up ahead about two miles. More soldiers than I've ever seen in one place. Tents for miles to see."

After the women were out of view, Conroy ordered the squad into the woods. "Dismount," said Conroy.

"It seems we've come upon a major part of the Southern forces, none other than Robert E. Lee's Army. Tarback, Cummings, you two stay here with the horses. The rest of us will go ahead on foot to see what we can find out."

That woman wasn't exaggerating, thought Conroy, as he saw the camp in the distance. It was a sea of tents. He could also see what appeared to be an ammunition dump area next to a vast artillery section.

They continued through the woods to get a better view. Conroy dictated his observations into his recorder just as he did on the first reconnaissance mission almost three months ago. "I need your eyes and ears, guys. Just tell me what you see, and don't forget to take pictures with your phones."

They walked through the trees to get a view of a large field. An infantry company was going through a combat drill. They were arranged in platoons of sixteen soldiers and then further spaced apart into eight man squads. Conroy was amazed how the men stood, marched, and even ran shoulder to shoulder. This is the concept of the firing line, a military doctrine that lasted for centuries. By modern military analysis, the tactic was as deadly as it was dumb. The idea was to enable an officer to see a hole in the line and plug it with a fresh soldier. Their rifles were antique by twenty-first century standards, but they were not inaccurate. From what he had read, Conroy knew that those muskets now had rifling in them and could shoot a bullet with accuracy from 300 yards. From where he stood behind a tree, Conroy figured he could pick off soldiers one by one. If he had 25 other riflemen with him they could leave a pile of bodies in minutes. But even without soldiers shooting from behind trees, a few cannons firing canister shot could shred a formation of men. That's what happened (will happen?) in Pickett's Charge at the Battle of Gettysburg. It all looks very brave and honorable, but it's also stupid, thought Conroy. Where's the honor in offering your body up to be killed.

Conroy wanted to get a better view of the ammunition and artillery area. Besides the cameras on their phones, Conroy had a Nikon camera with a telephoto lens. Conroy climbed a tree and settled on a couple of crossed branches. He had a perfect view of the artillery and the ammunition wagons. He knew the wagons carried ammo because he saw a soldier retrieve bags of gun powder from behind the door.

He did a rough count of the artillery, which was neatly parked in rows and columns. He counted 25 caissons, the two wheeled carts that transported ammunition. Each caisson carried two ammunitions chests. He also counted 50 twelve pounder howitzers and 55 twelve pounder Napoleon cannons. Looking further to his left he saw a battery of 45 twenty pounder Parrott rifles, which were cannons that had rifling in their barrels. Next to the twenty pounder Parrotts were 50 ten pounder Parrotts. Although these weapons may be primitive compared to the artillery Conroy was trained in, they could pack a punch.

As Conroy surveyed the enormous encampment his eyes came upon a man on a horse who Conroy recognized from countless old photographs. There he was, on his faithful horse Traveler, Robert E. Lee himself. Just as he appears in the old photos, Lee always looked as if he knew a picture or sculpture was about to be taken of him. Maybe that's how he got his nickname, *Marble Man*. Conroy focused his camera, steadied it, and snapped about a dozen pictures of Lee.

After Lee went back inside his tent, Conroy returned his gaze to the artillery and ammunition carts. Including alleyways between the rows and columns of guns, Conroy estimated the area to be about the size of a football field. The ammunition carts took up about a quarter acre. This is one mother lode of ordnance, thought Conroy.

Conroy planted a laser tracker at the edge of the trees to enable a drone or missile to track on the area.

The second part of their mission was already a success. Without expecting to, the SEALs found Robert E. Lee's Army. Now it was time to proceed with the first part of the mission, to capture Bradley.

# Chapter 72

At 9 a.m. on July 8, Phillip Bradley sat in the waiting room outside of Jefferson Davis' office in Richmond. Stephen Mallory, the Secretary of the Confederate Navy, had been with Davis for 45 minutes. Both men had been briefed by General Beauregard about this mysterious naval officer. They had also been given an extensive report of the huge explosion near Beauregard's headquarters.

Bradley hated cooling his heels, but he didn't have much control over the situation. At least the waiting room was comfortable. A large awning outside the window blocked the direct rays of the easterly morning sun. The temperature was in the high 70s, and the humidity moderate. He sat on a comfortable leather chair looking at his notes. The cruise missile attack on the weapons camp changed Bradley's narrative, to say the least.

Beauregard suspected, a suspicion he shared with Davis and Mallory, that Bradley may have lured the General to the camp only to have him killed by the rocket fired from the ship. Had it not been for his insistence on lunch at his headquarters, Beauregard would have been blown to bits. Bradley could have jumped behind a rock at the last moment, Beauregard speculated.

Finally, Bradley was escorted into Jefferson Davis' office, although not as the conquering hero that he had hoped to be.

Davis and Mallory greeted Bradley and shook his hand. Missing was the typical smile when a person meets another for the first time. Davis gestured toward a chair, and Bradley sat.

"General Beauregard told us about your interesting story in some detail," said Davis. Bradley imagined Beauregard telling them that this nut job thinks he's from the twenty-first century.

"Clearly, Commander," said Davis, "the story as recounted to us by General Beauregard is a strange tale indeed. Because we only heard it second hand, please give us your summary of who you are and how you got here."

Bradley summarized of the strange days of the USS *California* and her travel through time. "Gentlemen, I realize that the story sounds unbelievable. Not one person on my ship would disagree with that. But we found evidence beyond a doubt to convince us that we had traveled, somehow, through time."

Bradley then told them that Captain Patterson, along with other officers from the *California*, had already met with Lincoln and Navy Secretary Wells. He did not mention the *Operation Gray Ships* deception.

"Because we have the hindsight, or better stated, the foresight of history, we know that a major battle will take place at Manassas, Virginia on the 21st of this month, near Bull Run Creek. Three months ago we were able to predict the attack on Fort Sumter to the minute. The Battle of Manassas, or the Battle of Bull Run as it's known in the North, will happen, gentlemen, less than two weeks from today."

Davis and Mallory were well aware of the upcoming battle, but were surprised that this man knew the exact day.

"Tell us, Commander, from your knowledge of history," said Davis, "how did the battle go?"

"What was expected to be a Union victory turned out to be a triumph for the South. Both sides were inexperienced, but the Confederacy won the day, primarily by destroying Union artillery."

"And how does this involve you, sir?" Davis asked Bradley.

"History will change, Mr. President, because of the involvement of a *Gray Ship*, the *USS California*. The gigantic explosion that destroyed the weapons I had offered to General Beauregard was caused by a weapon known as a Tomahawk Cruise Missile. I believe the General told you about its destructive force. At the Battle of Manassas, that weapon and many more like it will be used against the Confederacy, or at least that is the Union's plan. But I have put into motion an alternative plan."

"Please give us the details of your alternative, Commander," said Mallory.

"I have a colleague on the ship, another man of the South, who is in charge of all of the major weapons. He knows how to disable them, and will do so before July 21st. Manassas will occur with no *Gray Ship* assistance."

"So history will unfold as it has been written," said Davis, his skepticism starting to wane.

"More than that, sir," said Bradley. "I have studied the Battle of Manassas in great detail. I can advise all of the Generals involved just what the Union maneuvers will be. The Southern victory will become a smashing triumph."

Mr. Secretary," said Davis, "see to it that this man is sworn in as a Confederate naval officer with the rank of captain."

"Yes, sir," said Mallory. But can we trust this man? Mallory wondered.

I hope Chief Ray is being cautious, Bradley thought.

# Chapter 73

Near Bali, in the Dutch East Indies, Malcolm Holmes, an English wildlife artist, painted his favorite subject, the monarch butterfly. He drew a sketch first, making sure to capture the beautiful coloration of the butterfly's wings. It was tricky, of course, because the wings were flapping. Holmes noticed a cloud of pollen as the butterfly's wings disturbed the air. He made a note on his sketch to make sure to put the pollen cloud into the painting.

On July 9, 1861, off the Northwest coast of Africa, a zone of low atmospheric pressure formed. At the same time a light wind developed in the upper atmosphere. The combination of low pressure near the surface of the ocean and the upper atmospheric wind resulted in a tropical depression, which soon became a tropical storm.

The storm began its journey toward the East Coast of the United States.

\* \* \*

On the morning of July 12, 1861, Lt. Kathy Cooney, the *California's* meteorologist, asked to speak to the Captain. Wind driven rain pelted the windows on the bridge, and the howling of gusts sounded throughout the ship. The sea was turning rough, with white capped waves growing to eight feet. Cooney had two observations, neither of which was good. The cloud formations the night before and at sunrise foretold a large weather front heading toward the *California* from the Southwest. What really concerned her was that both of the ship's barometers, the instruments that measure atmospheric pressure, were dropping fast. Like rocks.

"Captain, it's time to duck for cover," said Cooney.

Lt. Wayne Bellamy, the ship's navigator, was on the bridge. "We're not far from Baltimore Harbor, Captain," said Bellamy. "ETA one hour if we can maintain 20 knots."

"Make for Baltimore, Lieutenant," said the Captain.

"Recommend you come to course 098 and maintain a speed of 20 knots," Bellamy said to the OOD.

The OOD then called for the boatswain's mate of the watch to sound his pipe over the PA system. "This is the officer of the deck. All hands prepare for heavy weather. Stay off weather decks unless absolutely necessary."

Ashley called Nick Wartella, the Engineering Officer. "Nick, we need to do a fast costume change."

Wartella called Jeff DeLouker and Nancy Forsyth, the "costume designers. "I've put out the call to the *Gray Ship Gang*," said DeLouker. "We've drilled for this and everyone knows where they have to be. I'm going down now to supervise."

"Be careful, Jeff," said Wartella.

The *Gray Ship Gang* heavy weather drill called for each team to report to their assigned places. The *California* cruised under the name of USS *New York* that day, and she would soon be the *California* again. The nameplate USS *New York* was removed and the two large boards with the ship's number were to be taken down. The large fore and aft structures that were designed to look like gun turrets were trickier. Forsyth had designed them so that the walls could be folded in on one another like the sides of a box. The long water pipes that were made to look like guns were removed and lashed to the deck. After the gang folded down the walls of the wood structures, they draped heavy chains across each resulting pile of wood and secured it to the deck. During drills, the entire operation could be accomplished in less than 20 minutes. But this was not a drill, and the winds were gale force, with a sustained blow of 40 mph gusting to 60.

The four man team assigned to take down the wooden number boards was having a difficult time. They had just taken down the starboard number when a gust picked up the board like a paper envelope. One of the sailors fractured three ribs as he tried to hold onto the board and was dragged into a rail. The board sailed past the missile batteries and took a downward trajectory as it approached the stern. Jeff DeLouker was on the stern supervising the nameplate removal. The number board smashed into his back, knocking him overboard. Everyone screamed "man overboard," and hurled life rings toward DeLouker. He waved his hands, confirming that he was conscious. Nancy Forsyth sprinted to the rail, having just seen her friend hurled into the ocean. "Hang on Jeff," she screamed.

The word reached the bridge in less than 15 seconds that someone was in the water. The quartermaster of the watch reached for the ship's horn and sounded six short blasts, the man overboard signal. The officer of the deck gave rudder commands to the helmsman, steering into a Williamson, or Life Saving, turn. This maneuver was invented by a navy man during World War II as a way to turn a ship and end up in the same spot facing in the opposite direction. With a bit of luck, the overboard officer would be there. Because of the building seas, the turn was difficult, the bow of the ship rising and crashing back to the water as the ship made its agonizing maneuver. When the turn was completed, a lookout spotted DeLouker 30 yards off the starboard bow. The OOD guided the ship toward DeLouker, bringing her hull against the wind and sea to create a "lee," an area of calm to make it easier to haul the man aboard. It also created a gut wrenching sensation on the ship as the heavy seas crashed against the hull, causing her to take nauseating rolls.

After DeLouker was plucked from the sea, the ship turned once again to steam toward Baltimore. They had lost valuable time with the man overboard incident, time that enabled the storm to worsen.

The entrance to the harbor was deep enough so that running aground wasn't a major concern. The *California* entered the harbor at a speed of 10 knots. The wind was still fierce, blowing at 50 knots with gusts over 75, but at least the embrace of land at the harbor entrance made the seas less frightening. The Captain ordered the anchor dropped, and the *California* was finally safe.

Damage control reports to the bridge gave Ashley a sense of relief. The ship suffered no major structural problems, just a few bent rails. The weapons, and the platforms they were mounted on, were not damaged, and the costume change equipment made it through the storm.

It was a fast moving storm and within an hour, the winds had calmed down. It was 1400 hours. Ashley decided to stay the night anchored in the harbor to give the crew a break to nurse bruises and contusions from slamming into bulkheads. The cooks in the mess were most appreciative.

Nick Wartella and Nancy Forsyth were at DeLouker's bedside in sick bay. As he was hurled overboard, DeLouker's ribs made furious contact with the ship's rail, fracturing four of them. He was in a lot of pain. "If you guys are here to cheer me up," said DeLouker, "please do not fucking make me laugh."

The *California* dodged a bullet, Ashley thought, but she knew there were more storms to come.

# Chapter 79

On July 11, at 0930 hours, Union Brigadier General Irwin McDowell and his aide, Col. James Burns met with Marine Major Richard Carrubba in CIC to begin preparations for the upcoming Battle of Bull Run. The Captain had ordered Carrubba and Conroy, upon his return, to be the key ground combat contacts since Col. Bingham had been killed. They had a map of the area around Manassas spread out in front of them, as well as earmarked books from the ship's library that described the battle. The purpose of the meeting was to pick targets for cruise missile strikes.

The consensus was that the *California* would concentrate its firepower on the Confederate artillery and ammunition placements. General McDowell was given a radio, and would communicate with the *California* during the battle. Drone pilots Lt. Bob Nathan and Lt. Andrew Cinque attended the meeting, along with Lt. Russ Colombo, the pilot of the Apache Attack Helicopter.

McDowell felt chastened that the history books showed that his efforts at Bull Run would result in defeat. Did he really need these mystical weapons from another century to win the day, he wondered. But the practical military man in him trumped his thoughts of romantic martial glory. It was his job to defeat the enemy, and to defeat him by whatever means possible.

"Gentlemen, are you confident that these weapons can turn the tide of battle in our favor?" McDowell asked. Rather than go into lengthy detail, Conroy thought, why not just show this guy what will happen. He asked McDowell and Burns to move to a computer in the corner. He inserted a Navy training video into the CD-ROM drive and hit play. The video was an instructional film all about the Tomahawk Cruise Missile. They watched as the Tomahawks obliterated target after target before their eyes. Conroy then put in a video of drones and the Apache Helicopter firing Hellfire missiles. He looked at McDowell. The General said nothing, he only smiled.

The Battle of Bull Run was 10 days away.

# Chapter 75

The SEALs arrived at the outskirts of Richmond on the morning of July 12. Conroy ordered the men to tie up the horses in a wooded area, leaving Tarback behind to tend to them. They would proceed on foot and patrol in three groups. Their orders were to take photographs and to dictate comments, especially about possible missile targets. If stopped, the protocol was to say that they were to deliver a message to the War Department. Each pair of SEALs had one two-way radio. They all had simple code words to report to Conroy.

Their main target, Phillip Bradley, had suddenly stopped transmitting the beacon signal of his location. Conroy correctly assumed that Bradley had taken his batteries out of his radio to conserve power. Without that beacon, he would be almost impossible to find. Their orders were to call off the search no later than July 13, the next day, if they hadn't found Bradley.

Conroy, who patrolled with Petty Officer Jordan, sent out a message to the others. "Need more hay," meaning, patrol and gather information.

Two major targets in Richmond were easy to find. Their locations were prominently noted in history books. One was the Executive Office Building, the structure that housed the Confederate administration, including the office of Jefferson Davis. As they walked past the imposing building, a former US Customs House, Conroy planted a laser tracker in a bush near the entrance.

Less than a half mile away, near the James River, Conroy and Jordan came upon the Richmond Arsenal, also known as the Armory. It was easy to spot because the word "Armory" was prominently carved on its facade. Jordan planted a laser tracker in a grassy spot in front of the building.

Conroy sent a code to the other SEALs, "Hometown," indicating that they were to go to their rendezvous spot where the horses were tied up.

"We didn't find Bradley," said Conroy, "but we've gathered excellent intelligence. We didn't accomplish everything, but this mission is a success. Okay, move out."

They passed Lee's Army as they trudged through the woods. Conroy ordered them to stop while he double checked his map so he could pass the information on for drone surveillance. Earlier he had placed a laser tracker at the edge of the encampment.

The SEALs made it back to the location of their hidden Zodiac without incident. They gave the horses water and set them off on the road, where they would soon be found. They pumped air into the Zodiac with an inflation canister and climbed aboard.

SEAL Squad Bravo arrived back at the *California* at 1700 hours on July 14. Conroy reported to the Captain's office immediately.

Conroy told Captain Patterson how they lost the signal beacon from Bradley's radio, and were therefore unable to find their number one target.

"But I consider the mission a success, Captain. We found Robert E. Lee's Army."

# Chapter 76

shley radioed Navy Secretary Wells to tell him about the SEAL's mission, being cautions not to mention specifics because Bradley still had a radio. Bull Run was six days away, and Ashley recommended a meeting at the Navy Department.

"We will meet on the *California*, Captain," said Wells. "I will be with President Lincoln. He wants to see the *Gray Ship* with his own eyes." Ashley felt dizzy and sat down. She had hosted many a distinguished visitor aboard the *California*, but this was beyond anything she had imagined.

\* \* \*

As President Lincoln stepped from the motor launch onto the ladder's base, the boatswain's pipe sounded throughout all compartments, "United States of America, arriving."

Ashley greeted Lincoln and Wells on the quarterdeck. She, along with all department heads, wore dress whites, uniforms they hadn't worn in a long time. They all saluted while a recording of "Hail to the Chief" played throughout the ship. Lincoln felt overwhelmed with this respectful ceremony by the people from another century. He pondered that a woman like Ashley Patterson would be lucky to find a job as a maid in his day.

He walked up to Ashley, who extended her hand. Lincoln cupped it in both of his, looked her in the eyes and said, "So good to see you again, Madam Captain."

They were escorted to Ashley's office, preceded by a tour of the ship. Lincoln shook the hand of every sailor he encountered. Cell phone photographs would provide the crew with memories they would never forget. Along the way Wells pointed out to Lincoln a few of the things he remembered from his tour. Lincoln was especially impressed with the Combat Information Center.

They arrived in Ashley's office where coffee, tea, and snacks were waiting. Besides Campbell and Conroy, Ashley invited Father Rick and Lt. Jack, for no other reason that she wanted to share the moment with them.

Lt. Conroy gave a summary of the SEAL mission from Manassas to Richmond. The highlight of his talk was the discovery of Lee's Army near Richmond. He handed Lincoln and Wells two copies of photographs of Lee that Conroy had taken. Neither Lincoln nor Wells had ever met Robert E. Lee, but he was immediately recognizable from the numerous photos of him taken with mid-nineteenth-century cameras. He also showed them photos of the artillery park and the weapons depot.

"Do we know he's still there?" asked Lincoln.

Ashley was waiting for this moment. She asked them to look at the wide screen monitor on the wall of her office. Her computer was networked with the drone images in CIC. Lt. Bob Nathan, one of the drone pilots, had been alerted to the timing of this meeting, and he had launched a drone earlier. It circled above Lee's Army.

"Gentlemen," said Ashley, "the Army of Northern Virginia, as we see it this very moment."

Both Lincoln and Wells asked how long a drone can patrol overhead. Ashley explained that they can fly overhead for over 30 hours. One would return to the ship, and the other could be overhead in a short while.

"So," said Ashley, "if Lee moves his Army we will know when, and we can see where it's going."

Ashley then asked Conroy and Carrubba to review their discussions with Union General McDowell, who would command the lead Army in the Battle of Bull Run.

Everyone in the room was impressed by how much Lincoln and Wells had studied the *California*'s armaments. All one needed to do was point to a spot on the map and say "Tomahawk," and both of these nineteenth-century warriors knew its significance.

\* \* \*

As the meeting drew to a close, everyone left the room except for Ashley, Lincoln, Wells, and Campbell.

"Do you have any other specific thoughts for us Madam Captain?" asked Lincoln.

"Yes sir, I do." said Ashley. "You may be ahead of me on this, and I know I'm speaking way over my pay grade, but here's what we should do immediately after Bull Run. And I mean *immediately*. We should attack the artillery park, the ammunition depot and the headquarters at Lee's Army encampment. We should then attack the Armory in Richmond."

Lincoln smiled and nodded his head, as if he just heard a witness give him an answer he wanted.

"But why the immediacy?" asked Wells. "Won't the drones give us ample opportunity to gather forces and attack Lee?"

"Where I come from, Mr. Secretary," said Ashley, "a successful military operation depends on winning the hearts and minds of the enemy, as well as the hearts and minds of the people who support the enemy. Simply stated, within two, maybe three days, I think we will sap the Confederacy's will to fight. A clear victory at Bull Run, followed immediately by the destruction of Lee's Army and a missile attack on Richmond, and we should see a peace delegation riding into town."

"My friend," Lincoln said as he looked at Wells, "Captain Patterson, as usual, has shown us her wisdom."

How will I do without this woman? Lincoln thought.

# Chapter 77

"Lieutenant, would you please come up to my office," said Ashley to Jack Thurber. She referred to him as lieutenant when she called him, and switched to Jack in her office.

"Jack, I'm nervous, and I admit it. We have so much riding on Bull Run, not only the Union but the crew of this ship. Put your investigator hat on. Have we missed anything with the Bradley conspiracy?"

"I've been thinking about little else, Captain. We know that his major accomplice on the ship was Chief Ray. We also know that Ray's job was to disarm the major weapons systems. He was caught with a circuit board in his hand. We also know that Bradley's unaware that Ray has been killed. Bradley is looking forward to Bull Run, so he can prove to the Confederacy that he disabled one of the great *Gray Ships*. It will win him admiral's bars."

Ashley asked Jack to come over to the conference table. It was covered with sheets of notes she had taken from her prior talks with Jack.

"Is there anything we haven't thought of?"

"Let's connect the dots." Jack said. "Suppose, just suppose, that Bradley gets cold feet and yells to the rebels to call off Bull Run because he can't guarantee the *California* is harmless. We know where the rebel forces are. The Union Generals can force a battle, whether it's called Bull Run or not, just using our drones and heavy weapons. And, we know where Lee's Army is. This war will be over soon."

"You've become quite the military strategist in the last few months, Jack."

They were still looking at the table, their hands flat down on the surface.

As Ashley gestured toward one of the documents, their hands touched. Neither made a move to break contact. Jack moved his hand from the table surface and placed it firmly on top of Ashley's. Ashley looked up into his eyes. Their faces came closer together, slowly but deliberately.

"Captain to the bridge, please, Captain to the bridge," screamed the squawk box.

Ashley squeezed Jack's hand and started for the door. She stopped suddenly, spun around, and walked back to him. She wrapped her arms around his neck and kissed him on the lips.

\* \* \*

"What is it Lieutenant?" Ashley asked Kathy O'Gara, the officer of the deck.

"A rebel gunboat has been looking at us for awhile, about 300 yards off the port bow."

"Has he closed his distance in the last half hour?" asked Ashley.

"No, Captain," said O'Gara. "The only reason I called you is the protocol we've been following."

"Very well," said Ashley, also acting according to protocol, "if he gets any closer or shows any sign of hostile intent, sound general quarters and fire a warning shot from one of the five inch gun batteries."

When Ashley returned to her office, Jack had gone. He didn't know how long Ashley would be on the bridge, and he thought it would be inappropriate for him to stay, and he was right. Ashley realized she had crossed a line with that kiss, ratcheted things up to a different level, and probably violated a few dozen Navy Regulations. *I don't care*, thought Ashley. *Let's just finish this and go home.*

# Chapter 78

The First Battle of Bull Run, known in the South as the First Manassas, saw two inexperienced armies facing each other. As the day of battle approached, Northern leadership expected a solid thrashing of the rag tag rebels. Even in the South, few believed that the Confederacy would win the day. The North expected a major start and a quick finish to the Southern rebellion. Manassas, Virginia was only 25 miles south of Washington D.C. Wealthy folks from the upper crust of Washington society as well as high placed government officials, saw the battle as a chance to witness the uppity rebels get their comeuppance. Picnic blankets were spread on a hill to afford a good view. This battle would show the rebels a thing or two.

It didn't happen that way. A certain Union victory, according to the history books, turned into an embarrassing rout of the Northern forces. Because of the inexperience of his troops and especially of his officers, McDowell's forces couldn't execute coordinated movements that would have insured a Union victory.

The *USS California* would change all that.

\* \* \*

Confederate President Jefferson Davis had made the 80-mile train trip from Richmond to Manassas early on July 20. He wanted to see his forces in action first hand.

That same day, the day before the actual battle, one of the *California's* drones spotted a train advancing toward Manassas. The train carried a brigade of General Joseph Johnston's Army of the Shenandoah to reinforce Beauregard's forces. As the train approached a railway bridge, the drone unleashed a Hellfire missile at the locomotive. The missile exploded inside of the locomotive's engine, sending a plume of smoke and fire in all directions. The cars carrying the troops collapsed over the bridge in an accordion of death. Captain Patterson then ordered the launch of a Tomahawk cruise missile at the bridge itself. The missile smashed the bridge into a jumble of steel girders and exploding railway cars. It would be the last of Beauregard's plan for reinforcements from General Johnston in the Shenandoah Valley.

McDowell's troops began their advance in the early morning hours of July 21. The first drone had been replaced by another. It hovered over an area that showed a Union artillery emplacement of 11 guns facing off against a Confederate battery of 13 guns. The Confederate cannons were smooth bore, unlike the more advanced rifled barrels of the Union. This was an advantage for the South because smooth bore guns are more effective at close range. Another Tomahawk missile came screaming into the battle. All of the Confederate cannons were blown into small pieces, along with dozens of Confederate soldiers.

At 12:30 in the afternoon, a cavalry brigade led by the dashing Colonel James "Jeb" Stuart, prepared to rush a Union infantry brigade with a head-on charge. As Stuart raised his sword and shouted "Charge," Lt. Russ Colombo, pilot of the Apache Attack Helicopter, unleashed a barrage of bullets and two Hellfire missiles at the amassed cavalry. Men and horses scattered over the huge field. The survivors, deafened by the explosions, retreated in disarray.

An hour later Bob Nathan, the drone pilot saw a battery of 20 Confederate artillery pieces being wheeled around a hill. He could see that they were 10-inch Napoleon guns, fearsome weapons against an infantry unit. Another Tomahawk cruise missile roared from the *California*. It decimated the artillery battery and left a deep crater in the hillside.

Shortly after that, the drone spotted 12 caissons loaded with ammunition boxes. They had been hidden under a stand of trees because someone in the Confederate force had quickly learned about the danger of overhead drones. The drone was out of Hellfire missiles, so Captain Patterson ordered a Tomahawk fired at the munitions. The explosion was deafening, compounded by the gunpowder in the boxes.

Jefferson Davis was almost blind with rage. He had been assured by Bradley, that heathen Yankee bastard, that the weapons of the *Gray Ship* had been silenced. Bradley supposedly had a colleague aboard who was in charge of that mission. Davis and Beauregard had discussed cancelling this battle weeks ago. Bradley's words of assurance had changed his mind and possibly the future of the Confederacy itself.

\* \* \*

Phillip Bradley reported to the Confederate Navy Department to discuss the Union naval blockade with Navy Secretary Mallory. That morning he wore his new uniform as a captain in the Confederate Navy. A full-length mirror hung in the room adjacent to Mallory's office, and Bradley looked at himself approvingly. He had begun to grow a mustache, which he would train into a handlebar. He began to feel comfortable in the nineteenth-century. Bradley was confident that Chief Ray had ensured a Southern victory at Bull Run, and the battle would soon be as good as over.

An aide escorted Bradley into Secretary Mallory's office. Mallory listened to his ideas. He was curious that the *Gray Ships* only appeared one at a time, and asked Bradley to give an explanation. Bradley's response was confusing and convoluted, as Mallory expected it would be.

Suddenly, Mallory's aide burst into the room.

"Sorry to interrupt, Mr. Secretary," said the aide, "but this message has just been wired from President Davis."

Mallory read the cable. "Arrest Bradley," said the message.

\* \* \*

At Manassas Junction, the day was not going well for Beauregard's Army. With little artillery left and no reinforcements as expected, General Beauregard ordered his Army to retreat. Jefferson Davis, having stationed himself at Beauregard's command tent, objected with fury. Beauregard repeated the grim details of their circumstances. No artillery, no reinforcements, a weakened cavalry.

"Sir, my men must live to fight another day," Beauregard said to Davis, who hesitated but then agreed.

The Battle of Bull Run was an overwhelming tactical and strategic victory for the Union. The history books had been rewritten.

# Chapter 79

Phillip Bradley looked out over the Richmond waterfront toward the James River. It was a pleasant summer morning, with a temperature in the mid 70s and a gentle breeze off the river. The humidity had yet to percolate. The river ran fast on the incoming tide, sparkling in the bright sun.

He watched a flock of seagulls loudly greeting an arriving fishing boat, swooping and squabbling over the morning's offerings.

"Ready!" shouted the young Lieutenant.

Bradley wondered why seagulls set up such a commotion when they spotted food. Why squawk so much, why not just eat?

"Aim!"

Maybe they're yelling at their friends, worried about being betrayed, Bradley thought.

"Fire!" shouted the Lieutenant.

Bradley's body slumped toward the ground, held up by the ropes entwined around the execution post.

The young Lieutenant ordered the firing squad dismissed. The burial detail began their grim assignment.

# Chapter 80

At 1700 hours Captain Patterson ordered the *California* to steer toward Richmond and the encampment of the Army of Northern Virginia. The ship would arrive at its destination after darkness and would attack at dawn.

Ashley walked from her office to the bridge. As she rounded a corner in the companionway, Jack Thurber was heading the other way. They almost collided. They looked into each other's eyes, and they both wished they could resume where they left off.

"Well Jack, we've changed history," Ashley said softly. "Pretty soon we'll commence *Operation Wormhole.*"

Jack laughed. "Why does everything we do need to have the word 'operation' in front of it?"

"It's the Navy way, Jack," Ashley said, smiling. "It helps us to focus on our mission. And I've just come up with another operation."

"And what would that be?"

"It will be a very exciting mission, Jack, one that I've been thinking about for quite a while. I'm calling it, "Operation Jack and Ashley Take Some Time Off and Get to Know Each Other." *And show each other the love that we both feel*, she thought.

"May I volunteer to take command of that operation, Captain?"

"I think you're the perfect man for the mission, Lieutenant."

Ashley looked both ways. Seeing no one, she leaned over, held Jack's face in her hands and kissed him. She then continued on her way to the bridge, stroking his face as she walked away.

\* \* \*

Ashley entered the bridge smiling from ear to ear, wearing what a vulgar sailor would call "a shit eating grin."

"You look happy this evening, Captain," said Ivan Campbell.

"Oh, yeah, Bull Run and all that," Ashley mumbled. *Not to mention Operation Jack and Ashley.*

# Chapter 81

At 0515, just after sunrise, the *California* was on location off the southern coast of the Delmarva Peninsula, about 110 miles east of Richmond, Virginia. Captain Patterson was in CIC, along with Lt. Conroy. The sky was clear except for a line of clouds moving from the southeast. Ashley knew they would need to act soon because laser homing technology is affected by clouds. She had ordered a drone launch three hours before.

Lt. Bob Nathan, one of the drone pilots, stared at the screen. Ashley had chosen him specifically for the job because of his experience and skill. He also showed a steely professionalism. Piloting a drone, especially one armed with missiles, is a stressful job. It's not like playing a video game. The pilot knows that he can pour death from above with the click of a button.

"You did a hell of a job yesterday at Bull Run, Bob. I'm putting you in for a medal and a promotion." Hopefully it will take place in the twenty-first century, Ashley thought.

Nathan flew the drone over the camp of the Army of Northern Virginia. Conroy confirmed what he saw on the screen from the photos he had taken while on the SEAL mission. In front of them appeared the artillery park the size of a football field.

"Isn't it dumb to place artillery so close together to make such a convenient target?" Ashley asked Conroy.

"Yes, ma'am, it is. The idea is to enable the guns to be closely guarded against sabotage. But that idea is out the window with aerial warfare. Even as late as December 7, 1941, people still thought that you should cluster your assets for security. Dozens of American planes were destroyed on Ford Island during the attack on Pearl Harbor, clustered in groups, using that same outmoded doctrine. Yes, it's dumb. I guess Robert E. Lee hasn't heard of our capabilities."

"He'll hear soon," said Ashley.

She told Nathan to lock his laser sights on the upper third of the artillery park. Because of the size of the field she would launch three Tomahawks at the park.

"Battery three, advise when ready," said Ashley

"Battery three ready, Captain."

"Fire one!"

The ship rumbled as the cruise missile screamed toward its target.

The Tomahawk scored a direct hit on the upper section of the field. The Captain waited until the smoke cleared to get a view of the damage. What had been neat rows and columns of artillery pieces looked like tooth picks.

Ashley then ordered another missile launch, this time toward the bottom of the field. Same result. After they viewed the damage from the third Tomahawk, they could see that Robert E. Lee had virtually no artillery left.

Ashley told Nathan to focus on the huge area of ammunition carts. She ordered a fourth Tomahawk fired at the ammo. The explosion, which they viewed on Nathan's screen, was fearsome. It was almost 15 minutes before they could assess the damage because of so much smoke. When it finally cleared, they saw that the ammunition dump was now a very large crater.

As a parting shot at Lee's Army, Ashley ordered Nathan to shoot his Hellfire missile at the command tent. The tent went up in a confusion of fire, smoke, debris, and canvas. Lee was not in the tent at the time, although no one could tell.

* * *

The final part of their mission was to attack the large Armory in Richmond. The drone hovered over the site within a few minutes. The clouds had not yet moved in, so their laser guidance was still good to go.

Based on planning with both Conroy and Andrea Rubin, the weapons officer, Ashley decided to use two Harpoon ship-to-ship missiles and one Tomahawk on the target. The Harpoons are made to penetrate the hull of a ship, and would work their destruction on a building as well.

An actor named John Wilkes Booth walked in front of the Armory on his way to a rehearsal for a play in which he would soon star. He heard an odd sound in the sky and looked up. In the final moments of his life he admired the beauty and speed of the strange machine as it rocketed over his head toward its target.

The resulting explosion was so large and dramatic it almost looked like a nuclear blast. The Armory and its contents were reduced to rubble, as was a large part of the Richmond waterfront. At the old Customs House, the Executive Office Building a few blocks away, the Armory attack spread its violence. The shock wave smashed the windows along the side of the building facing the Armory, and large cracks appeared in the walls. The impact on the building was similar to the after effects of an earthquake. On Lincoln's specific orders, the Executive Office Building was not targeted. Lincoln wanted to have plenty of Confederate government officials to bear witness to the Armory's destruction.

A British blockade runner had dropped anchor in the middle of the James River, having made it through the Union blockade to deliver its cargo. Not far from the British ship were three Confederate gunboats, also swinging on their anchors. All four vessels were destroyed by the firestorm of debris hurled from the Armory.

After the last two days, Ashley thought, can the South possibly want to continue this war?

# Chapter 82

Jefferson Davis got his first hand view of the war at the Battle of Manassas. A graduate of West Point and former United States Secretary of War in the Pierce Administration, Davis was no dilettante in military affairs. Known for his stubbornness, he was nevertheless a realist.

He witnessed the awesome destructive power of a *Gray Ship* and its terrible weapons. If he had known in advance of the *Gray Ships'* existence, he would not have gone to war against the Union. In one battle he saw an army stripped of its artillery and ammunition, and its cavalry decimated.

Davis, in a horse-drawn carriage, approached the capital. He couldn't take the train that had brought him to Manassas because the *Gray Ship* had destroyed it. On his way to Richmond he stopped to inspect what was left of Lee's Army. His journey had taken three days. He met with Lee in the General's new command tent, the other one having been destroyed by an object from the sky. Davis had received a detailed report of the attack on Richmond by a rider while on his way to the capital, and he shared the information with Lee. He always thought of Lee as a man of granite, a person whose resolve never weakened.

What Davis saw was a shaken man. Lee, with a military record of bravery and leadership, was always ready for whatever an enemy could throw at him. And he always prepared to strike back, only stronger. But Lee had no training, no experience, or even imagination for what he saw on the morning of July 22. It was an enemy that came out of the sky, an enemy that had no face, an enemy that hurled destruction in a way that was almost casual.

Lee was both a strategist and a tactician. He saw the big picture of vast armies and the small picture of a supply list. He was a planner who knew how to execute the plans he made.

But in the past few days Lee could come up with no plan, no strategy, not even a guess. He simply had no idea how to fight the *Gray Ships* and their strange captains.

Neither did Jefferson Davis.

# *Chapter 83*

*I*t is 10 a.m. Eastern Time on April 10, 2013 in Washington DC. The *USS California* has been missing for seven hours. President Obama is about to address the nation and the world.

"My fellow Americans," the President began, "I'm here to talk to you about 630 people, 630 Americans, who are lost, 630 lives who have touched others. Moms and dads, sisters and brothers, sons and daughters, boy and girlfriends. Now these 630 people have touched the lives of all of us, here in the United States and around the world. It has been just over seven hours since the *USS California* disappeared from our radar and satellite scopes. A massive search and rescue operation is now underway, one of the largest ever conducted, looking for our 630 friends. We're using the most sophisticated technology available, and we will continue our search. For anyone listening to me I ask you, if you know anyone who is a friend or relative of a *California* crew member, please reach out. Reach out with a call, a kind word, a hug."

An aide with a five-year-old girl in her arms approached the lectern from the left. She put the girl in the President's arms.

"I hear you made a card for your mom," said Obama.

She held the card up. It read, "I miss you Mommy." At that the little girl broke down and cried.

Obama then cried. Not the cry of a skilled politician who knows how to turn it on for effect, but the cry of a father who feels helpless to make a child's pain go away.

"God Bless the crew of the *California*, and God Bless America." Obama concluded his address, his voice barely under control.

When the President went behind the curtain at the end of his talk, he looked at Bill Daley, his Chief of Staff, and said, "I just hope to God that I didn't make it look hopeless."

"It just may be hopeless, Mr. President," said Daley, tears running down his face. "You spoke for all of us."

* * *

On CNN, the camera panned to Wolf Blitzer, the veteran anchorman.

"If what you just saw doesn't summarize everyone's feelings this morning, nothing does," said Blitzer, his own voice choking. "As the minutes and hours go by, our hearts are with those families. We will break in with any new developments, any developments at all. In other news..."

# Chapter 84

General Nathan Bedford Forrest, also known as the *Wizard of the Saddle*, was in Jefferson Davis' office along with Robert E. Lee. Forrest was renowned as a daring horseman who used cavalry charges with strategic and tactical brilliance. Forrest had requested the meeting. It was July 29, 1861, eight days after the Battle of Bull Run/Manassas.

"Sir," said Forrest, "the word is all over the South about the events at Manassas, at General Lee's camp, and here in Richmond. If I may be so bold I would summarize the thinking of many people, perhaps most, that the South cannot win a war with the *Gray Ships* on the Union side."

"I would agree with that summary, General," said Davis. Davis looked at Lee, who nodded in agreement.

"What we have to do gentlemen, is to challenge our notions of an army, throw away the history books, and start anew. I recommend that we take every one of our armies, corps, divisions, regiments, and brigades and break them down into cavalry battalions. We should then set up small headquarters throughout the countryside. An army may control a city, but will be useless against countless small battalions of raiders. Not only will an army be useless, but a *Gray Ship* will be useless as well."

"What you're talking about, sir, is guerilla war," said Lee.

"That's exactly what I'm talking about General, guerilla war. It's the Spanish word for "little war," and it's been used for centuries. It's a way for small units of soldiers to defeat large forces. I believe it's the only way to wage war against a fleet of *Gray Ships*. We won't fight the *Gray Ships* — we'll ignore them."

Lee didn't like what he heard. There had been elements of guerilla warfare throughout the country even before secession. Kansas and Missouri were almost torn apart by raiding bands of "bushwhackers." None other than the James brothers, two murderous lunatics, participated in those horrible attacks. Lee expressed his concern that these "battalions" could degenerate into bands of armed hooligans, subject to no authority.

"Gentlemen," said Forrest, "it is not that we have much choice. If we continue a traditional war, the South will be annihilated. The *Gray Ships* will turn the tide of any battle before the first bugle sounds. They will target our artillery, our munitions, and our command headquarters. Future battles will have nothing to do with bravery or resolve, things that we have in abundance. No, gentlemen, future battles will be determined by terrible weapons falling from the sky."

"The alternative," Forrest said, "is to take to the hills. We can enforce discipline on the guerilla battalions, although that may not be easy. But it is easier than continuing this conflict toward an inevitable defeat, a defeat that will leave us no possibility to negotiate. We will be forced into unconditional surrender. If we wage a guerilla war, the North will want to end it. The *Gray Ships* will be useless against small, fast moving cavalry battalions."

Davis and Lee, both crushed by what they had seen at Richmond and Lee's camp, looked at each other. Davis got out of his chair and paced the room. He looked again at Lee. Lee slowly nodded his head. Forrest was right, they both concluded. The Confederacy will have to wage a guerilla war.

Davis sat down and drafted an announcement to the press. He stated that the Armies of the Confederacy would soon be reorganized, concentrating on small cavalry battalions. He didn't use the word "disband" when he referred to reorganizing the Armies, a word that sounded defeatist.

The Confederacy would not give up; rather it would "reorganize."

Davis saw the wisdom of this idea, as did Lee. He also saw the potential tragedy. He would make the announcement to the press.

But he said to Lee and Forrest, "Absolutely no steps will be taken reorganize the armies until some time goes by. I want to assess the Union response to the announcement."

# Chapter 85

On the morning of July 31, Lincoln called a hasty meeting with Navy Secretary Wells, Secretary of War Cameron and Secretary of State Seward.

As they were ushered into his office, Lincoln stood behind his desk holding a copy of yesterday's *New York Times*. The headline read:

**"Confederacy to Reorganize All Armies into Small Cavalry Battalions"**

It was a headline that Lincoln hoped he would never see. His advisors were stunned. The headline of one newspaper had changed everything. It made the difference between what was supposed to happen, and what would happen.

With the help of the *California*, the Battle of Bull Run was a resounding Union victory. It was followed up by the attack on Lee's Army, which decimated his artillery and munitions. Then the missile attack on the Richmond Armory was the final straw, or should have been.

"Gentlemen," said Lincoln, "my worst fears have come to full fruit. We know what 'small cavalry battalions' means. It means a guerilla war of attrition, of lightning fast strikes against our larger forces, a war of endless bee stings. All of our military plans called for us to eventually occupy key Southern cities. But now, instead of occupying cities, we shall have to occupy a vast land area, an area the size of France, Germany, Italy, Poland, Spain, and Switzerland combined. Instead of dealing with a central government, we shall have to deal with countless bands of warlords. Our numerical superiority as well as our industrial strength will be sapped. Our plans call for us to engage large armies. Now there will be no armies to engage, just bands of marauding cavalrymen. The *California* was to be the key to forcing the South to come to its senses. Captain Patterson and her crew performed beyond our expectations. But instead of bringing the South to its senses, our recent victories have caused it to lose its senses."

"We have seen no reports that the Confederacy has realized that *Operation Gray Ships* was a ruse," said Wells, trying to be helpful. "They still think that we have a vast fleet of terrifying ships."

"But," continued Lincoln, "the *Gray Ships* deception is what caused the South to reorganize. After they saw what happened at Bull Run and Richmond, they knew they were fighting a force they could not resist. Our success is what has cornered them into their only option, guerilla warfare. Not only is the *California* at a disadvantage in a guerilla war, she is only one ship, as we all know. Captain Patterson has advised me that they are beginning to run low on munitions. They only have three Tomahawk missiles left, and a dwindling supply of other arms. They are also running low on the fuel they need to fly their aircraft, fuel that we cannot provide. We have deceived the enemy. Let us not deceive ourselves."

Lincoln went on to say that even the naval blockade would lose its power, because the South would no longer worry about provisioning large armies. Small guerilla groups can live off the land. The *California's* blockade assistance will become less important because of her constantly diminishing firepower.

Abraham Lincoln, in addition to his qualities as a great leader, also suffered bouts of depression, his "black moods." His mood had never been darker. They had achieved great military success, but they failed in the most important goal of all, to win the minds and hearts of the enemy.

"Gentlemen," said Lincoln, "I need to look at new war plans as soon as possible, because we suddenly have a new war."

# Chapter 86

Ashley kept a heavy boxing bag suspended from the overhead in the corner of her office. It was a great form of exercise, doing wonders for upper arm strength and agility. It was also a great way to let off steam, to give anger a way to vent, a way to punch the face of an opponent without causing trouble.

When the news of the Confederate "reorganization" got to Ashley, she suddenly developed a lot of steam to let off.

Ashley put on her gloves and started to work the bag. As she punched the bag, the image of Jefferson Davis was on her mind. After 20 minutes of the most intense workout she ever had, she steadied the bag and removed her gloves.

Ashley felt better, or at least calmer. She took a quick shower, toweled off and changed into fresh fatigues. She needed to meet with her brain trust, her Time Travel Brain Trust. She picked up the phone and called Father Rick and Jack to her office. She then stood up, walked over to the bag and gave it one last punch. Maybe two.

Father Rick and Jack showed up within moments of each other. Father Rick noticed the punching bag swaying on its chain, and Ashley's boxing gloves hanging on the bulkhead.

"Having a nice morning, are we?" said Father Rick with his usual smile and chuckle.

Ashley walked over to each man and gave him a hug in place of a salute. Jack's hug was a little longer than his, thought Father Rick with a smile.

They sat around the conference table, with Father Rick and Jack on one side and Ashley on the other.

"No, we are not having a nice morning, to answer your question, Father."

"As we steamed away from Richmond I ordered the navigator to lay out a course for our last position on April 10, 2013, the wormhole, our doorway to home. I don't know if he's done it yet, but suddenly there doesn't seem to be a rush. Soon I'll be meeting with President Lincoln, I'm sure. My guess is that he'll see the strategic use of the *California* reduced to blockade duty. We'll be back to 'costume changes' and firing warning shots, with our dwindling supply of ammunition. I can only imagine the shock that went through the White House when they heard of the Confederate 'reorganization.'"

"The bottom line is that we achieved military success beyond our expectations," Ashley continued. "From Bull Run to Lee's Army to the Richmond Armory, we showed the South the new face of warfare. Our job was to scare the shit out of them, and their job was to come running and waving a white flag. We did our job, but they have rethought theirs. Instead of surrendering, they decided to make warfare a continuing part of the future for both the North and South, a guerilla war that will have no real end. I never saw this coming, and I don't think President Lincoln and his people did either."

"Jack, you have an amazing talent for pulling together a bunch of facts strewn all over the place. How do you see our situation?"

"In a way, it's simple," said Jack. "Not pleasant, but simple. I agree that Lincoln will probably want us to continue blockade duty. But with scattered forces all over the South, fresh supplies are less important. Fresh armaments are not as critical either. Guerilla actions don't take up a lot of materials or ammunition. Strike and run. Disrupt and seek cover. So we'll steam up and down the coast until we run out of ammo, not to mention aviation fuel for our drones and the Apache. I heard the weapons officer say at the meeting the other day that we're down to three Tomahawks, about 25 Harpoons, 30 Hellfires and enough gas to keep the drones flying for maybe 500 hours. It seems that everyone aboard the *California* will want to find a nice large target and fire everything we have in one big turkey shoot, and then start searching for the wormhole. That's the way I size it up."

"Father Rick," said Ashley, "your perspective?"

"I see a diplomatic problem," said Father Rick. "The South has no incentive to talk to the North until they try out their new plan. They think that guerilla war may be a way of getting a peace they can live with. The problem is that it will probably take years. Right now, they have nothing to talk about. The North and South are at an impasse, and the *California* is stuck in between."

"Father, anything new to report on your meals with the crew?" asked Ashley.

"Yes, there is. I see a lot less sadness, sullenness, or anger. What I see are glimmers of hope. It's been an open secret that we were going to make an impact at Bull Run, and that the battle would be our key to the door marked home. Your public speeches over the last few months, Captain, have given the crew a stake in the battles. I can't see how any of them will see a stake in a long protracted cruise on blockade duty. If I could summarize the crew's thinking it would be this: 'We've done our job. Let's go home.'"

"And we *have* done our job," Ashley shouted as she slapped the table. "But our journey home has been delayed by some rat shit, swaggering assholes who want to continue their elite lifestyles and keep their slaves in fucking chains. Sorry about the language, gentlemen. Maybe I should take a few more shots at my bag."

"But I think I have a solution," Ashley said, after she took a deep breath..

Both Jack and the chaplain leaned forward, expecting to hear something bold. They weren't disappointed.

"The three of us are going to visit Jefferson Davis and Robert E. Lee as a delegation from the future. From my reading about both of these guys, they're men of honor, or at least they think they are. This is especially so of Robert E. Lee. Have you ever seen one of those old photographs of him when he didn't appear to be posing for a marble statue?"

"I couldn't agree more, Captain." said Jack. "Duty and honor are steeped in their DNA. That's why Lee gave up a successful career with the Union Army so he could defend his beloved Virginia."

"We'll probably violate a few hundred federal statutes," Ashley said, "but we're going to form a diplomatic team and try to talk some sense into their heads by appealing to their sense of honor. It's not only their honor that's at stake, but the honor of the entire South. I suspect that's an angle that will get their attention. I want you two with me, Father Rick for your historical knowledge and Jack for your time-travel experience. You two are brilliant. You're also my good friends."

"I'm going to send a preliminary delegation ashore, led by SEAL Lieutenant Conroy, to set up the meeting and to have a carriage waiting for us. Even though the Executive Office Building is a just few blocks from the edge of the river, I don't want to walk. We'll be wearing dress whites and I don't want to arrive in a sweat. Also, a colored girl dressed up like a naval officer may cause an unnecessary stir. We'll travel in daylight in the motor launch, and we'll fly a white flag to show that we're looking to talk under rules of truce."

"And what if they find your message unconvincing, Captain?" asked Father Rick.

"Then we immediately steam for the wormhole. One way or the other, we're going home."

# Chapter 87

O n August 3, at 0900, Petty Officer Donizzio guided the *California's* motor launch up to one of the few remaining docks in Richmond. The destruction along the waterfront was on grim display. Both he and Marine Corporal Falanga were in their dress uniforms. As the boat touched the dock, Donizzio leaned over to Falanga and whispered, "Isn't this the town that we blew the shit out of a few days ago?" Falanga nodded. "I hope you have plenty of ammunition," said Donizzio.

Ashley, Father Rick, and Jack got into the waiting carriage. In two minutes they were in front of the Executive Office Building. All three of them noticed that repair crews were replacing windows all along the front of the building.

They were escorted into a large entrance hallway. Jefferson Davis' office was on the third floor. They trudged slowly up the stairs, trying to keep perspiration to a minimum in the sweltering building.

An aide opened the door and the three walked in. President Jefferson Davis, Navy Secretary Stephen Mallory and General Robert E. Lee sat on one side of a long table. The three men stood when the delegation entered. None of the men offered their hands. None of them knew what to do in the presence of a woman in a captain's uniform, especially a colored woman. Ashley was pleased with the chilly reception.

She seethed with anger, not the kind of anger that makes you punch holes in a wall or kick things over, just a low burn feeling of being pissed off. She was glad that she felt this way. It focuses one's attention and avoids distractions. It's the kind of anger that propels you to get a job done and to send a message. She realized what made her angry. These people are bullies, she thought.

"My name is Ashley Patterson and I'm the Commanding Officer of the USS California." *And if you have a problem with that, eat shit. Stop, calm down, make nice.*

"You're not the first delegation from your ship to visit us," said Jefferson Davis coldly.

"I assume you are referring to Commander Phillip Bradley, sir," said Ashley. Davis nodded. "Simply stated, the man was a traitor. He betrayed us, he betrayed you. I understand that you put him before a firing squad. I thank you for saving us ammunition."

Ashley then recounted the events of April 10, now almost four months ago. She talked about the *Daylight Event* and their discovery that they had travelled through a time portal, and came from the year 2013 to 1861 in an instant. *Whether you assholes believe it or not. Stop, stop, don't blow it.* She talked about the photos of Charleston in the twenty-first-century and the view they saw when the SEALs went ashore.

She then asked Jack Thurber to speak about his studies of time travel. Jack concluded his talk, saying, "So, the scientific possibility of time travel has always existed. We just experienced it in reality."

Ashley continued. "Because we come from the future, as strange as that may sound, we have a unique perspective on history. We know what happened, or to be more accurate, what will happen. I personally witnessed the bombardment of Fort Sumter, and consulted my time piece when the first shot was fired. It was exactly the time that the history books said it would be. We also knew what would happen at Bull Run, or Manassas if you will. For the first time a *Gray Ship*, my ship, intervened in history. The books told us that the South would have a resounding victory. Instead, the *California* turned it into a Confederate defeat. Then, as you know, we attacked General Lee's Army and destroyed his artillery, and finally we blew up the Richmond Armory."

Davis pounded his desk and yelled, "And you have the gall to stand before us after unleashing such violence a mere matter of days ago."

Ashley stood, put her hands on the table, and locked Davis in a full Ashley Patterson Eye Job. Jack thought she was going to punch him.

"We are at war, unless you haven't noticed," Ashley said in a loud voice. "Did you not expect your enemy to fire on you?" And then an amazing thing happened. Robert E. Lee, old *Marble Man* himself, laughed.

"With all due respect, Mr. President," said Lee, "I believe the Captain has a point. When I have superior firepower, I do not hesitate to use it against the enemy."

Davis said nothing, just frowned, realizing that he had made an ass of himself.

Ashley then introduced Father Rick to go through a history lesson of the Civil War.

"Commander Richard Sampson is an Episcopal priest, our ship's Chaplain," Ashley said. Both Davis and Lee were Episcopalians, and Lee was a devout worshipper. This, both Ashley and Father Rick had agreed, was another reason that he should be on this delegation.

"Father Sampson is also an expert on history, specifically the history of the Civil War," said Ashley.

Father Rick then gave a rundown of what the history books said. But unlike the history lesson he had given the Union high command, this lesson had to include the revised Battle of Bull Run and the attack on Lee's Army, both events that would likely change history. As Ashley had insisted, the chaplain would leave it to her to discuss guerilla war.

"But that has now all changed, has it not?" Jefferson Davis asked.

Ashley gestured to Father Rick to sit down. She would handle it from here.

"To answer your question, Mr. President," said Ashley, "yes, it has changed. The question for you to consider is whether the change is for the good. We've read the newspaper reports about the 'reorganization' of the Armies of the Confederacy into small cavalry battalions. It is your obvious intention to wage a guerilla war."

"Our history books about the Civil War, gentlemen, have one theme that runs through them. The theme is bravery and honor, on both sides. The South eventually loses the war, according to these books, but the sons of Dixie can hold their heads up high." *And the Academy Award for best actress in a drama goes to...Stop it, you're doing just fine.*

"Guerilla war," Ashley continued, "a war without end, but most important of all, a war without honor. The Confederacy is about to disband its armies and send the men into the hills to fight. You, gentlemen, have access to the history of guerilla wars, and that history is sickening. The South is about to take its courageous armies, armies like the Army of Northern Virginia," she nodded toward Lee, "and turn them into bands of roving brigands. In the time I come from we would call them thugs, gangs, criminals."

"Diplomacy," Ashley continued, "gets thrown out the window, because the opposing government has to negotiate with countless bands of warlords, like the Shoguns of feudal Japan. The greater good is determined locally, by the warlord in charge of his fiefdom. It will begin as a story about these cavalry battalions protecting the people from the evil Yankees. Soon, and you know this as I speak, the people will begin to wonder who will protect them from the local warlords. Of course, there will be a central government, the Confederate States of America, but that government will soon find itself trying to exercise some semblance of discipline over the bands of criminals in the hills."

Ashley sensed that she was making an impression. She appealed to their honor, something these men cherish. She chose not to touch on the issue of slavery, because that was not her mission today. She noticed that Lee, especially, looked uncomfortable.

"Gentlemen, I do not stand here with any mission from my government," said Ashley. "I'm a naval officer, not a diplomat. I did not seek permission to speak to you, nor was any granted. I have nothing to offer, nothing to negotiate. I stand here to appeal to your love of your people and your sacred duty to them. I, like General Lee, am a professional military person. I believe in honor, but not honor just for myself. I believe in honor for my fellow citizens, and I think that you do too."

Ashley sensed it was time to go for the big point, a point that, if not taken, would make this meeting useless.

"Gentlemen, I appeal to your sacred honor," Ashley said. "I don't just appeal to your personal honor but to the honor of the South, to the honor of your ancestors and loved ones. End this war. Negotiate a peace. The alternative is to turn the South into small bands of roaming criminals. It's in your hands."

She couldn't believe it. Were those tears streaming down Robert E. Lee's cheeks?

"How can we contact you?" asked Davis.

My God, Ashley thought. He wants to contact me.

"Through the Navy Department in Washington, sir," Ashley said.

Davis then said, "Please give me until tomorrow morning, Captain. Kindly send your boat to the dock. I shall have a communication for you that I request you personally deliver to President Lincoln."

"I shall indeed, sir."

The meeting was over.

# *Chapter 88*

On the morning of August 4, 1861, Petty Officer Donizzio piloted the motor launch up the James River to Richmond, still flying the white flag. A Confederate soldier stood on the dock waiting for him, holding two envelopes.

"Nice boat, Yankee," said the soldier, smiling.

"If this war ends soon, maybe I can take you out fishing," said Donizzio.

"I'd like that, I really would," said the soldier as he handed the two envelopes to Donizzio.

\* \* \*

Ashley called Secretary Wells on the radio to request a meeting with Lincoln. He called her back a half hour later, saying that a meeting had been scheduled for 9 a.m. the next morning. She had some thinking to do, fast thinking. Lincoln would be more than curious to know how she came into possession of a letter from Jefferson Davis. Maybe she should just tell the truth, Ashley thought. She had two fellow naval officers as witnesses who could swear that she divulged no secrets and offered nothing. She didn't know what the envelope contained, but thought that it may offer a glimmer of hope.

At 0845 on August 5, Ashley's carriage pulled up to the White House. Ashley was alone, except for Corporal Arnold Nesbitt, her aide. She wondered if this would be the last time she visited the White House of Abraham Lincoln. Nesbitt opened her carriage door and extended his arm to assist Ashley. This time she didn't trip.

Lincoln sat in his office along with Gideon Wells. He got up and strode across the floor to welcome Ashley, succumbing to the strange twenty-first-century custom of shaking a woman's hand. Wells followed and shook Ashley's hand with both of his. My nineteenth-century friends, Ashley thought.

Lincoln sat down at his desk, Ashley and Wells seated before him.

"You executed our plans for the Blockade and the Battle of Bull Run perfectly, Captain," said Lincoln. "Your attack on Lee's Army and the Richmond Armory were brilliant. You and the crew of the *California* have given us a stunning success. But, as we have all learned in the last few days, it has also given us a terrible setback. Instead of the expected Confederate surrender, we now look at years of a damnable guerilla war. May I have your thoughts, Madam Captain."

Ashley figured now was the time to explain her unauthorized diplomatic efforts.

"Mr. President, I too was shocked at the Southern announcement of 'reorganization.' I felt like I'd been hit by one of my own Tomahawk missiles. I realized that I had to take some action, any action, to try to correct a grave historical mistake." She took a deep breath. "Although it was not authorized, I met with Jefferson Davis and Robert E. Lee."

Lincoln and Wells glanced at each other. Yes, thought Lincoln, this was a serious violation of government protocol. Diplomatic contacts are authorized only by senior command. But, Lincoln recalled, he had actually considered appointing Ashley Deputy Secretary of State. So, although her meeting with the Confederate President may have been unauthorized, he was sure that Ashley conducted herself with competence.

"Captain," said Lincoln, "yes, it was unauthorized, but we can discuss that later. Please tell us about the meeting."

"Mr. President, I, along with my fellow officers Commander Sampson and Lieutenant Thurber, tried to convince Davis and Lee of the disgraceful and dishonorable future that would unfold if they left the future of the South in the hands of marauding bands of guerilla fighters. Whether our meeting had a positive impact, I don't know, but I believe I may have the answer here." She reached into her pocket and took out the letter from Jefferson Davis to Lincoln.

"Jefferson Davis had this letter delivered to me yesterday morning, the day after our meeting. As you can see, sir, it is addressed to you." She handed Lincoln the letter.

Lincoln walked over to the window. Before he began to read the letter, he looked out over the White House lawn. A weather front was moving in from the Southeast, and he heard the distant rumble of thunder. It sounds like cannon fire, he thought.

Wells suggested to Ashley that they get some fresh coffee. Ashley got the point. Wells wanted to give Lincoln the privacy of reading the letter by himself. Wells and Ashley mumbled small talk by the coffee service while Lincoln read. When Lincoln asked them to take their seats, they returned to his desk.

Lincoln looked at them and smiled. He covered his face with his hands and then removed them, still smiling.

"I shall read the words of President Davis."

My Dear President Lincoln:

The calamitous events of the past several months have caused me a surfeit of anguish for the suffering inflicted on both sides of our conflict. We have recently detained three officers of your naval forces, and discussed with them matters of recent import. Although they held no diplomatic pouch, they comported themselves ably and well. One of them, especially, with admirable eloquence, prevailed upon us to dwell on our recent announcement to reorganize our armed forces. The words of that officer weighed upon us. After the meeting we released the three without harm."

Lincoln looked at Ashley, and they both smiled. Jefferson Davis was covering her ass.

Lincoln continued reading.

"Sir, as President of the Confederate States of America, I wish to present for your consideration the following steps that may lead toward peace:

There shall be no arrests of any Confederate citizens for treason.

The soldiers of the Confederacy shall be allowed to keep their weapons.

The United States Government shall render financial assistance to the states of what shall formerly have been the Confederate States of America.

Slavery shall be abolished in all of the Confederate States of America.

Lincoln looked at Ashley after this last point. Ashley lost it with dignity. She didn't break down and sob, or jump up and fist pump. She just closed her eyes and let her tears wash down her face onto her uniform.

Lincoln continued to read Davis' letter:

The United States Government shall make interest-free loans, for a period of time to be determined, to enable farmers and plantation owners to make a transition to employment based enterprises.

I shall welcome the opportunity to discuss these matters personally.

I am, very respectfully, Jefferson Davis

Ashley, concluding that composure was overrated, broke down and sobbed. Gideon Wells, his great white beard looking like a slushy ski slope, also wept. Lincoln joined in, although with a handkerchief over his face.

"It's over," Ashley choked, "it's over."

Lincoln knew, of course, that it wasn't over. Feathers would need to be smoothed, factions to be satisfied, appointments to be bargained for, and deals to be cut, both North and South. There would be fiery oratory, calls for recriminations, and demands for arrests. But all that is the stuff of politics, something Lincoln knew he could handle. He would have his work cut out for him, and so would Jefferson Davis. But the alternative is young men in blue and gray uniforms slaughtering each other for years.

"With malice toward none, with charity for all..."

Those words just popped into Lincoln's head. He'd have to work them into a speech some day, he thought.

# Chapter 89

*F*riends never say farewell. They say, see you later, until next time, catch you around the campus. They say, ciao, aloha, later babe, fuggeddaboutit, don't be such a stranger, don't forget to write, or let's do lunch. They don't say farewell. It's too final. It's too painful.

But sometimes it's time to say farewell.

Abraham Lincoln and his entire cabinet stood on the dock to see Ashley off. Both Lincoln and Wells decided to try something from Ashley's time. They both hugged this amazing Captain from the twenty-first century. Lincoln held it together. Wells cried, as did Ashley.

Petty Officer Donizzio had grown accustomed to his role as boat captain for the famous and powerful. As he assisted Captain Patterson aboard, he switched on the boat's powerful Bose stereo system.

"The Battle Hymn of the Republic" sounded off both banks of the river as the launch motored down the Potomac.

# Chapter 90

Ashley radioed ahead to speak to Father Rick. As prearranged, she gave him a simple message.

"It's a go, Father."

The boatswain's pipe screeched throughout the ship, followed by the boatswain's mate of the watch saying, "Attention all hands, attention all hands. Attention to Chaplain Richard Sampson."

Father Rick leaned into the microphone and said, "I have just spoken to Captain Patterson who is on her way to the ship. My friends, we're going home."

The launch was about two miles from the *California*. Ashley and Donizzio would later swear that they could hear the cheering from the ship. Donizzio looked at the Captain and shrugged his shoulders. "That means we're going home, Mike," Ashley said. "We're going home."

*  *  *

"*California*, arriving."

For those who still had a voice after Father Rick's announcement, they let out a cheering scream that could probably be heard at the White House. Executive Officer Ivan Campbell grabbed the microphone and led the crew in a few stanzas of "For she's a jolly good fellow."

Ashley stepped onto the bridge and saluted as the officer of the deck yelled, "Attention on deck."

She walked over to the navigator, Lt. Wayne Bellamy and said, "Wayne, let's go wormhole hunting."

"Aye aye, Captain." said Bellamy. He then gave the course setting to the OOD.

Ashley then looked to the OOD, and gave him a jerking thumbs up motion to raise the anchor.

As the *California's* anchor cleared the bottom, the Navy theme "Anchors Aweigh" blared throughout the ship.

\* \* \*

Ashley couldn't wait to gather her diplomatic brain trust together to tell them about her meeting with Lincoln and Wells. She called Father Rick and Jack to come to her office.

"The White House photocopy machine was on the blink," Ashley joked, "but Lincoln let me transcribe Davis' letter." She read the letter out loud.

Father Rick and Jack were especially impressed that Davis had intimated in the letter that the three of them had been arrested, to cover their butts in case they faced punishment for unauthorized diplomatic activity.

When she read the part of Davis' letter about abolishing slavery, the emotional impact on the Chaplain and Jack was the same as it had been on Ashley, Lincoln, and Wells. She always knew her friend Father Rick was willing to let go of his emotions, but, before now, she had never seen Jack cry. She reached across the table and they squeezed hands.

"Father Rick, Jack, I honestly don't know how I can thank you two," Ashley said.

"Now let's find that wormhole. I'll see you guys later."

"Oh, one thing, Captain," Father Rick said. "Mike Donizzio, the motor launch captain, gave me this for you." He pulled an envelope out of his pocket. "A soldier gave him this letter from Jefferson Davis to you. Davis specifically asked that it not be given to you until after your meeting with Lincoln. I think Jack and I should let you read the letter in private."

"No, I want you and Jack to hear it as I read it."

Ashley began to read Davis' letter.

My Dear Captain Patterson:

As you read this letter, you shall already have met with President Lincoln and have given him my letter. I trust that my entreaties to him shall put us on a course toward peace. But in this letter, Madam, I wish to express to you my personal thoughts on your diplomatic mission along with your two able colleagues. I wrote this letter after I retired to my home for the evening. I was greeted at the door by my trusted servant, the head of our household servants, Mrs. Ida Mae Bardwell. Yes, Mrs. Bardwell is a slave. As I looked at the woman, who my wife and I hold with affection, and I believe it to be likewise with Ida Mae, my thoughts went back hours earlier to my meeting with you, Captain. Ida Mae is, I believe, about your age. You, Madam, if I may be so bold, are a courageous and talented woman of proven deeds. Your Nation has entrusted you with the command of a powerful warship, and I am sure that such trust was not granted lightly. I looked at Ida Mae, and realized that she would never have the opportunity to achieve your accomplishments, for one reason. She is my property.

I have long been uncomfortable with the institution of slavery. You, Captain Patterson, have turned my discomfort into action. As you read this letter, Captain, I am pleased to inform you that Ida Mae Bardwell is a free woman, no longer my slave. It is because of you that I made this decision. Ida Mae is pregnant with the child of her husband, Joseph, also my property until this morning. I have freed Joseph, as well as all of my other slaves. I am happy that Ida Mae and Joseph will stay on with me as salaried employees. I told them about you. They asked me to tell you that their child, whether boy or girl, will be named Ashley.

God bless you.

Jefferson Davis

Father Rick looked at Jack, gave him a squint and a sideways shake of the head, indicating that they should give Ashley some privacy.

Ashley hugged each of them before they left.
Ashley walked to the door leading to the weather deck. She wanted to breathe in some fresh salt air, to be alone and let her thoughts wander, and to be with her friend, the ocean.

# Chapter 91

At 0800 on August 5, Ashley met with the ship's navigator, Lt. Wayne Bellamy, in her office. She also invited XO Ivan Campbell to the meeting.

"We're going to do a bunch, and I mean a bunch, of modified Williamson turns," said Bellamy. "The Williamson Turn is the good old fashioned lifesaving turn that we used to pluck Lt. DeLouker from the water during the storm. We turn the rudder on specified and timed commands and wind up where we started, but facing 180 degrees in the opposite direction. I call it modified, because we don't want to wind up in the same spot, but a spot a few yards to starboard. We then steam for three miles and do it all over again. We don't have satellite navigation, of course, so we'll be plotting by dead reckoning, marking a fix based on our known speed and compass heading."

"I know you two have worked on this plan, but tell me," said Ashley, "are there any downsides?"

"Yes, Captain, there are two big downsides," Bellamy said, "monotony and seasickness. We're going to be spinning in the ocean like a top until we hit that sweet spot of a wormhole that Lt. Jack is looking for. I recommend that we have a quartermaster next to the OOD at all times with a stop watch so we can execute the turns correctly. I also recommend that we have two people qualified as OOD on watch and that the watch be two hours, not four. I can't overemphasize the monotony of these repeated maneuvers. The Williamson turn is designed to get the ship to the approximate spot of the guy who fell overboard. It wasn't designed to be executed every three miles."

"Nobody ever said getting home would be easy," Ashley said. "I accept your recommendations gentlemen. Ivan, post the watches accordingly."

"Aye aye, Captain."

\* \* \*

After the navigator and the XO left, Ashley met with Father Rick and Jack. She told them about the navigator's warning of monotony as they carved circles in the ocean. She wanted to talk about morale, and what could be done to help during long and sickening maneuvers.

Father Rick talked about his most recent meal with the crew, which was yesterday after he made the announcement that the *California* was heading for home. It was a different experience from the sad, sullen and angry emotions he had seen.

"Handling periods of monotony and a rocking ship should not be a problem," said Father Rick.

"I don't want to throw cold water on people preparing for a big party," said Jack, "but I want to talk about something we have to face. Nobody on this ship, and that includes me, can guarantee that we'll ever find the wormhole. We've been making our plans based on my book research and my personal experiences. Find the place where you crossed the threshold and just cross back. It sounds easy and logical, but, as I've said before, I've never heard of this being done on the ocean. All of my interviews as well as my own experiences have always involved a specific spot on land. I recommend that we don't put out a lot of 'any day now' reports. Truth is, we don't know what's going to happen. We've all heard stories of the

Bermuda Triangle. What if all of those lost ships, boats, and planes went through a wormhole and could never find a way to get back."

Ashley looked at him.

"Jack, I want you on the ship's TV. I'm thinking of a sort of *call in show* where you tell the crew what you know, including a sprinkle of reality like you just gave us, and then take calls from the crew."

"I couldn't agree more, Captain," said Father Rick. "Jack is the obvious person to talk about hunting for a wormhole."

"We'll arrive on location where we start our search tomorrow," said Ashley. "Jack, could you be ready to go on tonight?"

"No problem, Captain."

The ship's TV station operated throughout the day. It was a valuable outlet for the Captain to get word out to the crew. Ashley called Petty Officer Wally Cabrerra, the host of *TV California*, and told him to start announcing that tonight's special show will be entitled, "Lt. Jack Thurber Talks About the Hunt for the Wormhole."

# Chapter 92

"This is Petty Officer Wally Cabrerra, host of *TV California*. I realize that I haven't been much of a Leno or Letterman substitute these last four months, but hey, you get what you pay for. Tonight, however, you will get a break from my endless bad jokes. You will get to listen to a man who has a lot to tell us about something we're mildly curious about – How the hell do we get home? Lt. Jack is a highly accomplished author of ten non-fiction books and three novels. He even won a Pulitzer Prize for an article he wrote about the Gulf of Tonkin Incident, something that happened before a lot of us were born. The book that we're really interested in hearing about is *Living History – Stories of Time Travel Through the Ages*, which was on the *New York Times* Best Seller List for 48 weeks. This guy is no slouch. I think this is a man we should listen to. Lt. Jack has agreed to take calls from our viewers, which means I get to do my Larry King, *Murray from Sheboygan, Michigan, You're on.*" Cabrerra prided himself with his excellent imitation of Larry King.

"Ladies and gentlemen, Mr. Time Travel himself, Lt. Jack Thurber!"

"Good evening, Wally, and good evening to my shipmates," said Jack. "Some of you know me as Seaman Jack, some as Lieutenant Jack. In a pinch, Jack works fine. The Captain has asked me to talk to you about something I have done a lot of research on for the book that Wally mentioned. When I reported aboard the *California* I never thought I'd get the opportunity to plug my book, so I figure this is just a hidden Navy benefit."

Jack discussed his book, especially the interviews with the six time travelers, how they crossed the portal and how they got back. He also went into detail about the time lapse in past and present time, and how when they got back to the present, they were amazed that so little time had passed.

"So the good news, folks, is that we may have been gone a short period of time, maybe hours or days from 2013. But Captain Patterson has asked me to be frank with you. I have never, in all of my research, encountered a person, not to mention a ship, that crossed a time portal or wormhole in the middle of the ocean. As I said before, the way to get back seems to be to find the way you got in. But the ocean presents something new to me. Now, I'll be happy to answer any questions."

"Lieutenant Cheryl Goveia from the engineering department — By any chance are you from Sheboygan? I love that word. You're on Lieutenant," said Wally the showman.

"I'd like to ask Lt. Jack if there is any chance that we may not make it back," said caller Goveia.

"No," Jack lied. "In all of my research and interviews there was a way back in time and a way back to the present. Sure the ocean complicates things a bit, but I'm absolutely confident that we'll find our way back to 2013." My lips to God's ears, thought Jack.

"Yes," said Ashley as she slapped her desk. She was watching the Jack Thurber show with Father Rick. "That's leadership. That's called taking command."

It occurred to Father Rick that Jack could have belched and Ashley would have thought it was wonderful.

"Here's a caller on line 2, Lieutenant Tom Lawlor from CIC. Talk to us Lieutenant," said Wally.

"It seems to me that we changed a lot of history in the last few weeks," said Lawlor. "Will the world be different when we get back?"

"I don't know," said Jack, "I really don't know. We're still in 1861. Whether our actions changed all history going forward or whether we carry our own time with us is something I don't have an answer for. Some people believe that there is such a thing as a parallel universe, two realms of existence separated by a wormhole. We'll find out soon."

"Caller on Line 1 — Lieutenant Donna Perricone from Personnel. Go ahead Lieutenant Perricone."

"I realize that this is a tough question, Lieutenant," said Perricone, "but do you have any idea, any guess, how long it will take us to hit the portal?"

"I wish I did," said Jack. "Once we hit the wormhole, it will be a matter of moments, but how long it takes us to find it is anybody's guess. Our navigation department has plotted a well thought-out series of maneuvers to try to get back to our last position in 2013. But I can tell you this. It may be a good while before we get there. On the other hand, it may be a short time. It won't be comfortable. We're going to be making circles in the ocean every three miles. It's likely to get rocky, maybe even rough. But we're going to do what we need to do."

"We have a caller on line 3, Warrant Officer Phyllis Ozarin from Personnel. Fire away, ma'am."

"I'd like to ask Lieutenant Thurber if we can expect the same event that got us here, a bumping followed by bright daylight," said Ozarin.

"All we have to go on is what happened before," said Jack. "Whether we cross the portal in daylight or darkness is something I can't predict. In April, we experienced that strange bumping sensation and then the *Daylight Event*. My guess is that we'll feel it again, but it's only a guess. I hate to be evasive, but there's no book out there called *Time Travel for Dummies*.

We can only take guesses based on the small amount of data that I've found in my research."

"Caller on line 2, our very own favorite Chaplain, Father Rick Sampson. Talk to us Padre."

"Lieutenant Jack," said Father Rick. "I'm going to be holding a special prayer service at 0730 every morning. Will you join me?"

"Count me in, Father. I'll be there."

"We have a special caller on line 3, the Commanding Officer of the *California*, Captain Ashley Patterson. Please go ahead, Captain."

"I'd like to ask Lieutenant Thurber if he could share with the ship his personal thoughts on the last four months," Ashley said.

"That's a tough question, Captain, but I'll give it a try," Jack said. "I think, like everybody on the *California*, that the last four months have been a time of fear, sadness, fascination, and wonder. But my most intense thoughts on the last few months involve the friendships that I've made. Some of those friendships are very deep and I have no intention of ever letting go. Whatever happens, these friendships will last."

Both Jack and Ashley knew that they were having a personal conversation on the ship's TV. Ashley thought of saying *I love you*, but concluded that it would be too adult for this viewing audience.

"It's a wrap, ladies and gentlemen, another Emmy Award quality show from the *TV California*," Wally said. "Remember, the early bird gets the wormhole." A collective groan was heard throughout the ship.

# Chapter 93

Lt. Cmdr. Frank Orzo has been the watch officer at Naval Operations at the Pentagon since midnight. He volunteered to extend his eight-hour watch because he thought it was important to have continuity in the search efforts for the *California*. Lieutenant Talierco agreed to extend her watch as well. Orzo had served a lot of time at sea and had stood many watches as officer of the deck. Sometimes those watches could be emotionally draining. They were nothing compared to this.

Orzo and Talierco had been on emotional high alert for over seven hours, and they were beginning to feel it in their muscles. Warrant Officer John Chinnici, who worked in the physical therapy office at the Pentagon, walked into the room. He had orders from the Vice Chief of Naval Operations.

"Somebody tells me that massages are in order," Chinnici said.

He first walked behind Orzo and said, "Just relax, Commander." After five minutes of muscle manipulation, Orzo was grateful that this guy was on duty. Chinnici then went to Lieutenant Talierco and did the same.

At that moment, neither Orzo or Talierco had any more information than anyone else in the world about the *USS California*. But looking at a display screen and knowing that the *California* should be there brought on a special kind of stress.

Orzo went to visit the head. There's something about taking a leak that seems to make things happen. If you're in a restaurant waiting for your dinner to be served, going to the john is a great way to make your meal show up. Orzo realized that he was just playing mind games with himself, but there was little else to do.

Petty Officer Dirkson, one of the screen watchers said, "This is hopeless. This is fucking hopeless."

"Secure that talk, Sailor," Orzo barked. "I can't control what you people think, but I can goddamn well control what you say in this room. Stow the word 'hopeless.' "

Everyone in the room knew that Orzo was right. The guy may be a pain in the ass, but he's right. All they can control is their attitude, and it may as well be positive.

\* \* \*

At the White House, Chief of Staff Bill Daley entered the Oval Office.

"Mr. President, the Coast Guard Sector Commander wants to know if we should convert the operation from Search and Rescue to just Search.

"No!" shouted Obama, smacking the desk. "Until further notice this is a Rescue operation. Any change will only be on my direct order."

Obama knew that, of the many tasks of a Commander in Chief, one of them is to give the people hope.

\* \* \*

Janet Sampson is at the beginning of a busy day. Besides being choir mistress at church, a job that took a surprising amount of time, she taught a few courses at a local community college. She has classes at 11 A.M., noon, and two more in the afternoon.

She's glad that she's busy because she is frantic about her husband Rick, the Chaplain of the *California*. Cancelling classes and sitting in front of the TV is a stupid option, Janet thought. Rick, a man she both loves and looks up to, had long ago convinced her of the power of surrendering to God things that you can't control. "Give it up to God," Rick would say. Still, the tension wrapped around her like a python. She thought of Rick, and of their mutual friend, Ashley Patterson. It's in Ashley's hands, and God's, she thought.

\* \* \*

The comedy writers for the Leno and the Letterman shows were having a tough morning, and so were the writers at *Saturday Night Live*. It's an unbreakable rule of comedy that you can't make jokes of a bad situation until the situation is resolved. Not only couldn't they create humor from the *California* situation, they were wondering if they could write jokes about anything for the upcoming show. Like the days after 9/11, laughter was temporarily on hold.

\* \* \*

Daytime TV anchors were earning their large salaries. "There's nothing new to report" is not journalism, not entertainment, and not worth watching.

CNN's Wolf Blitzer was interviewing yet another sea captain on the dangers of life on the ocean.

Fox News anchor Sheppard Smith interviewed people who had been lost and almost given up for dead. These segments were good, judging by the ratings, because viewers remember those days of waiting for miners to be rescued, a lost skier to be found, or a boy scout who got separated from his camp. All of these segments had one thing in common: hope. It's what the country wants. It is also something the country is starting to lose.

\* \* \*

Commander Hester, skipper of the Coast Guard Cutter *Gallatin*, pondered the old saying, "ignorance is bliss." He wished he had some of that, some ignorance. But he didn't, he had knowledge. He is an expert in sonar, and he knows the situation is hopeless. As a military commander he would never say that to anyone in his command, but he didn't have to say it to himself. He had lost hope. He was just going through the motions. He awaits word from Washington, and he knows what the word will be: suspend operations. He just doesn't know when the word will come.

As the *Gallatin* passed over the target coordinate one more time, he felt a rumbling, a slight bumping against the ship's hull. The sky started to turn dark, as if a storm cloud suddenly rolled in. The bumping stopped, the sky brightened, and he thought the same thought that went through the minds of the entire crew: "What the hell was that?" He checked all systems. Satellites okay, radar okay, sonar okay. He put in a call to Washington. No problem with communication. He checked his email on his phone. He had just gotten a message. No problem.

Decades into the future, theoretical physicists would label what the *Gallatin* had just gone through as "skirting the wormhole." Of course that would be just a label. The actual phenomena would be explained by pages of mathematical formulas.

The *Gallatin* had just skirted the wormhole and remained in 2013.

It was 10:30 a.m. on April 10, 2013.

The *California* has been missing just over seven hours.

# Chapter 99

O n August 14, 1861, the *California* had been executing seemingly end-less circles in the ocean off Charleston, South Carolina. They had been doing this nonstop, day and night, since August 7, a full week. The weather was typical of South Carolina at that time of year, hot and humid. The ship's speed was 15 knots, the exact speed she was doing when they hit the wormhole and the *Daylight Event* four months ago.

Seasickness is a chronic malady; you either have it or you don't. Modern science over the last few years has worked marvels to combat the problem, with patches you stick behind your ear, stuff you put under your tongue, or pills you swallow. But even salty veterans of sea duty on the *California* were feeling queasy. The turns every three miles were relentless. At 15 knots the ship turned every five minutes. Five minutes of relative steadiness before you had to brace yourself for another turn. Cheese and crackers was the meal of choice in the crew's mess and the wardroom. One sailor, seeing a stew sloshing around in a pot on the chow line, had to make a dash for the nearest head.

In his morning report over the loudspeaker, Ivan Campbell tried to lighten things up a bit. "The uniform of the day will be service fatigues and barf bags."

To relieve tension, Captain Patterson ordered that a Rolling Stones song be played over the PA system every 45 minutes. *I KNOW, IT'S ONLY ROCK & ROLL, BUT I LIKE IT.*

Would it ever end? Five minutes, lurch to port. Five minutes, lurch to starboard.

SEAL Petty Officer Pete Campo suspended his martial arts classes until further notice. Instead he organized a line dancing class. Hundreds of sailors discovered that, on Campo's timed command, when they switched their weight from one foot to the other, it compensated for the ship's roll. Petty Officer Simon Planck, the hero of July 2, joined the class. He was healing from his shoulder wound. Planck thought he may have a future in ballroom dancing, maybe with the lovely young Marine corporal he always lined up next to.

Ashley took her exercise bag down from its chain. The constant swaying nauseated her.

\* \* \*

Commander Joseph Perino, the ship's medical officer, attended to Petty Officer Bill Jordan, the man who suffered a severe heart attack in April. His condition has steadily worsened since then. His immune system is compromised, and he suffers one infection after another. He recently contracted pneumonia, and his condition is grave. Having lost over 40 pounds, he barely has the strength to speak. Perino had taken a liking to this poor guy, and the feeling was mutual. They would talk for hours about their mutual love, carpentry.

At 1035 hours, Jordan drew his last breath. Perino called the Captain to inform her. How sad, thought Ashley. The poor man would never see his old century again, not to mention his family. She called Father Rick. The chaplain's office handled all arrangements for burial at sea.

\* \* \*

At 1040 hours, on a bright morning, everyone aboard felt it, a soft but distinct bumping below the hull. There wasn't a sudden cheer. It was like watching a basketball game when the guy for your side just threw what could be the game winning shot. You hold your breath, not wanting to distract him.

Ashley was on the bridge.

"How's our depth, Jim?" she asked the OOD.

"Perfect, Captain," said the OOD, smiling, "300 feet. No ma'am, we're not going aground!"

Suddenly it was pitch dark. *Yes, yes, yes* could be heard throughout the ship.

After two minutes, the darkness returned to daylight.

The reaction on the *California* was not a crowd reaction. It was 630 individual reactions. Some screamed. Some prayed. Some cried. Some laughed. Some danced. All reached for their cell phones.

\* \* \*

Medical Officer Perino stood next to Jordan's body writing a Death Certificate for his friend. Jordan sat up and shouted, "What was that, did we go aground?"

"Are you okay, Bill?" asked Perino, as he dropped his clip board to the deck, his eyes like saucers.

"I feel great. What am I doing here?"

\* \* \*

Any crew member of the Coast Guard Cutter *Gallatin* who was standing on the starboard side of the ship yelled, in unison, "Holy shit!" as if it were an official greeting.

There, not 200 yards off the *Gallatin's* starboard beam, was the *USS California*. Hester, the *Gallatin's* Captain, laughed. Then he cried. Then he laughed again. He grabbed his phone and made a call to Naval Operations at the Pentagon, a call he thought he would never make.

"Frank," he shouted to the NavOps Duty Officer, with whom he had become friends in the last few hours, "the *USS California*, I say again, the *USS* fucking *California*, is steaming 200 yards off our starboard beam!" Orzo ran to Fran Talierco's screen. There was that lovely blip they'd been looking for over the last seven hours.

# Chapter 95

*A* story in the world of 24-hour news cycles takes on a life of its own. With live TV newsfeeds available as apps on various computers, smart phones, and tablets, word gets out fast. The debris of the first plane to hit the World Trade Center had not yet hit the ground when the event became *THE STORY*.

News stories, like the stories in novels, can break different ways. There can be tragedy, as in a natural disaster or a plane crash. There can be heroism, where an individual or group saves the day. There are courtroom dramas, which, like sporting events, are riveting because we don't know the outcome. The same can be said of political elections. There are scandals, which we love because they're so shocking. Of course, there are war stories. Vietnam, the first "TV war," was a story that was with us for five years, Afghanistan and Iraq for over 10.

But there is one kind of story that the world loves, a story of someone or some group that's lost and in peril. When stories like that have happy endings, it's as if the world has been given a treat. It's a report that makes you want to clasp your hands, call a friend, fist pump the air, or shed a tear.

The safe return of the *USS California* was a story like that, a story like the lost baby who is found safe, or the injured hero who makes it home. It gave the world a break from the daily yada yada of life, and let everyone, if only for a short while, be happy.

TV news producers, writers and anchors had a special reason to be happy. They were happy because the BIG STORY had now broken down into a zillion small ones to talk about, angles to look at, people to interview, experts to book. The big story of the *California* was no longer one of finding creative ways to say, "nothing new to report." It had now become, in a matter of hours, a story that could be its own TV series.

There was an even bigger reason for the news industry to be happy about the *California* incident. An 11,000 ton warship disappears for seven hours, and nobody knows why, or if they do, they're not saying.

Now, *that's* a story.

# Chapter 96

*A*shley realized that there was a detail she forgot to think about. Her last orders were to proceed to Charleston Harbor, South Carolina and participate in the Fort Sumter reenactment ceremonies on April 12, two days from now, now being the year 2013.

Ashley called Naval Operations at the Pentagon. Duty Officer Orzo answered the phone. "Naval Operations, Lieutenant Commander Orzo speaking."

"This is Captain Patterson of the *California*. How are you this morning, Commander?"

Orzo's last few stressful hours were taking their toll on his nerves.

"Holy shit!" said Orzo. "Excuse me, Captain, I mean Wow, I mean *fuckin' A*, I mean I think I better patch you in to the Chief of Naval Operations."

Admiral Roughead answered the call.

"I suppose, Captain, if I ask you where you've been, you're going to tell me it's a long story," said Roughead.

Ashley bit her hand, and managed to let out a respectful chuckle. What she was inclined to do was collapse on the deck in hysterical laughter.

"Yes, Admiral, it is a long story, and I'm sure I'm going to be telling it to you very soon."

Roughead said that he wanted her to give him a short explanation for now.

Ashley knew that if she said they went through a time portal, arrived at the beginning of the Civil War, hung around with Abraham Lincoln, kicked Confederate butt at Bull Run, and all that, he would think she was an insubordinate wise ass.

"We encountered a very strange sea anomaly off Charleston Harbor, Admiral, which affected our navigation and communications ability," Ashley said.

"But just tell me how you could have disappeared from our communications, radar and satellite systems," said Roughead.

"Sir," said Ashley, "I don't have an answer for that. We will need to do a lot more investigating." Ashley knew that she had just told the Admiral the absolute truth. She did not have the foggiest idea how a wormhole works. He seemed mollified by her answer, if only temporarily.

"Admiral, as you know we're scheduled to be in Charleston Harbor the day after tomorrow, after which we are to deploy to the Persian Gulf for six months. If I may, sir, I recommend that we return to the *California's* homeport in Norfolk."

"Captain," said Roughead, "the thought of deploying a ship that disappeared for no reason is just not on my radar screen. Yes, set your course for Norfolk. Future deployments are on hold."

# Chapter 97

As soon as Ashley got off the phone with Admiral Roughead, she walked quickly to her office to meet with Father Rick and Jack. The three of them huddled around Ashley's computer screen.

"Destination, Wikipedia," said Father Rick.

They were nervous, armpit moistening nervous. They had just spent four months in another century and actively intervened in the Civil War. They all had a list of items they wanted to look up.

Father Rick typed in "*USS California*." There was the standard Wikipedia history of the *California*. Date of launch, gross tonnage, length, weapons. The article mentioned that Ashley is the current captain. Nothing about disappearing on April 10, 2013. "They probably haven't updated the article yet," Said Father Rick.

"Put in 'Battle of Bull Run,' " said Jack. Father Rick typed it in. Some of the familiar history of the historic battle was there, the problem of inexperienced troops and officers. But then came a an amazing change. The article discussed the missile attack, indicating that it probably came from the *Gray Ship*, the mysterious *USS California*. Instead of the old entry that Father Rick remembered, the article then summarized and concluded with the words, "The Battle of Bull Run, or First Manassas as it was called in the South, was a resounding Union victory, and hastened a quick ending to the Civil War."

"Try *Gray Ship* and *Gray Ships.*" said Ashley. He entered the terms. Pages of entries on various historical websites, besides Wikipedia, discussed the *Gray Ships,* and how it was the greatest example of PsyOps, or psychological operations, in the history of warfare. One article concluded that there was only one *Gray Ship,* and that was the *USS California.*

"I have to talk to the crew," Ashley said as she stood up.

"I have a special project for you guys for the next few hours," Ashley said. "I don't expect you to write a *History of the World from April, 1861,* but it would be great for the entire crew if you could summarize the parts of history that have changed from what we know it to be. We made it back to 2013, but it's a different 2013."

# Chapter 98

The boatswain's pipe got everyone's attention, as it was designed to do. "Attention all hands, attention all hands. Stand by for Captain Ashley Patterson. The Captain will be on both TV and loudspeaker."

"Good afternoon everyone," said Ashley.

"The last time I spoke to you I said we were going home. Well, I guess I got that right." Those who still had voices screamed and cheered. She then announced that their visit to Charleston had been cancelled as well as their deployment to the Persian Gulf. She said they would tie up to the pier in Norfolk at 0800 the next morning, and that the word had been put out to their families. More cheers.

"When you return to your families, your homes are likely to be surrounded by TV, radio, and newspaper reporters in brigade strength. Don't be surprised if they aren't sympathetic and understanding of what you've been through in the past four months. They think you've been gone for only a bit over seven hours."

"A few of you have asked me what to say when questioned by the press, by the Navy, or by anybody. I have one suggestion and one suggestion only. Tell the truth, the truth as you saw it, the truth as you understand it. Everybody will want an explanation of what happened. They don't know our dirty little secret. We want to know what happened too! There is no official position of the *USS California*. I have my story and you have yours."

"To repeat," said Ashley, "the people who will question you for the next few days or weeks or months, have not gone through what we've been through, the fear, the boredom, the anxiety, the sadness, the anger. And God knows they didn't go through two weeks of barfing and dry heaving as we hunted for the wormhole." That brought laughs and groans.

"Speaking of telling the truth," Ashley continued," I'm going to tell you the truth. I have never served with a finer group of human beings than the crew of the *USS California*. We've all been through four months of living without a future, wondering if our lives would ever return to normal. What you people showed me was courage, patience, dedication, and maturity. You people are what this great Navy is all about."

Ashley then said something that the crew of a warship would never expect to hear, especially from a commanding officer.

"I love you." *And especially you, Jack,* Ashley thought

# Chapter 99

Father Rick and Jack Thurber sat in the ship's library for the next four hours collaborating on their outline of the new history of the World since April 1861. They agreed that the outline would be a randomly picked list of major world events and the characters who shaped them. The details were from articles in wikipedia.com.

## The American Civil War — 1861

The American Civil War was one of the shortest wars in world history. It began with the South firing on Fort Sumter, South Carolina on April 12, 1861 and effectively ended three months later with the Battle of Bull Run, known in the South as the Battle of Manassas. Total casualties on both sides were 942. The turning point in the war was the appearance of a strange Union vessel that came to be known as the *Gray Ship*, also known as the *USS California*. After her heavy weapons turned the Battle of Bull Run into a complete rout of the Confederate forces, the ship then attacked the Army of Northern Virginia, which was camped near Richmond. Next, the ship fired a missile at the Richmond Armory, completely destroying it along with a valuable cache of weapons and munitions. Part of the Richmond waterfront was also destroyed.

The Confederate administration briefly considered waging a guerilla war against the Union, but the plans were abruptly abandoned. Robert E.

Lee would later write in his memoir that the nation could thank a persuasive colored woman for the South's capitulation. No historian has been able to decipher what he meant, or who the woman was. The Confederate States of America declared a truce, and Davis presented a plan of peace to Abraham Lincoln on August 5, 1861.

## Slavery

On August 5, 1861, the same day that he delivered a plan for peace to Abraham Lincoln, Confederate Jefferson Davis freed all of his slaves. The next day he announced that slavery was abolished in all of the Confederate States. The Thirteenth Amendment to the United States Constitution formally abolished slavery in all of the United States. It was ratified unanimously by a vote of the state legislatures.

## The Presidency

Barack Obama, a former United States Senator, took the oath of office for his first term on January 20, 2009. He was the third African American to be elected President of the United States. In 1921 Virginia Governor Ashley Bardwell had become the first black president and also the first woman to be elected. Her parents were once slaves, owned by Confederate President Jefferson Davis. In her memoir Ashley Bardwell wrote that her parents named her after a sea captain who they had never met.

Abraham Lincoln died of natural causes in 1899 at the age of 96. The most important part of his legacy was his diplomatic and fair treatment of the Confederate States after the brief Civil War in 1861. He was also instrumental in reconciling the racial animosities that existed because of slavery. He appointed seven former slaves to high posts in his second administration.

## The Gray Ships

*The Gray Ships* are shrouded in historical mystery. They were sleek modern vessels that supported the Union in the American Civil War. Much about them is still unknown. Many accounts held that the *Gray Ships* were not a fleet, but only one vessel, the *USS California*, and that the ship changed appearance and names every night as a ruse to confuse and strike fear into the Confederacy. It, or they, suddenly disappeared on August 10, 1861 and there were no further records of a *Gray Ship* sighting.

## Japan

In November 1941, the Roosevelt Administration negotiated a treaty with the Japanese Empire. In exchange for Japan's abandoning its claims in China and Korea, the United States would end its oil embargo of the Japanese Empire. Japan also agreed to remain neutral in case of hostilities between the United States and Germany. Yoshuri Yamato, one of the Japanese negotiators, was an historian and an expert on the brief American Civil War. Relying heavily on the memoirs of Robert E. Lee, he wrote a book entitled, *Strategic Capitulation: When Peace Overpowers War.*

## Germany

After Japan signed the treaty with the United States, Hitler declared war on America. Germany had been secretly working on an atomic bomb. The United States had abandoned its Manhattan Project after signing the treaty with Japan. In May, 1943, a German battleship off the United States East Coast fired a V2 rocket bomb with a nuclear warhead. It was targeted to hit Washington D.C., but, because it had a rudimentary guidance system, the rocket missed its target and landed in a rural area of Pennsylvania. The officer in charge of the operation, Luftwaffe Colonel Kurt Schweightkopf, was a history buff. He had always been fascinated by the stories about the *Gray Ships* in the American Civil War, and how the use of swift and violent force could bring about peace. As a result of Germany's action, all neutral nations declared war on Germany, including Switzerland, Belgium, Ireland and Japan. In July, 1944, Hitler was assassinated by one of his own body guards. The Third Reich was disbanded, and the new German government sued for peace.

\* \* \*

"But there was no surrender at Appomattox," Father Rick said to Jack. "I wonder how Great Grandpa Sampson made it to Iowa. If he didn't, how am I here?"

"We're all amateurs when it comes to time travel, Father. Maybe there is such a thing as a parallel universe. We left 2013 and returned seven hours later local time. But even though the calendar says 2013, it's not the same one we left."

# Chapter 100

Any time an unforeseen major event involves a ship of the United States Navy, a Naval Board of Inquiry is convened to sort out the facts. Typical events that would result in a Naval Board of Inquiry would be a grounding, a fire, a sinking, or a collision. When a ship goes missing for over seven hours, that event more than qualifies for the appointment of a Board.

*The Naval Board of Inquiry into the Disappearance of the USS California* convened on April 24, two weeks after the *California* came back to 2013. The Secretary of the Navy appointed Retired Rear Admiral Floyd "Hoss" Miller, the first Commanding Officer of the *California*, to chair the Board. Eight other admirals served on the panel.

Ashley had met Admiral Miller once, at a Change of Command ceremony. She admired and respected him. At a dinner with him and his wife Kay, and Miller regaled her with stories about the early days of the *California*. Retired admirals can sometimes be stuffy, even pompous. That wasn't Hoss Miller. He is the kind of person you think of as an old friend after meeting him once.

The Board convened behind closed doors in a conference room at the Navy Department in Washington. A team of investigators fanned out to interview each sailor on the ship. Because there were over 600 stories to be told, if each crew member testified it would go on for months. They would call witnesses as they deemed necessary.

The first witness was Captain Ashley Patterson, as she expected. She didn't feel nervous at all. Maybe these guys can help figure out what happened, because she sure as hell can't.

According to procedure, a lawyer from the Judge Advocate General's office was appointed to sit next to Ashley and advise her. His name was William Braden, and he held the rank of Commander. He immediately got on her nerves when he whispered in her ear. Do these guys feel important by whispering in people's ears, she thought. But she realized that it was his job to look out for her legal rights. If he'd only stop whispering.

Promptly, at 0915, Ashley began her testimony. She told *THE STORY*.

As the hours went by, she was interrupted several times by questions. Everyone was impressed by her simple, direct answers.

Ashley didn't hold back. She told everything. Well, she did edit out a few scenes with Jack Thurber. Ashley was at the microphone for seven hours, including a one-hour lunch break.

When they returned from lunch, Admiral Miller thought he would break the tension with some humor.

"Do you have your flux capacitor with you, Captain?" asked Miller.

"Yes sir, I do," said Ashley without missing a beat, "but it's on the blink. I'll have to get it to a flux capacitor repair shop."

The room broke out in laughter.

"To summarize, gentlemen," Ashley said, "at 0309 on the morning of April 10, 2013, the *California* slipped through a time porthole, a wormhole, and found itself in the year 1861. We spent just shy of four months in 1861, going through all of the experiences I've discussed today. Then, at 1040 hours on April 10, 2013, we came back."

"Captain," said Admiral William Ferguson, "there is one thing that concerns me, well, one of many. You engaged in combat operations. You fired nine Tomahawks and dozens of Harpoons and Hellfires. But Captain, you had no orders of engagement. You had no authorization." Braden, her appointed lawyer, leaned over to whisper in Ashley's ear. Would it be inappropriate if I broke this jerk's nose, Ashley thought.

"I'll be happy to answer that Admiral," said Ashley, interrupting Braden's whispers. "I acted on direct orders from the President of the United States, Abraham Lincoln."

"Captain, if I may," said Admiral Dwight Bushley, "I've read your personnel record, and I've been listening to you all day. You are one remarkable officer. But you've been telling us that you met with Abraham Lincoln, Jefferson Davis, and Robert E. Lee, engaged in wartime naval combat operations, and you did this all within seven hours, local time. Captain, I'm having a very hard time believing this story."

"You're not alone, Admiral. I have a hard time believing it too. Sometimes I expect that I'll wake up from a dream like Dorothy in Kansas. But it did happen, and it wasn't a dream."

Admiral Miller called the day's meeting to a close.

# Chapter 101

The Naval Board of Inquiry reconvened the next day, April 25 at 0900 hours. The Board would continue its investigation for a month, until May 24. They heard from 175 crew members, both officers and enlisted. The only ones they didn't call were those who had no operational contact with the events in question.

They focused on the testimony of Lt. John Thurber, and admitted his book, *Living History — Stories of Time Travel Through the Age*, into evidence. Jack described his research for the book and his own experiences with time travel.

Jack was followed by Father Rick, who stunned the Board.

"Great to see you again, Padre," said Admiral Bushley. The chaplain had served under Bushley on the *USS Independence*, and they became friends. "A straight shooter if there ever was one," Bushley whispered to Admiral Miller.

Father Rick held up two books, *The Battle Cry of Freedom* by James McPherson and the one volume set of Bruce Catton's *The Civil War*.

"Have any of you gentlemen ever heard of either of these books?" asked Father Rick. Everyone at the table shook their heads.

"I can't believe anybody could write an entire book on the Civil War. It was such a small part of our history," said Admiral Ferguson.

"I suppose you could say that, sir, because your understanding is that the war lasted only three months and total casualties were only 942 on both sides," said Father Rick. "I had these books with me on the morning of April 10, 1861 and 2013. In the 2013 that we left, both of these men were famous as were their books, and the authors earned fortunes from the book sales. The history of the Civil War was different before we hit the wormhole. It lasted for four years and there were over 620,000 casualties on both sides. Just after the end of the Civil War, Abraham Lincoln was assassinated. You never heard of these books because they were never published, post wormhole, in the 2013 in which we find ourselves. These books are relics from a different time, a different 2013."

"I need a drink, Hoss," Admiral Ferguson whispered to Admiral Miller, "I need a fucking drink."

The Board also heard from expert witnesses, people with no personal knowledge of the facts they examined, but who could explain phenomena, both physical and psychological. They struggled to find an explanation for the unexplainable.

One expert, NYPD psychiatrist Dr. Benjamin Weinberg, was the man who had corroborated with Jack Thurber on his book on time travel. "Benny the Bullshit Detector" sat in front of the microphone.

"Dr. Weinberg, thank you for joining us today," said Admiral Miller. "We've asked you to testify because you have a reputation for judging the veracity of witness testimony, and you've also had input into Lt. Thurber's book on time travel. So let me ask you a flat out question. You've heard the testimony of dozens of crewmembers of the *California*. Do you find their testimony to be honest and straight forward?"

"Admiral, I look for signs of lying. I have about a dozen things that I look for, including perspiration, voice, physical mannerisms, and eye contact. I've developed a reputation for spotting lies and helping prosecutors put together cases."

"Is that why you're known as the "bullshit detector?" asked Miller.

"Yes," said Weinberg, chuckling, "it's my favorite title. But to answer your question Admiral, not one person I've observed and listened to in these proceedings is lying. That's my opinion. If they're not telling the truth they are amazingly talented psychopaths, and you don't find that many psychopaths together in one place, or on one ship."

"Dr. Weinberg," said Admiral Miller, "do you believe these stories?"

"It isn't my job to believe stories or not to believe them, Admiral," said Weinberg. "It's my job to assess whether the *witness* believes his own story. But I will say this. I don't know much about this time travel stuff, but ever since I worked on that book with Jack Thurber, I've noticed that I've developed an obsessive compulsive disorder. I never step on a crack... it may be a wormhole."

"Thank you Doctor Weinberg," said Miller. "We may ask for more of your help."

The next expert they called to the stand was a Dr. Jerome Suydam, a professor of Psychiatry from the University of Chicago. His specialty is group hysteria. He testified that large numbers of people can show signs of hysterical reaction when faced with traumatic events. He discussed eyewitness testimony from groups who witnessed an accident, only to find that actual taped evidence contradicts what they believed they saw. It was his opinion that the crew of the *California* suffered from mass hysteria, causing all of them to believe a strange story.

"Doctor," said Admiral Blake Jones, who also held a law degree, "we have heard testimony from 175 different individuals and over 400 written affidavits from crewmembers of the *California*. These people have talked about hundreds, maybe thousands of experiences over a four month period, and you're saying that they're thinking the same thoughts?"

Suydam mumbled about his long experience, the classes he's taught, and the books he'd written.

Jones leaned over to Admiral Miller and put his hand over the microphone. "Where'd we get this asshole, Hoss?"

Miller just chuckled and said, "Thank you Dr. Suydam. We have no further questions."

After Suydam stepped down, the Board heard from a MIT physicist who testified that a wormhole was a theoretical possibility. The man was obviously more comfortable with numbers than words, so he was excused after 30 minutes of testimony. But he did make an impression. Time travel is a theoretical possibility.

\* \* \*

Lt. Jg. Nancy Forsyth was called to testify. It was the most dramatic testimony to date. Because of her expertise in design and presentation, she was asked to show selected photographs and video clips taken during the *California's* four months in 1861. On a large screen, she displayed dozens of photographs, including pictures of Abraham Lincoln and his cabinet with Captain Patterson and her fellow officers. She also showed a video clip of Lincoln talking to Captain Patterson. She then clicked to photos of Robert E. Lee taken by Lt. Conroy. Forsyth also discussed architectural photographs. Using pictures taken by the SEALs on their recon mission, she highlighted the Charleston waterfront, comparing them to current day photographs.

Forsyth's slide presentation was so dramatic no one asked questions. The drama increased when the next witness was called.

Professor Thomas Pendleton of Cal Tech is the nation's most recognized expert on photographic evidence. He has testified many times before Congress and government investigatory bodies. Pendleton had examined every photograph from Forsyth's presentation as well as hundreds of other photographs taken by *California* crewmembers. He compared photographs of Lincoln to the existing photographs taken with nineteenth-century cameras.

"Gentlemen," said Pendleton, "the person you saw in those photographs is Abraham Lincoln, not a likeness, but Abraham Lincoln himself. And the people Lincoln is shown with are Captain Patterson, Lt. Thurber, Chaplain Sampson, and Commander Campbell. I'm a man of science, so I can't give you a clue as to how this happened. All I can tell you, as an expert on photography, the photos are real."

\* \* \*

After a month of listening to testimony the Board began their deliberations. Admiral Miller arranged for a large photograph to be displayed on the screen for the duration of their discussion. It was the photo of Abraham Lincoln and Captain Patterson.

Admiral Miller set the stage for their deliberations. "Fellas, our job is to come up with findings of fact and to make recommendations. I want to be clear on something. Remember the testimony of Dr. Weinberg, Benny the Bullshit Detector. He said it wasn't his job to believe the stories or not, only to assess whether the witnesses believed them. Well our job is different. We have to determine, as a factual finding, if this incredible story is true. I've drafted a summary finding of fact that I believe to be the truth. If you disagree, let's hear it. Here's my summary.

*The Naval Board of Inquiry into the Disappearance of the USS California*

**Summary Finding of Fact.** On April 10, 2013, off the coast of Charleston, South Carolina, the *USS California* encountered a wormhole, a phenomenon that modern science has not been able to explain. The ship was transported through time to April 10, 1861 and participated in the Civil War. The *California* engaged the naval blockade of the South, the Battle of Bull Run, the destruction of Robert E. Lee's Army, and the missile attack on the City of Richmond. After four months, 1861 time, the ship again encountered the wormhole and was transported back to 2013. The ship had been missing for just over seven hours, 2013 time.

"So that's the summary as I see it, gentlemen," Miller said. "The actual record, consisting of hundreds of pages, will be attached. So this summary, if you agree, says that we believe the story. Does anyone disagree with the summary?" Not one hand went up.

"Well, since we all believe the unbelievable, I have a few other findings that I suggest we answer."

Hoss Miller passed around a sheet of questions.

"Do you find any evidence of wrongdoing by any fact witness who appeared before this Board?" The unanimous answer was NO.

"Do you find any evidence that Captain Ashley Patterson did not execute her duties to the best of her ability?" The unanimous answer was NO.

"Do you have any specific recommendations to avoid a similar occurrence from ever happening again?" This wasn't a yes/no question. It was a question to solicit ideas from the Board members. All Miller saw was shaking heads and hunched shoulders.

"Well, I have a recommendation," said Admiral Miller.

He held up a large card, which simply read:

STAY AWAY!
N 32° 41' 41"
W 78° 34' 27"

"What's that, Hoss?" asked Admiral Ferguson.

"The coordinates of the wormhole," said Miller.

"This Board of Inquiry is officially closed."

# Chapter 102

$\mathcal{A}$shley and Jack left the ship at different times. Ashley was concerned about appearances. This crap shall soon end, she thought.

They were both on a 30-day leave, 30 days of relaxation, freedom from stress, and also 30 days to get to know each other. They met for lunch at an out of the way diner near the rental place where they'd pick up a car. Jack owned a vacation home on a lake about two hours away. As Jack drove, they passed the time telling jokes and guessing the states of passing license plates. No decisions, no boatswain's pipe, no uniform of the day, no meetings. Their mission was to relax and be in each other's company. They were both dedicated to the mission.

"So, *Operation Jack and Ashley* has begun," said Ashley. "As I recall I put you in command of the operation, Lieutenant. A house on a lake is a commendable start."

"I take this operation very seriously, Captain," said Jack, as he reached over and squeezed her hand.

"Jack, isn't it about time you started calling me Ashley?"

"Aye aye, Ashley. How about Sweetheart?"

She leaned over and kissed him.

They drove down a winding road to the house. Jack's caretaker had arranged things for their visit.

Ashley drew her breath as she looked at the house and the view of the lake. The house rose two stories high with dark shingling and a roofline inspired by Frank Lloyd Wright. In front was a gravel parking area, marked off by logs and surrounded by wild flowers. They walked out onto the huge mahogany deck. In the distance, two small mountains converged, providing a viewing frame for the lake. They inhaled the fresh air blowing across the water. A stairway led from the deck to a floating dock, to which was tied a shining antique wooden Chris Craft powerboat. The boat was named *Wordsmith*. They sat down to take in the view, Ashley in an Adirondack chair, Jack stretched out on a lounge.

"Where do you live when you're not at this beautiful place, Jack?"

"I have a place on East 66th Street in Manhattan."

"You own an apartment on East 66th?"

"Well, it's a Brownstone."

"What do we pay Lieutenants these days?"

Jack smiled. "Book royalties do add up."

"Speaking of books, I think you should write another novel after you're done with the big *Gray Ships* book. Maybe something inspired by the last few months."

"I have been working on an idea for a novel, and I've been looking forward to bouncing it off you."

"Fire away," said Ashley. "I'll play the part of your literary agent."

"Okay, but try to act short, fat, and bald."

"Here goes. Two lonely people meet on a ship at sea in a scary and troubling time. They're frightened and confused, and they don't know what will become of them. As the time passes, they become closer. They fall in love, and with all the uncertainty they know one thing. Whatever happens, their love will never go away."

Ashley brushed a tear from her eye, reached over and touched Jack's hand.

"Now that's a book that deserves a big advance," Ashley said softly.

"How big?"

Ashley got up from her chair and lay next to Jack on the lounger. They embraced as if trying to squeeze away the events of the last few months. Their lips met, and they both lost track of time.

A loud screech interrupted them. Ashley sat up with a bolt, expecting to hear, "Captain to the bridge."

"Relax Hon, it's just an osprey." Ashley collapsed back into his arms, laughing.

\* \* \*

The sun was setting behind the mountains, and a gentle breeze came off the lake through the screen doors of the master bedroom suite. Jack was taking a shower. As he lathered up, he heard a soft tapping on the shower door.

"Don't you believe in conserving energy, Lieutenant?" Ashley said as she opened the door and stepped in.

"Wow, I've never seen you out of uniform before," Jack said as he wrapped his arms around her. "Did I mention, *Wow?*"

"You're not too bad looking yourself, sailor."

They caressed amid the steam, water, and soap.

Although they both needed sleep, there was little to be had that night. They recalled the months of longing, the months of wanting to reach out, to touch and embrace. Those months seemed like an eternity ago. But that night there was no tentativeness or timidity. There was no looking both ways, no listening for footsteps. They abandoned themselves to passion and made love into the wee hours.

\* \* \*

Ashley awoke before Jack. She took a quick shower, threw on a robe and went downstairs. As she walked into the kitchen she had a great idea. She would cook a country breakfast for herself and Jack. She rummaged through the well stocked refrigerator, piling ingredients on the counter.

A thought intruded. She had no idea how to cook. Anything. Can't be that hard, she figured. Just common sense, right?

Jack came down a half hour later. Ashley placed a folded napkin over her left forearm, bowed and gestured toward the table with her right hand. She didn't identify the offerings, which was just as well. They were unidentifiable. She and Jack leaned over and kissed, and then began eating.

The food was inedible.

At first they chuckled. Then they laughed until tears rolled down their cheeks.

"I'll just toss this stuff in the lake," Ashley said, still laughing. "Biodegradable, right?"

Jack envisioned hundreds of dead fish floating along the shoreline.

"That's okay, Hon. I'll just put it out in the trash."

\* \* \*

"I've got a place in mind that you'll love," said Jack. "There's a great little restaurant down the lake. The food's great and the view is almost as good as it is here. We'll take the boat."

As they boarded *Wordsmith*, Ashley ran her hand over the mahogany decking and the leather upholstery. Jack stood behind the wheel and turned the key, the boat's inboard diesel engine growling to life. Ashley tossed off the lines and they motored down the lake. Rather than sit, Ashley chose to stand next to Jack as he steered the boat. For months on the *California*, they stole glances, blew kisses, and occasionally touched hands. Now, neither of them wanted to be apart from each other. She put her arm around his waist.

Jack maneuvered *Wordsmith* next to the dock at the restaurant, aptly named *Lakeside.* Ashley jumped onto the dock and secured the lines. I can't cook, she thought, but I sure as hell know the ropes.

They were seated on the open deck, shaded by a stand of tall deciduous trees. The waiter brought two cups of steaming coffee while they perused the menu. Jack was right. The place was beautiful, and the view even better. They could almost see Jack's house at the far end of the lake. Two snowy egrets patrolled the flats as if it were a buffet line, plucking fish and pointing their beaks skyward to swallow. Along the shoreline to the left, a great hawk circled, looking down for inattentive prey. A sailboat rocked in the distance, her sails luffing in the light morning wind.

The waiter came to take their orders.

They finished their breakfast, sat back and sipped coffee, while taking in the view and holding hands. Jack glanced down at an advertisement on the placemat.

"Hey Hon, it says here that there's going to be a nineteenth-century antique fair at the old farm just down the road from my house. Sounds like fun. It'll be like a trip to the past."

"Shut up, Jack," Ashley said, as she leaned over and kissed him.

"Let's talk about the future."

"Aye aye, Captain."

# About the Author

Russ Moran is the former CEO of Moran Publishing Company, a publisher of legal periodicals. He is a Navy Veteran, having served aboard the aircraft carrier *USS Wasp*. He has written two books of non-fiction, *Justice in America: How it Works, How it Fails*, and *The APT Principle — The Business Plan that You Carry in Your Head*.

He is the former Chairman of the Board of Trustees of the Long Island Maritime Museum.

Russ lives on Long Island, New York with his wife Lynda.

CPSIA information can be obtained at www.ICGtesting.com
Printed in the USA
LVOW07s1156300314

379528LV00021B/985/P